Masquerade of Finches

Angelio, Book Two

Elizabeth Hopkinson

Winnipeg, Canada

Developmental editor: Margaret Larson
Proofreader: Francisco Feliciano

Published June 2025 by Deep Hearts YA, an imprint of Story Perfect Books.

Deep Hearts YA
PO Box 51053 Tyndall Park
Winnipeg, Manitoba R2X 3B0
Canada

Visit deepheartsya.com for more great reads.

To Anna and Charlie

Characters

Tammo Capell - a young bird-charmer, in possession of a magic flute

Carlo Bianci (Seraphini) - a young castrato singer, Tammo's sworn twin

The Archangel Michael

Pageno Mansion

Celestina - daughter of the house and Carlo's special friend

Count Pageno - Celestina's father and the Duke's right-hand man

Countess Pageno - Celestina's mother; very ambitious

Orlando (deceased) - Celestina's brother, who died in childhood

Rinaldo - Celestina's spoiled younger brother

Maestro Loreto - a music teacher from the conservatorio

Teresa - Celestina's body-servant and former governess

Fenice - a sassy laundry maid with a smutty sense of humour

Pompey (Olusegun) - a footman; Fenice's on-and-off boyfriend

Caesar (Kayode) - another footman

Signor Plattini - the major-domo

Signora Rosamunda - the housekeeper

Vittori - Count Pageno's personal manservant

Leonardo, Guilio & Roberto - footmen

(Unnamed) - the porter, laundry maids, seamstresses etc.

Giacomo - an extremely mischievous monkey

Carlino - a rosefinch
Canella - a horse

Teatro di Palazzo

Maestro Sarastro - the Duke's Master of the Art Musical; short-tempered

Signor Contarini - director of the Teatro

Herr Wilhelm - stage director

Signor de Rosa - ballet master

Signor Croci - bursar

Signor Verdi - artistic designer

Signora Narni - wardrobe mistress

Stephano - head groom (horses)

Claudio - bird handler

Alfredo - head carpenter

Marcello - candle snuffer

Singers

Morestelli (soprano) - former primo castrato, who is mysteriously absent

Il Cupide (alto) - a ladies' man

Parnasso (Giovanni, soprano) - Carlo's old schoolmate; very femme

La Bellina (soprano) - the prima donna; owner of pugs

L'Amoricana (alto) - a new, young singer

Scipione (Uberti, bass) - former Conservatorio boy; friendly to Carlo

Dancers

Angelo - Parnasso's sometime lover
Marie - also attracted to Angelo

Singer's apartments

Citizeness Aldo - the housekeeper; very chatty with few teeth
Citizen Aldo - her husband
Casale - Carlo's personal manservant
Orpheus - a song thrush, once a gift to Carlo from Tammo

Caffe Armide

Armide - the host; loves to gossip
Michelangelo - an undersized serving boy
(Unnamed) - various clients, including a merchant from Mingguo

Angel's Wood

Grimaldi - a reclusive blacksmith, Tammo's foster father
Coronis - Tammo's crow companion

Pamina Mansion

Marchesa della Pamina - an alluring aristocrat
Florian - a footman

He asked me first if I am
Man or woman, where I came from,
If people like me are born
with this voice and skill, or rain down
from the sky. In confusion I reply:
If I say "man", I lie,
"Woman" I certainly shall not say
and "neuter" would make me blush.
~ Filippo Balatri (1676-1756)

Well, alas! How will it be heard,
the chaste desire that burns the interior of my heart
by those who in others see only themselves?
~ Michelangelo Buonarroti (1475-1564)
to Tommaso Cavalieri

Masquerade of Finches

1
The Carnival Ring

A crow sat on the bell tower of Piazza Giustizia. It jerked its beak toward the Poor School belonging to the Michael di Giustizia monastery. Then it turned toward Caffe Armide across the courtyard, with a look that, even when seen from the ground, resembled scorn.

"Give it up, Coronis. I don't need that from you." Tammo rubbed his freshly-shaven chin and scowled. He gave a sharp whistle. "To me, girl!"

The crow opened its wings and swooped, a funereal fan in flight. Tammo felt the talons grasp his shoulder. He readjusted the weight of the cage in his left hand. Inside it, two living jewels flittered and twittered.

"And you've been more trouble than you're worth as well." He grinned at the whirring green and gold of the birds within. "But you're worth a fair ducat and more besides." He tugged at his cravat. "I need coffee."

The smell of coffee from the open doors of Caffe Armide reached Tammo long before he had crossed the piazza. At the back of it was the stale smell of tobacco and sweat. Tammo rubbed his chin again. The barber had nicked him with the razor, and it itched. He hated shaving. He hated wearing the wig and the broadcloth suit, too. His head got too hot and the huge cuffs on the sleeves kept catching on things. It wasn't what he'd had in mind when he'd dreamed of being a bird charmer. He hadn't thought then that the job might involve charming patrons, too.

Before Caffe Armide stood a tiled portico, where a few citizens who wished to enjoy the last of the summer sunshine took their morning chocolate around circular tables. Tammo walked past them, and past a whole row of doors and windows, through which his own trade card looked back at him. *Tammo Capell. Purveyor of Fine Singing Birds.*

Tammo nodded in satisfaction and went through the door of the caffe's least fashionable booth. Oval mirrors, religious scenes and engravings of past castrati beamed from dark wooden panelling. In a corner, three merchants were arguing over a news sheet. Two were foreigners. One had the full beard and turned-up shoes common to the Caliphate Empire. The other had almond eyes and a bald forehead, with a pigtail down his back. A visitor from Mingguo, if Tammo wasn't mistaken.

Tammo put the birdcage on a table next to a carafe of cloudy water, picked up a news sheet from a rack, and sank into a seat beneath a painted Annunciation. Coronis perched on the dado rail behind him, wiping her beak close to several existing beak marks.

Tammo squinted over the news sheet's tiny print.

Today, our correspondent heard of yet another instance of the ongoing quarrel between the Duke and his heir, the Nobilissimo. It seems that Their Excellencies were attending mass in the ducal chapel, when...

Tammo sighed. Not more court gossip! Why couldn't news sheets concentrate on something more important, like the price of iron ore or the likelihood of severe weather over the winter? He glanced again at the foreign merchants, who were still arguing furiously, then squinted back at the news article. Had he missed something? He suspected the merchants of spotting some connection he couldn't fathom between trade prices and the Nobilissimo's temper tantrums. He scratched the back of his neck under the wig. He needed Carlo for stuff like this. Intrigue wasn't his style. He tossed the news sheet into the corner.

"Michelangelo!" Tammo's harsh croak sounded above the arguing merchants.

A waiter came running from the service entrance. He couldn't have been over thirteen, and his apron looked bigger than he was.

"Citizen Capell." The boy scratched his nose. "Will it be the usual this morning?"

"Yes," said Tammo. "And tell Citizen Armide I'm here."

"Right you are, citizen." The boy gave a nervous smile. "Anything for your crow this morning?"

Tammo grunted. "Just bring the usual."

The coffee was black and bitter; the coffee dish white with ivy leaves. It came with a tiny almond confection, which Tammo fed to Coronis. The crow cawed and flapped her wings in appreciation. The feathered jewels in the cage trilled in response.

"Not for you, little beauties." Tammo ran a finger down the bars of the cage. The twittering subsided. "Or else you'll end up as fat and spoiled as this ill-omened creature." He tickled the back of Coronis' neck.

"Citizen Capell! God save you."

A man it was hard to ignore came through the service entrance. He strutted into the coffee booth in his red wig: a cheery cockerel amid his roost. He clapped his hands and held out his arms in a gesture of embrace. Tammo nodded stiffly at the caffe host, and the arms went back down again. Armide was learning not to attempt embracing Tammo, unless he wished for Coronis to use his arms as she used the dado rail. He leaned over the birdcage and whistled.

"That's a remarkable delivery you have there, citizen. What do you call those? They don't look big enough to be real." He peered closer. "They never stop moving, do they?"

"Flamecrests. You get them from deep in the forest." Tammo swallowed another mouthful of coffee.

"Well, you do, Citizen Capell. You do. I wouldn't have the first idea where to find the things. To each his own gifts, that's what I say."

"Yes."

"And for whom are these fine specimens destined, if I might ask?"

"The Cavalier Argante. An anniversary gift for his wife."

For a moment, it looked as though Armide was about to launch into a recitation of more tedious gossip. But suddenly his face changed, and he fumbled in his apron pocket.

"I almost forgot, Citizen Capell. Two letters came for you this morning."

At last! Tammo held out a hand, trying to conceal his impatience.

"The ink was barely dry when the runner brought this first one. It can't have come far. And the second one has a noble seal."

"Thank you." Tammo prised the letters from between Armide's fingers. The proprietor carried on standing where he was. "That will be all. God save you."

"You don't… Will you be wanting your room tonight?" Armide's eyes were still on the letters.

"Not tonight."

Tammo's fingers twitched over the seal of the top letter. When was the lackwit going to leave? Doing business from Caffe Armide was generally a good arrangement. It was easy to pick up custom in such a fashionable meeting place, and messages could be passed via Armide much more easily than they could, had a messenger had to visit Tammo at Grimaldi's cottage in Angel's Wood. The only inconvenient part of the arrangement was that Armide was so infernally nosy. The last thing Tammo needed was a caffe host with a mouth that chattered like the River Harmonica, reading all his mail.

At last, a crash and a yelp from Michelangelo forced

Armide to hurry from the booth. Tammo held the letter up to the light and gave a wry smile. The handwriting on the outside was as familiar as flat bread and stew on a winter's night. It had been sealed with a ring, but the sigil wasn't that of any noble house. It was a six-winged creature, surrounded by stars. A seraph. Tammo took out a pocket knife and broke the seal in one movement. A scent of jasmine and rose petals wafted up to greet him. He shook the letter open. As he did so, a third letter fell onto the table. Tammo felt his throat narrow as he saw the single name written on it: *Celestina*. He snatched up the first letter and began to read.

Tamino, my dearest twin,

I cannot describe to you my joy on waking this morning to find myself home again in our beloved Angelio and near to you once more. We would have arrived sooner, but the roads yesterday were dreadful, and the poor horse became lame. Casale is busily unpacking as I write, but I fear it will be some days before my familiar surroundings emerge from all the trunks and packing straw. I have several gifts for you, and I will not allow you to refuse them this time, whatever protests you may make.

May I ask you a favour, dear twin? I find myself with an unexpected engagement this morning, which means I will be unable to call on Noblesse Celestina as soon as I would have liked. Could you possibly deliver this letter to the Pageno mansion for me? I would be eternally obliged, and I know she would be, too.

I will wait for you tonight in our usual spot at the hour of the evening stroll. How I long to see your face again!

Your devoted and loving twin,
Carlo.

Tammo let out a controlled breath. His friend was back. His sworn twin. It seemed only yesterday that he and Carlo had played together at the Conservatorio Archangeli. They had met quite by chance. Carlo was a pampered eunuch soprano and Tammo a charity pupil, when Tammo had tumbled through Carlo's dormitory window. What mischief they had got up to, climbing the lime tree, singing through windows, smuggling Orpheus, the song thrush, under Carlo's cassock!

Then came the miracle. Tammo and Carlo had been lucky enough to meet their city's patron, the Archangel Michael, in person. Carlo had bargained away a little of his health and strength to grant Tammo the ability to charm birds with his dark flute. Tammo had made a bargain, too. A companion for Carlo, so he would not be friendless and misunderstood in the aristocratic world he must inhabit as a sopranist. Celestina. How could Tammo have known at the time the sacrifice he must make for such a gift?

How he had longed to see her, the night he and Carlo sneaked out of school to visit the Carnival by night. That had been a disaster! Carlo had lost Count Pageno's patronage as a result, and Tammo had been forced to flee before the maestri sent him to Fiorentina. That was when Tammo had found his home in the woods with Grimaldi the blacksmith. It had taken a second miracle to put everything right.

Could you possibly deliver this letter to the Pageno mansion for me?

Tammo sighed. Only one day in Angelio, and already Carlo was stirring up matters Tammo would much rather leave alone. That was the trouble with having his sworn twin back home. When Carlo was on his travels, touring the theatres, churches and salons of the continent, Tammo could keep his head down and absorb himself in the birding business. Michael knew, it gave him enough work! But the moment his castrato friend came back to Angelio, everything came back with him. The opera, Carnival, and of course Celestina.

Beautiful Celestina! Noblesse of the House of Pageno. She was the companion he had begged the Archangel to give Carlo. The moment Tammo met her, he understood the sacrifice he must make so Carlo could enjoy that gift. To have her always before his sight, an angel on this earth, knowing his love must forever remain unrequited.

It wouldn't be so bad if it weren't for the times Tammo and she had come so close. For example, the night he and Carlo had saved Celestina's life. Was that really two years ago? She had been deathly sick, and they had broken into her chamber to sing and play the flute at her bedside, attracting Michael's presence with their music. Michael had healed Celestina, and restored everything Tammo and Carlo had lost.

Later that night, while Carlo was speaking with the Count, Tammo and Celestina had been alone. He had played his flute for her, and she had smiled and clapped her hands. He had given her a ring. A carnival face in a black mask, surrounded by jewels. The ring Carlo had given him when they pledged eternal twinship. True, Tammo felt some guilt on parting with it, but it was the only thing of value he possessed. The only thing worthy of a lady. Did she still have it, he wondered? Did she ever wear it and think of him, just for a moment?

He read the letter through again. *I would be eternally obliged, and I know she would be, too.* Damn Carlo! Tammo struck the table, making the flamecrests flutter against the bars of their cage. How could he possibly resist such a plea? It was as if Carlo was there in person, simpering and fluttering his eyelashes.

"Here we go again, Coronis." He put his coffee dish down upon the papers, as if to neutralise their power. "Let's see what's in this other letter."

It was sealed with a shield, marked with three bells and a rose. Tiny bits of pale green wax crumbled to the table as Tammo sliced with his pocket knife, releasing a scent of gardenia. The handwriting was even more effeminate than Carlo's. The message was brief and to the point.

The Marchesa della Pamina would be pleased to have Citizen Capell call on her at his earliest convenience, with an appropriate sample of his wares, to discuss a possible commission.

"Ha! This is the one, Coronis!"

Tammo ruffled the crow's feathers. She cawed and flapped to the table, then back to the dado rail. Tammo leaned back, running his thumb over the rounded script with its delicate flourishes. The Marchesa della Pamina. He had heard a rumour (probably from Armide, he hated to admit) that she was becoming quite the leader of fashion this season. Strange. Tammo shrugged. The Paminas were an old family, going back to the days of the second duke, but they hadn't been fashionable since before his grandfather's time. There was no accounting for fashion. That was another thing Carlo understood much better than he did.

He leaned out from his seat to bring into view the bell tower with its triple-dialled clock. A quarter to ten. He ought not to linger too long.

"Good news, citizen?"

Tammo started. Armide had appeared at his elbow again, wiping his hands on his apron in a too-obvious gesture of nonchalance. He leaned forward slightly, trying to read Tammo's letter upside-down. Tammo scooped all the papers from the table and stuffed them in his coat pocket.

"I'll be on my way."

He downed the last drop of coffee and flung a handful of centesimi on the table.

"God save you, Citizen Armide. Come, Coronis."

He had almost reached the door when a soft "Excuse me," stopped him. The pigtailed foreigner was at his shoulder.

"You must not leave without your birds, young citizen." He spoke good Angelian, with almost no accent. "Your skill with them means a great deal to you, I'm sure."

The man held the cage of flamecrests toward Tammo.

There was a smile on his lips that suggested he was withholding secret knowledge.

Tammo scowled, hoping his scar was enough to scare the man off. Interfering busybody! Standing there with his Ming robes and his insufferable politeness. Tammo would have realised his mistake soon enough. He didn't need it pointing out.

He snatched the cage from the foreigner's hand. The man had soft skin and manicured nails. Might as well be a eunuch, Tammo thought. Maybe he was. The Ming had court eunuchs, didn't they?

As if one eunuch in his life wasn't trouble enough. Look at the scrape Carlo had already landed him in. Two aristocratic women to deal with. And it was not yet noon.

"God save you," he growled, and went out into the piazza.

The flamecrests were delivered. The Cavalier Argante had been pleased with them and, even better, had instructed his agent to pay Tammo there and then. He could feel the weight of silver in his pocket as he made his way along the tree-lined avenue toward the Pageno mansion. The very first leaves were beginning to turn yellow. As Tammo passed under a maple, one fluttered down and brushed his shoulder, making Coronis croak.

He cleared his throat and straightened his cravat as he gazed up at the burnt umber façade of the Pageno mansion. The golden pheasant that was the family crest spread its wings over the portico, overlooking the flight of stairs that led up to the main entrance. The back of Tammo's head prickled with sweat. Ought he to use the back entrance? This wasn't really a tradesman's errand, but Tammo preferred to be greeted by lower servants who would treat him with respect, than to face Caesar or Pompey at the front door with their footmen's faces on.

"And you can shut up," he said, as Coronis gave a caw and flapped into the branches of a maple tree. "I am not a coward. Just prudent, that's all."

He made his way down the paved walkway to the left-hand side of the mansion and knocked on the wicket gate set into the high double doors. A red-nosed face looked out and grinned.

"Oh, it's you, Citizen Capell. God save you."

Tammo gave what was supposed to be a lordly nod, glad of the extra dignity the wig and broadcloth suit gave him. He had worked hard over the last two years to make sure the porter saw him as Bird Charmer to the Nobility and intimate friend of Signor Seraphini. Mostly, it worked.

He followed the porter into the courtyard at the back of the mansion, past the stables and coach houses, past the well where a scullery maid was drawing water and chatting with a stable boy. Close by, a laundress was pegging out linen. A little child tottering round her skirts threatened to trip her up. There was a smell of lye in the air. It must be a washing day.

A familiar voice brought Tammo up short. "Don't you

dare scrub those petticoats like that! Have you any notion how much that lace cost? Lackwit!"

There was a yelp as though someone had been struck, before the laundry room door banged open and a very short person in a white cap and apron came storming out, her hips leading the way. She raised her hands to the heavens.

"Sweet Michael, help us! Am I surrounded by bottle-heads?"

Tammo made a quick calculation of the distance to the servants' entrance and the time it would take to reach it before he was spotted. Too late. The expression on the woman's face changed to that of a horse trader who has spotted a prize stallion. She sidled over to Tammo, hands on hips.

"Well, well, if it isn't Tammo Capell, come to brighten little Fenice's day."

"God save you, Fenice." Tammo tried to ignore the amount of bosom directed at his waistcoat buttons.

Fenice tossed her head. "Well, I must say, I expected better than that. Don't think I've forgotten last Victory Day. You were more than keen to show me your flute that night. So, don't come snubbing me now."

"Fenice!" Tammo's face flared red. He glanced about to see whether the laundress and scullery maid had heard Fenice's words. "It wasn't like that and you know it."

Tammo had only a hazy memory of what it was like. The truth was that he had drunk an unwise amount of port wine during the feast of Saint Michael of Victory, and found himself climbing through the window of the belvedere tower to Fenice's sewing room. The rest was a rather jumbled impression of stays and ribbons and Fenice's bare chest. It wasn't the first time such a thing had happened, but Tammo was determined it was going to be the last. Fenice wasn't even his type. And he certainly wasn't in love with her.

He tugged his cravat and tried to feel like Bird Charmer to the Nobility. "Aren't you back with Pompey, anyway? Strangely, I have no taste for getting my face smashed in. I'm ugly enough."

Fenice snorted.

"Oh, him, the great lump! He's taken up with the new chambermaid. Mincing little creature! I'm well done with him. Any time you care to call, I'll be waiting."

"I told you…" Tammo began, but Fenice thumped him on the arm and burst into throaty laughter.

"Oh, the look on your face! You are so easy to gull!"

"What's going on here? Is this his lordship's courtyard or a public tavern? Less chattering and more working. Fenice, her ladyship needs you upstairs. Citizen Capell. I would appreciate you not distracting my staff."

"Signor Plattini. God save you." Tammo made a bow to the count's major-domo, who was standing in the servants' entrance, veins throbbing in his temples. Seriously, every time Tammo saw that man, he was in a fluster. It was a miracle he didn't have an apoplexy. Tammo held up the letter. "I have a message from Signor Seraphini to Noblesse Celestina."

"Then why didn't you come to the front door and give

it to Caesar?" Signor Plattini wiped his forehead with a handkerchief. "Come in. I'll give it to a footman."

Tammo followed the major-domo through the door and down the long service corridor. At the end of it was a dining room, where two men in maroon coats and white wigs were laying out silverware. Each fork was being carefully turned face-down so that the large cuffs of fashionable coats would not catch on them. As ever, Tammo found himself wondering why so many different forks were needed. That was another matter Carlo would know about.

"Leonardo." One of the footmen looked up at the sound of Signor Plattini's voice. "A letter has arrived for the noblesse. She's in the music room. Now, if you please," the major-domo added, as the man hesitated over a silver cruet. "Giulio can finish here."

The footman bowed, picked up a silver salver from the sideboard, and left with Tammo's letter balanced on it. Signor Plattini beckoned Tammo through the breakfast room and into a gallery hall.

"Wait here," he said. "There may be a reply. I'll send Leonardo back to you." He strode out of sight.

Tammo clasped his hands behind his back and tried not to feel as out of place as a fish on a fruit stall. The walls were covered in paintings, gods and saints and Pageno ancestors, and he felt like they were watching him, criticising his serviceable coat and pinched features.

He tightened his grip on the leather case that hung from his hip in place of a sword. The dark flute was inside.

Touching it, Tammo convinced himself that he could feel something of the Archangel's power. He ought to have felt confident, a successful tradesman with his pocket full of silver. But standing here made him feel as if he was fourteen years old again, a charity boy with a voice like a crow and a scar on his face.

"Just Carlo's messenger. That's all I am."

He turned his face toward a friendlier painting, a little boy around eight years old, wearing a blue velvet suit and spotless stockings. A greyhound sat at his feet, and on his shoulder was a monkey that Tammo recognised as the mischievous Giacomo. The boy gazed into the distance, as though he was itching to run off and have adventures, although Tammo knew this boy's adventuring days would be over not long after the painting was complete. This was Orlando, Celestina's late brother, who had died in childhood. Carlo had been a cherub child at his funeral, and there met Celestina for the first time. Looking at the painting, Tammo could see the resemblance between brother and sister. The heart-shaped face and soft, brown hair. And something about the expression around the eyes. Tammo felt his throat constrict, and hastily looked for another picture to inspect.

A smile came to his face as he noticed a small portrait hanging over the doorway. That was Carlo. It must have been painted shortly after Count Pageno became his patron. He looked barely fourteen years old. His face was soft and full-cheeked, like a cherub, and there was a smile hovering over his Cupid's lips. How proud he must have been, to be painted in the house of his patron! A sudden yearning came over Tammo, to see his friend again. The hour of the evening stroll couldn't come soon enough. It would be like old times, the two of them laughing and joking together, just as they had as boys.

He was so absorbed in memories that he didn't immediately register the whirring, cranking sound coming closer. The moment he did, he whirled round, his palms sweating. Celestina was in her house carriage. The lacquer and gold glinted in the morning sunlight. She was turning the handles to drive it forward, the wheels running smoothly over the marble floor. Tammo took off his hat and made an awkward bow. How did she manage to become more beautiful every time he saw her? He scarcely knew where to look.

Celestina clasped her hands in delight. "Tammo Capell the bird charmer! When Leonardo told me you were waiting in the gallery, I simply had to come. These things are so much better face to face, don't you think?"

That smile. Always that smile. Even though she was now eighteen years old, there was so much of the little girl in her expressions.

Tammo cleared his throat. "Noblesse. A pleasure." He hoped she couldn't hear the blood pounding in his head, as he could.

"And how is dear Carlo?" Celestina said. "Have you seen him yet? He was supposed to come here to call on Papa, but then something came up and they're meeting elsewhere. Do tell him I was glad to receive his note. I long to see him again, don't you?"

"Yes, Noblesse." Tammo was unsure which part of Celestina's speech he was answering. She flitted from one subject to another like a butterfly, and Tammo was never able to keep up. "I will speak with him this evening. I'm sure he looks forward to seeing your ladyship again."

Celestina put a hand to her mouth and giggled.

"You call me ladyship. How sweet!" She glanced up at the portrait of Carlo. "How long it seems since we were children together! Do you remember that time I lay sick?" She lowered her eyelashes. "You and Carlo came into my chamber to sing and play me back to health. Right into my chamber! Whatever would Mama say to that now?"

Tammo felt a tide of red creep up his face. He ransacked his mind for something else to say.

"Do you remember the carnival ring I gave you, Noblesse?" His voice came out as a strangled growl. "The night we…that Carlo and I…"

"But of course!" Celestina's eyes sparkled like opals. She pulled on an indigo ribbon at her neck and drew out from beneath her fichu, a black ring in the shape of a jolly face. It had jewels for eyes and a red mouth, and was surrounded by gemstones of topaz and garnet.

Celestina gave a smile. She dropped the ring back into her bosom and it disappeared. Tammo tried not to think about where it had gone.

"I wear it always. How could I not? Considering who gave it."

"That is most generous of you, noblesse. Most…er… generous."

She wore the ring always. Around her neck, close to her heart. She had worn it every day for the past two years. And why? Because of who gave it. Because of Tammo Capell.

Tammo could have sworn the saints and gods in the paintings began to sing.

2

Primo Castrato

The music box was playing, "Where are you, Beloved?"

Carlo smiled as he took a spoon and lifted the cream from his morning chocolate. Both the box and the chocolate recipe had been gifts to Carlo from the Kapellmeister of Festeburg, where automata-making was the chief industry. The song was one that Carlo had sung there, in a masque called *The Lonely Shepherd*. The front of the box showed a pair of lovers in a garden, who moved slowly from left to right as the music played.

The chocolate was a delicious concoction of whipped cream, sugar, spices and orange peel, well-known in Festeburg for its fortifying properties. It would be just the thing, the Kapellmeister had said, to stave off winter colds.

He held out his right hand. Orpheus the song thrush, who had been flying back and forth across the apartment in time to the music, alighted on Carlo's finger with a shiver of wings.

"You know who loves you, don't you, beautiful boy?" Carlo cooed, stroking his back. In response, many voices twittered from cages hanging from the ceiling. The nightingales and bullfinches seemed happier today; they hadn't enjoyed the carriage ride. Carlo dipped a buttered roll in his chocolate and winked at them.

It was just as he'd imagined it during childhood. An apartment of his own, with fresh flowers in porcelain bowls and pet birds filling the air with song. A soft bed. Beautiful clothes to wear. True, the apartment's window overlooked the stables, which meant that certain smells did battle with Carlo's array of perfumes, but at least there was a ready home for all the packing straw that Casale still hadn't cleared away. They'd had to un-nail another box this morning to retrieve Carlo's songbooks and spare writing paper. The music box had been with them.

Carlo let the tune play on, slowing, slowing, as he finished the bread roll and lifted the chocolate dish to his lips. There was work still to do before the apartment became home. A curtain at the window would be pretty, and a few rugs would keep his feet warm in winter. He wished there was room for a harpsichord, but the spinet he'd bought in Fiorentina looked well under the window. Hopefully, while Carlo was out today, Casale would find time to hang his engravings.

"Your daily draught, Signor. And the washing water you asked for."

"Thank you, Casale."

Carlo put down the dish. Casale, his long, tawny face a picture of concentration, attempted to make room on the circular table for a tray. Its contents rattled as they slid into each other: a bowl, jug and soap, a glass vial of something rosy, and a metal spoon.

Carlo tactfully ignored his manservant's struggles by cooing to Orpheus again. He knew better than to offer assistance. Casale treated his duty toward Carlo as a matter of religious devotion. From what little Carlo knew of Casale's background (his almond eyes and coily hair suggested it involved a meeting of nations) Casale was the first person in his family to rise to the lofty position of personal manservant. It would damage the poor man's dignity for Carlo to perform domestic tasks for himself, even if that did sometimes mean that the tasks took twice as long.

Eventually, Casale managed to put the tray down without losing the towel that hung over his arm, and poured Carlo a spoonful of mixture from the vial. Despite the Festeburg chocolate, Casale insisted that his master take a dose of rosehip syrup every morning. It was an irritation in his otherwise balmy life, but sadly necessary. Carlo had always felt the cold more than most. But ever since his bargain with the Archangel, and especially since that first illness after Carnival, he tired easily without regular rests and was particularly susceptible to catching colds in the winter. He turned to his manservant, who was now struggling to lather up a piece of oatmeal soap.

"What do they say in the markets about the weather this season, Casale? Have you heard these rumours of a cold snap?"

Casale lifted his eyes, as if the recording angel of

weather might be found on Carlo's ceiling. "That's what they're saying, Signor. A hot summer and a cold winter. Il Cupide's manservant says his hollow tooth is aching, and that's a sure sign of cold weather to come. Would you like me to lay out the coat with the fur collar, Signor?"

"Not yet, Casale." Carlo smiled. It was still warm enough to eat breakfast with the window open. He wasn't going to wear fur until he needed it. "Just take away the breakfast things so I can wash." He sighed. "I hope this ink comes off."

Carlo turned up the sleeves of his dressing gown, to avoid wetting the blue and red floral embroidery. He hoped oatmeal soap with lavender would be strong enough to remove ink stains. Tammo still swore by good old lye, but that stuff took half your skin off and made you smell like a pigeon loft. A castrato should always have beautiful hands.

It was a pity the quill had broken when it did, right in mid-sentence. Carlo had been sleepy, not expecting to have to write letters so early in the morning. The one from Count Pageno had arrived before he got up. Carlo frowned, rubbing the soap into his fingernails. He'd almost forgotten what an early riser his patron was. Carlo had said goodbye to six o'clock starts when he graduated from the conservatorio to the life of a professional singer. Operas and late-night concerts left one needing a little more sleep in the morning.

He had intended to call upon Count Pageno as his first duty this morning, but the letter had changed that.

Please go directly to Maestro Sarastro's house. There has

been a development in the Duke's plans which I must convey to you both as a matter of urgency.

It was oddly mysterious.

Everyone knew that Count Pageno was regarded as the Duke's right-hand man, but to advise musicians of court affairs was unusual, unless it was something that affected the opera. Carlo pressed his lips together. Let him not lose his big opportunity! After two years of touring theatres and churches around the Apostolic Empire, Count Pageno had brought him back to the home of the art musical, to be secondo castrato on the boards of the Duke's own opera house.

Carlo had been longing for this chance. To be back in Angelio with his beloved Tamino and soul mate Celestina, and to sing for the Duke alongside his childhood idol, Morestelli. Surely Saint Michael would not tip his scales to reverse that fortune? He loved Carlo more than that.

Carlo dried his almost ink-free hands on the towel, as Casale came back to brush his hair. He had a couple of wigs for special occasions, but the younger castrati tended to wear their own hair, loose and flowing. Carlo's chocolate curls, so closely cropped at the conservatorio, now fell to his shoulders, soft and pretty as a girl's. When Casale held up the hand mirror for Carlo to inspect his handiwork, a grown-up cherub looked back at him. Full lips, peachy cheeks, long eyelashes. Perhaps slightly plumper than a twenty-year-old ought to be, but far from being a capon. He looked well. As he had in the dormitory as a boy, Carlo composed his features into a heroic expression, the sort

Hector might have assumed at the walls of Troy. He would meet his fate with courage and dignity.

"Nightingale!"

A voice stopped Carlo halfway down the staircase of the singers' lodgings. He paused and smiled. Nobody called him by his schoolboy nickname any more. The speaker could be only one person. Carlo had heard he was among the company this season.

"Where have you been hiding?" The voice meandered down the stairwell in a lazy stream. "There was a grand tournament at the billiard hall last night. Rossetti was playing. I kept waiting for you to walk through the door."

"So, I'm a ghost now, Giovanni, walking through walls and doors?" Carlo answered, looking up.

The eunuch following him down the stairs may well have been a ghost; he was powdered so white. He wore a beauty spot in the coquette position, and a whole cloud of ringlets, even more fastidiously curled than his one famous ringlet at school had been.

"Oh, lord, Nightingale! You're far too sharp for me this early in the morning." Giovanni gave an affected yawn.

Carlo smiled and shook his head. It was already after nine. He hadn't seen his old schoolmate since the opera of Perseus, in which Carlo, Giovanni and Giuseppe had played the Three Graces. But, sadly, this was not the time for conversation.

"Excuse me, Giovanni," he said. "I have a most pressing engagement. We'll speak soon."

He could not allow himself to be late for Count Pageno and the maestro. The sweet cream he had eaten with his chocolate was already churning uncomfortably in his stomach.

"Oh, let me walk with you for a while. I was just on my way to Caffe Armide."

"Very well." Carlo tried not to envy Giovanni the chance of seeing Tammo at the caffe. Or to mourn the loss of his quiet walk. Sometimes it was easier to go along with things.

At the foot of the stairs was a little vestibule with green painted walls. The keeper of the guest house was standing by the front door, chatting and laughing with a plump, bass-voiced man. Carlo was unsure what to make of the "house mother" so far. The woman had shocking red hair that was certainly not natural, and a scant number of teeth, but she seemed a friendly sort.

"Good morning, Signor Seraphini!" She beamed as Carlo approached. Carlo winced inwardly. Her breath stank, and it looked as if she had put on her makeup with a paint brush. He fixed a smile to his features.

"God save you, Citizeness Aldo. And what a delightful morning it is, when graced by your charming face."

The housekeeper cackled and reached up to pinch Carlo's cheek.

"Aren't you a little ray of sunshine? I could just eat you up."

The bass snorted into his handkerchief, trying to conceal laughter.

"Have you met your colleague, Signor Scipione?" Citizeness Aldo tried to assume the air of a fine lady, unaware that anything was amusing. "I believe he also attended the conservatorio."

"I did, indeed." Scipione gave a little bow and smiled, revealing teeth too small for his mouth.

"These are two of our sopranists, Signors Seraphini and Parnasso." The Citizeness was clearly enjoying her self-appointed role as hostess.

"Charmed." Giovanni bowed to the bass singer. There was something about the bow and the tone of Giovanni's voice that was faultlessly polite without being friendly.

Carlo felt a twinge in his stomach. Was it necessary to bring schoolboy hierarchy into the adult world? They were all singers in the Teatro now, and if a bass didn't rank as highly as a soprano, that was surely cause to be more gracious to the man, not less. "A pleasure to meet you," he told Scipione with a smile. "I look forward to singing with you. Now, if you'll excuse us, we must be on our way."

"Do you see anything of Giuseppe these days?" said Carlo, as he and Giovanni left the building and crossed the courtyard between the singers' apartments and the Teatro. At school, pale Giovanni and the florid Giuseppe had been a pair of inseparables, and constantly in trouble. It was strange now to see one without the other.

Giovanni made a languid gesture.

"I saw him once at Latinum. He sings in the cathedral

choir there. Such a dreadfully pious place; I don't know how he stands it. No women are allowed on stage at all, which is why the opera there required my touch…" He simpered.

"You must have been a very Diana," Carlo said. He raised an eyebrow. "I do hope you made the most of your cleavage." It had been a standing joke at the conservatorio, made whenever a boy had to play female roles.

Giovanni twirled a ringlet around his finger.

"Always, darling."

Maestro Sarastro lived in a yellow house, a short walk from the Teatro. Unlike most musicians, the Duke's Master of the Art Musical was able to afford his own property and a certain measure of privacy. Carlo pondered this, as he knocked on the door and was shown through to the rehearsal room by a manservant. Having one's own space might be pleasant on occasion, but Carlo had never known life without the bustle and chatter of other people close by. He certainly couldn't live out in the woods, as Tammo did. It would be like cutting off a stream at its vital source.

He found the maestro standing by the harpsichord. Before Carlo was through the door, Sarastro strode across the room, embroidered coat tails swinging, seized Carlo by the shoulders and kissed him smartly on both cheeks.

"Bianci! Good to have you back, my boy. You look well-fed. The Kapellmeister of Festeburg fill you up with sausage, did he?"

"God save you, maestro." Carlo smiled, wrapping Sarastro in a hug.

At six feet three, Carlo now towered above his old tutor. He stood back and let the maestro admire his lace cuffs, the fullness of his coat skirts, the intricate stitching around his buttonholes. Within minutes, Sarastro gave a snort and swaggered toward a doorway at the back of the room.

"Yes, yes. Very fine. No doubt you'll be trading it in for something finer by the end of the week. Now, don't be wasting his lordship's time or mine, Bianci. I have two lackwit copyists in there who couldn't be trusted to write out a laundry list correctly without supervision." He opened the door and yelled through it. "Make sure you get the bloody key signatures right this time!"

Carlo cast his eyes about the room. Count Pageno was sitting at a round table by the window. Carlo had not noticed him. How remiss of him not to greet his patron first! He made a deep bow. "God save your lordship."

The hint of a smile danced in the Count's grey eyes. There were more lines around them now, Carlo noted. The Duke's family problems could be to blame for that! Being right-hand man to the ruler of Angelio had many privileges, but many more challenges, and Count Pageno was not a man to shirk his responsibilities. Carlo wondered what had brought him to the maestro's house this morning, instead of waiting for Carlo to call on him at the mansion. There was something in the air that crackled with conspiracy.

"I'm glad to see you in good health, Carlo." Count

Pageno held out his hand. Carlo dropped to one knee and kissed his patron's ring. He was rewarded by a fatherly pat on the head.

"May the Archangel ever preserve and bless you, my Lord," Carlo said, and meant it.

The Count nodded and motioned for Carlo to stand. "I shall come straight to the point," he said. "Signor Morestelli will not be joining you at the Teatro this season."

Carlo's eyes widened. A Carnevale season at the Teatro without the great Morestelli! It was unthinkable. Morestelli had been Carlo's childhood hero. He had even sung alongside him once, at the Count's Twelfth Night banquet, when he was just a boy. Singing secondo castrato to Morestelli's primo this season was meant to be the highlight of his career so far. He glanced round to where Maestro Sarastro stood, but the maestro seemed perfectly composed. He must have already been told.

"Is he unwell, my lord?" Carlo allowed himself to say.

The Count touched a finger to his lip, running his thumb across his cheek. His signet ring winked in the sun. "Shall we say he is…indisposed? And leave it at that."

Carlo recognised that stern, charcoal tinge to his patron's eyes. *No further questions.* Maestro Sarastro cleared his throat and tucked his hands behind his coat tails. There was a conspiracy somewhere, possibly at the highest level. Carlo wondered if his maestro was in on the secret. There would be no way of telling.

"And therefore…" The Count rubbed his chin. "Oh,

you tell him, Sarastro. I can see you're about to burst with it."

"And therefore, Bianci, you will be singing primo in the Teatro di Palazzo. So, you'd bloody well better get practising. Five arias a night. With encores. At least there had better be encores or I shall want to know why!"

Carlo looked from his tutor to his patron and back again. His chest was swelling, larger and larger. His cravat tightened around his neck. "Primo? But I'm not yet one-and-twenty. That is to say…" His nose began to prickle. Tears welled in his eyes. He dropped to his knees before the Count again. "This is an undeserved honour, my lord."

"Nonsense." Count Pageno ruffled Carlo's curls, as though he was thirteen years old again. "I would not have sent you around the Empire if I didn't believe in your talent. The music lovers of Fiorentina and Vulcanetta have been praising you to the skies. You are more than ready for this."

Carlo nodded, trying hard not to sniffle before his lordship. Primo castrato. The most important singer in the opera. He had dreamt of this moment since he had sung for Signor Bernardi in the country church where he grew up. Worked for it every day at the conservatorio. But for it to come so soon…

"And by way of introducing you, his grace also wishes for you to return the hymn of thanksgiving at Homecoming Mass in the Sancti Michaelis."

"My lord?" Now Carlo's tears were really flowing. It was like a dream, a song. One more moment and he would explode with happiness!

"There, now." Count Pageno gave a fatherly smile. "Dry your tears. You represent the House of Pageno; never forget that."

Carlo felt in his pocket for a handkerchief, beaming like the sun on the clock face of Giustizia bell tower. There was only one thing that could make his happiness greater: the moment when he shared the good news with his twin.

Carlo's heart pounded as his footsteps echoed down the steps to the crypt. Six by the clock. The hour of the evening stroll. He had been waiting for this all day. He wanted to run, but the worn and twisted stairs were not made for hurrying. He would have to be patient. Just a few heartbeats longer. Surely, he could hold out that long after all these months?

At the foot of the stairs, he ducked his head under the low door lintel. Whoever designed the cathedral had clearly not considered the height of your average eunuch. Blinking in the dimmer light, he saw the familiar vaulted chambers of the cathedral's underbelly, the carven pillars lit by smoking flares, the sarcophagi and reliquaries guarded by wrought iron. Just the same as it was every year. The familiar meeting place. The familiar memories. And a familiar figure who turned to greet him as he ran with open arms.

"Tamino! My dearest twin!"

Carlo almost lifted his friend off the ground in the violence of his embrace. He held on tightly, drinking in the scent of the woodland and charcoal smoke, feeling the rough touch of woollen weave against his chin. His twin. His Tamino. He kissed his friend's scarred cheeks, once, twice, three times. A weathered face. A man's face. Tammo seemed to drift a little further from boyhood every time Carlo went away. He hugged tighter, reminding himself that Tammo was here, now. They were together again, with the whole opera season before them.

Tammo's shoulders stiffened. "Carlo, I can't breathe down here for all your bloody perfume."

"My apologies." Carlo laughed to himself. His Tamino. Just the same as ever. He released his embrace and took a step back.

Tammo was shrugging his shoulders, scratching at his neck. Trying to pretend he was as unmoved by the meeting as were the marble sarcophagi. It never fooled Carlo for a moment.

Carlo touched his fingers to his lips. "You need a shave, dear twin. I fear you have given me beard rash."

Tammo snorted. "What do you know about shaving? A lady could eat her dinner off that pretty cheek."

Carlo raised an eyebrow. "Perhaps she has."

Tammo gave him a restrained punch on the upper arm. "Cock-Robin! Besides, I had a shave this morning, if you must know. Not for you. For a customer. I have some dignity around here, I'll have you know."

Carlo tapped his friend on the tip of the nose. "Of course, you do, my dear bristle-chin." He looked around the crypt. "Where's Coronis?"

"Managed to persuade her to wait outside." Tammo wrinkled his nose. "For some reason, they don't take kindly to crows in the house of God."

"If they knew her, they would think differently." Carlo began to walk toward a particular reliquary. "Dear Coronis! I long to see her again. And I'm sure Orpheus does too. Ah, Tamino! You don't know what a gift you gave me, when you gave him. It's like having a little part of you with me everywhere I go."

"He still keeps his good health then?" asked Tammo, as they reached the grille which protected the holy relic from impious fingers.

"Remarkably so." Carlo crossed himself and knelt, his twin following suit. "And he's so intelligent. You know, Tamino, I hear tell that mistle thrushes can speak seven languages."

"Orpheus is a song thrush." Tammo narrowed his eyes.

"Details, details. Now, stop distracting me, Tamino. You know this is important."

Tammo shook his head and sighed. Carlo fixed his eyes on the reliquary. He was bursting to tell Tammo his good news, but this came first. This always came first. Every year, as soon as Carlo returned from wherever the Count had sent him. A sacred ritual. The renewal of a promise.

Carlo stared through the iron grille. The reliquary was said to contain the tears of the first Duke's sister, a godly maiden who had founded the convent of Michaelis Curationum. However, it wasn't the crystal vial with its gold and silver filigree that Carlo saw. His mind's eye had gone back to a day seven years earlier, and a man in lace with gold buttons, who had stood in this very spot and looked with eyes of wheeling fire at two frightened schoolboys.

"Are you ready?" he said to Tammo.

Tammo gave a barely perceptible nod, and both began to speak in unison the words they had rehearsed and refined over the years:

"Beloved archangel and patron, merciful Saint Michael. We, your unworthy servants, Carlo Bianci and Tammo Capell, renew our vows before you this day. As you have gifted us, so we pledge to ever remain friends and brothers. We dedicate ourselves anew to your service. Protect us from harm, we pray, and weigh us not in the balance of your justice. *In nomine Patris, et Filii, et Spiritus Sancti.* Amen."

Both young men held out their right hand, kissed it, and crossed themselves once more. Carlo gave Tammo a nervous smile as they got to their feet.

Tammo scratched his neck. "I don't suppose you've, you know, seen him recently, have you? The Archangel."

Carlo's smile softened. "My dear Tamino, I've only just returned to Angelio. It is I who should be asking you. Citizen Capell." His eyes twinkled.

Tammo sniffed and toyed with the clasp of his flute case. "Sometimes I think I see him for a moment. In the marketplace sometimes, walking among the hawkers, or in the woods at dawn before the mist clears. A face, a shadow, the echo of his voice. But when I look again, it's always just a fishmonger or a tree."

Carlo couldn't help but giggle at such a prosaic ending. He patted Tammo on the hand. "Never fear, dear twin. He is with us always. And maybe this will be the year when we meet him again." His eyes glowed in the light of the flickering torches. "Now I must tell you, Tamino, before I burst. The most incredible news."

His voice became more animated, his arms waving in a dozen gestures as he told Tammo about his visit to the maestro's house, his promotion to primo, the Homecoming Mass.

Tammo gave a low whistle. "That is astonishing news! Not that they'd pick you, I mean. You were born for the Teatro." He gave a half smile and patted Carlo awkwardly on the arm. "But Morestelli… That is mysterious."

He frowned. Carlo gave a resigned smile. Mysterious equated to unwelcome in his twin's book. Tammo stared at his shoes and scratched harder at his neck. "I…er…delivered your message this morning."

"Oh yes. I almost forgot." Carlo leaned closer. "How is dear Celestina? I was so sorry to disappoint her like that."

"She's…she's well." Tammo cleared his throat. His voice had gone huskier than usual. Which was saying something. His vocal chords had been damaged in the fire that killed his family. Boys at the conservatorio used to call him Crow. "Yes, she was glad that you got in touch and all that." He shrugged. "You know I can never remember all that girl stuff."

Carlo shook his head. "I should use Coronis as a correspondent next time. She might be more forthcoming."

They began to walk back the way they had come, through the crypt and up the stairs to the nave of the cathedral.

"Will you stay at mine tonight?" Carlo asked as they walked out into the expanse of white and gold. The myriad cherubs that tumbled from every arch and pillar were slowly being covered by evening shadows. "There's plenty to eat, and Casale can easily make up your bed. I have some plum brandy, all the way from Vulcanetta."

Tammo grinned. "Why not? I'll have to be away early in the morning, though. Wouldn't want the old man to worry."

Carlo smiled to himself as they walked toward the pink sunset pouring through the great west door. Although either of them would die before admitting it, Grimaldi and Tammo were like father and son. Carlo knew for a fact that Tammo had paid for repairs to the old blacksmith's woodland cottage out of his own purse. That was one of the things he loved about his twin: his quiet generosity. That and so much more.

"I am glad to be back," he said.

Tammo gave him a sideways look. "I'm glad too."

Carlo pressed his lips together and looked down before Tammo could see him blushing. Tammo might be glad, but he would never be as glad as Carlo was to see his twin again.

Would this be the season he finally found the courage to speak his true feelings?

3

The Rosefinch

The carnival ring came floating toward Tammo out of a pineapple sky. Its diamond eyes glittered; its red lips grinned amid its black, black face. Its halo of topaz and garnet revolved, first clockwise, then anticlockwise. The nearer it came, the larger it grew. He could touch it, if only he dared…

It was no longer a ring. It was a full-sized moretta mask. How could he have thought it a ring, when Celestina was wearing it on her face? She was sitting on the sopha in the music room, her skirts covered in peach roses. Tammo was kneeling at her feet.

"If only you knew," she was saying. "I've been trying to tell you for so long."

He wanted to touch her face. For some reason, it was a lot further away than it looked. His hand felt like it was pushing through water. His fingers brushed the edge of the mask. Black velvet. As soft as kitten fur. The mask floated from Celestina's face of its own accord. It gently grazed

Tammo's cheek and spiralled away, up into the moulded ceiling.

It wasn't Celestina's face behind the mask. It was Carlo's. He was weeping tears of white stage paint. His eyes were huge; you could drown in them.

"What have you done?" he cried at Tammo. "I'm naked. Naked."

Naked. Nake. Ake. Ake. No, that wasn't Carlo. That was Coronis.

Tammo sat up and bashed his head on the interior of the box bed. Damn. For a moment, he'd thought he was still at Carlo's apartment. He rubbed his sore head, gradually coming around to the smell of charcoal, the scratchy blankets, the throaty snore from the other side of the fireplace.

Of course. He was in Angel's Wood. He moved about so much nowadays, especially in the opera season, that he could sometimes go for weeks without sleeping more than one night in the same bed. He had been at Carlo's the night before last, playing *scopa* and drinking plum brandy.

Tammo had drunk rather more than his friend, he suspected. Either that, or Carlo was more used to fine liquor. At any rate, Carlo had swept the board a ridiculous amount of times and captured the precious seven of coins more times than Tammo cared to count.

"It's a good thing we don't play for money, dear twin." Carlo had assumed a superior smile. "Or you would owe me half the birds in Angel's Wood."

"I'll owe you a poke in the eye if you don't stop your eunuch preening," Tammo had muttered.

In the morning, Casale had mixed a concoction of raw egg and myrrh for his aching head. It had eased the grogginess, but tasted vile.

"I think your manservant is trying to poison me," he had said to Carlo.

Carlo had just laughed, but Tammo had scowled at Casale anyway. He knew that Carlo needed a manservant now he was a professional sopranist, but Casale always made him suspicious. It was his—Tammo's—job to take care of Carlo. That was what he had promised the Archangel all those years ago. He didn't need Casale muscling in, thinking he could do it better.

He had left Carlo's in the morning loaded down with gifts. When Tammo had tried to protest, Carlo had insisted that most of them were unwanted gifts from admirers. Tammo was not so sure about that. He had staggered back to Angel's Wood with a second bottle of plum brandy, a set of lace cravats, an exquisite miniature book of flute melodies in the shape of a heart, and an enamel patch box bearing the legend: *Accept this trifle from a friend whose love for thee will never end.* Carlo had also wanted him to take a jewel-encrusted snuff box with a mechanical bird that flapped its wings and twittered when you opened it, but Tammo had refused.

"What would I do with a thing like that?" He had given Carlo his most sarcastic look. "Impress my many society friends? Give alley-lurkers a good reason to ramp me, more likely!"

Neither of them took snuff. Carlo thought it disgusting and bad for the voice, and Tammo had heard a rumour that Celestina disapproved.

"I just thought it looked so sweet," Carlo had replied. "And I'm sure you could find something to keep in it."

But, in the end, the little box had gone back in Carlo's travelling trunk. Tammo had to put his foot down somewhere. He hated being beholden to Carlo when it came to worldly goods. He was glad that he had his own business and money to spend.

There was an almighty fart from the other box bed, followed by a yawn like a bellowing bull. Tammo suppressed a chuckle. It seemed Grimaldi was awake at last.

Tammo threw off the blankets, determined to stock up the firewood and get the porridge on to simmer before the old blacksmith was up and about. Tammo worried about Grimaldi. He wasn't getting as much custom as he once did. There were blacksmiths down in town now, and Grimaldi refused to take on a proper apprentice to help him keep pace with them.

Tammo couldn't be with him all the time now he had his own business. The landlord at Caffe Armide displayed his trade cards and took orders for him, which meant he had to spend at least some of his nights there. And of course, he couldn't neglect Carlo, when Carnival only lasted from the Feast of Seraphim until Lent. He was glad that, when there were birds to charm, he could come home to Angel's Wood and make sure the old man was all right. The charcoal burners and gamekeepers kept an eye on him, but Grimaldi never really trusted them. Stubborn old goat! Tammo thought, as he lifted the latch from the wooden door and let in the white September dawn.

He went to relieve himself behind the trees, sniffing the early morning mist. The forest had that earthy, dry leaf smell that said autumn to Tammo, as clearly as if it was written on a page. In a month or so, summer would have faded completely. After that, the ground would harden. Food would be scarce, for man and beast alike.

In some ways, winter was easier for catching birds. They were easier to spot without leaf cover, taking greater risks in their quest for survival. But many of the prettier kinds had disappeared by November. Tammo didn't know where they went. Grimaldi said they went into ponds and turned into fish until spring, but that sounded like a fairy tale. Besides, when he was calling them, Tammo sometimes caught a glimpse in his mind of somewhere hot and grassy, with cats the size of donkeys, somewhere the birds seemed to know and longed to return to. That seemed like a fairy tale too, but it was better than ponds. At any rate, he hoped there was something good out there today. Something that would impress the Marchesa.

He brought in a new bundle of firewood from the box outside the door, and hung the small cauldron on its hook over the fire. He poked and fed the embers for a while until it was warmer, and began to stir the cold porridge. The cottage looked a lot less of a hovel than it had done five years ago. There was the second box bed for a start, with heart shaped holes cut into its cupboard doors. New furniture. Rush-plaited rugs. The roof was mended. The windows had decent shutters. Of course, one wall still belonged to the old ruin it was built against. Tammo couldn't do anything about that; the ruin belonged to the Duke. But it looked a lot more like a home now. Even Carlo had visited occasionally.

By the time they came to eat the porridge, Tammo had taken a fire pot out to the forge, sharpened some of Grimaldi's tools for him and picked some mushrooms he'd noticed growing in a little clearing. The blacksmith made no comment on Tammo's labours. He limped over to the fire and ladled the porridge into two wooden bowls as he always did.

"Going bird-charming today?" he asked through a mouthful.

Tammo nodded. It was a pointless question to which Grimaldi already knew the answer, but conversation with the blacksmith never got any deeper than this. After Carlo's prattle, it was a blessed relief.

"Aye. Thought so. Be careful around Faun Dell. It's still a quagmire after those rains last week."

"I know." Tammo pushed the porridge into his mouth as fast as he could. Now the smell of the forest was in his nostrils, he needed to be out in it. The spirit of freedom was calling.

"Aye, you know everything, you young men. Always rushing about. Never stop to think."

Grimaldi wiped porridge from his beard. Tammo tossed his empty bowl into a bucket of water and picked his teeth with a stick. The other night, Carlo had shown him a little brush with horse hairs, so you could scrub your teeth like the front step, and a matching tool to scrape your tongue clean. He'd just laughed. Sticks were quicker.

"I'll be back to change before I go into town," he said, strapping on his flute case and grabbing a cage.

"Oh well, I'll lay out your clothes, then," Grimaldi said to his back. "Give me something to do, since the fauns have done my other chores. I'm not infirm yet, lad."

"God save you!" Tammo yelled to the closing door, before the blacksmith could say anything else.

He turned away from the pony path and picked his way along the deer trail to the little River Harmonica. He stepped over roots and stones, his woollen stockings tied up with gaiters, his boot-tips soaking up dew. Mist swirled and danced around the trunks of trees as Tammo negotiated the ground's sudden rises and falls. Careful now, he told himself. It was almost rutting season and, though the deer were usually timid, he had seen stags lock antlers enough times to know the damage they could do when riled. Coronis called from one bough and then another, weaving her own quest among the trees. Tammo could hear her voice, coming from further away each time, as she sought out prey.

This was real life, Tammo thought, breathing in the rich, brown smell. Out in the wild. One man alone with nature. It beat itchy wigs and endless waiting in reception rooms any day. Not that he wasn't grateful for the aristocratic clients he had gained, thanks to Count Pageno. But this was what it was all about! The dark flute in his hand and birdsong in the trees. He turned his feet outward like a duck to manage a crumbly slope, breaking into a trot before pausing to get his bearings again. Yes. He could hear water gurgling ahead. It was going to be a good day's charming.

The little river was running swiftly, brown, and bubbling over stones that chuckled when the current turned them over. Under the canopy, the year had progressed more slowly than it had in the glades. Grass and ferns hung low over the water. Most of the trees still had leaves of summer green. One twirled into the river and glided away as Tammo scrambled onto the low bough of a willow. It was a good spot for charming. Birds came to the water to drink, or to catch insects. The trees gave them shelter, and gave Tammo a little cover, too. He put the dark flute to his lips and began to play.

Some days, he knew exactly which bird he was seeking. Patrons asked for specific favourites. A nightingale. A goldfinch. A pair of doves. Often, they specified what they wanted the birds to do as well. Tammo had a few regular "behaviours" listed on his card at Caffe Armide. (He never called them "tricks"; that was a word for charlatan showmen and market criers.) Birds that came when called were always popular, as were those that sang tunes from the opera. He found that buyers would pay higher, the more recent the song. That was where friendship with a castrato came in extra handy. By staying close to Carlo, he could learn melodies alongside his friend, and so present a society lady with a bird that sang arias from a new opera, the same day it opened in the Teatro.

Some patrons wanted custom behaviours. That was more expensive, of course. Nobles believed birds could do the most bizarre things! A cardinal had once asked for a starling that could recite the Creed. A colonel in the Duke's Guard had wanted Tammo to provide a flock of green and scarlet finches that could demonstrate battle manoeuvres on his mosaic floor, with miniature cannons. It had taken the intervention of the Count himself to persuade the man toward something less fatal. Tammo might pride himself on granting his patrons' wishes, but he would never risk the lives of his birds. Once you had felt their souls, alert and buoyant, you could never condemn them to suffering or death.

Today, however, his thoughts were less specific. A bird for a lady. Something to demonstrate his skills. His fingers danced over the dark flute, as his tongue stopped and fluttered, harmonising with the music of the river. Tammo could feel the sense of yearning, reaching out from flute to birds. *Come to me. Be mine.*

It was hard not to think of Celestina with such a thought inside him. She still wore the ring he had given her.

Did that mean she had feelings for him? Was it one of those subtle female codes, like fans or beauty spots? Carlo seemed to understand such things instinctively, while Tammo was left floundering in ignorance, like a fish on shore. If only he could speak with Celestina. Alone. As himself. Not a messenger from Carlo. To prove himself a worthy admirer. A knight-errant, kneeling at the feet of his queen.

He let his passion spill into the music, swelling under his fingers. *Come to me. Be mine.* A bird for a lady. Beguiling and vibrant, like Celestina's laughter. Something to prove his worth. He played an extended flourish, gentle and breathy. It was answered by a shrill *twee-twitoo* from the further shore. Tammo echoed the call, note for note, on the dark flute. He could see his duetting partner now. A male rosefinch had alighted among the ferns on the riverbank, pecking at the earth between the drying leaves. He was a handsome creature and seemed to know it. His crest was scarlet, his breast the pink of Carlo's silk waistcoats. He turned his bright bead of an eye to Tammo and *twee-twitoo-*ed again.

Perfect. Tammo had not expected to find a rosefinch near water so late in the year. For the Marchesa, it was the ideal gift. Three bells and a rose was the Pamina family crest. She would appreciate Tammo's subtle sign of deference. He dipped his flute toward the open door of the cage he had brought with him. The flute's music copied the rosefinch's song, down the octave and very soft. The bird shivered its wings and took flight across the river.

That's a good boy, Tammo said in his head. Come and meet the Marchesa.

The Pamina family had one of the older mansions in Angelio, one overlooking a piazza, not purpose-built in its own grounds like the Pageno mansion. They were an old family, but not one that Tammo had heard much about. Not before the second Marchesa had come along, three years ago. Now it seemed all of fashionable Angelio was tripping over its red heels to reach the Paminas' door. Especially ladies. And ladies, Tammo knew, had an insatiable taste for cage birds.

He took a right turn by the Teatro di Palazzo. A groom was leading three bay horses toward the Teatro stables. One of them shied and snorted at the sound of Coronis' caw. Tammo took a wide step to the side and narrowly avoided colliding with a milliner and the two hat boxes he carried. He was followed up the street by a washerwoman, a butcher's boy and a girl carrying a basket of dried lavender.

Tammo wrinkled his nose at the combined smell of lavender and raw mutton. This crowd had most likely arrived in response to the return of the singers. Painters, carpenters, chandlers and firework-makers would all do business here in the next few months. Once Carnival began, they'd be joined by those in less savoury trades. Women of the street, liqueur sellers, purveyors of cheap news sheets filled with gossip about Il Cupide's latest amours. Tammo was glad that Carlo stayed above that sort of thing. Tammo would seek out and punch in the face any print-shop man who sullied his twin's reputation in the streets.

Tammo's path led him toward the river and the Bridge of Glories, where he and Carlo had spent that ill-fated Carnival five years ago. Without doubt, it was one of Angelio's wonders. The present Duke's father had had it built when Tammo was still in skirts and soil-cloths. It was made entirely of white marble. To cross it, you had to pay a toll and climb a staircase, grander than that of the Pageno mansion, with cavorting cherubs on every projection. At the apex, you found yourself looking down at the river's traffic from a vaulted cloister, with window after arched window to frame your view.

Tammo had no time to stop and loiter. He was more concerned with making sure his hat didn't blow away and spoil his appearance for the Marchesa. He gave a grin that was half scowl. Imagine him doing that as a schoolboy! He'd have thought himself a fop of fops.

He took a moment to get his bearings, then descended in the direction of the Piazza Saint Seraphiel, where the candlelit market was held on Justice Night. It looked different without the stalls and stages, somehow smaller in the light of day. The walls of the buildings were a soft saffron, with oleanders and dahlias growing on the many balconies. In one corner stood the bell tower of Saint Seraphiel's church. A loggia sheltered the shops of the mask makers, working to have their best wares ready by Carnival. On the opposite side of the square was the object of Tammo's pilgrimage. He looked up at its facade, picking out the symbols of three bells and a rose. He tugged his cravat straight for the hundredth time that morning.

"Wait for me here, Coronis," he said. "I'm about to make us lots of money."

Calling on a Marchesa was anything but an intimate affair. To be admitted to the upstairs reception room, Tammo had to present his trade card at three different doors, to three different footmen, each more self-important than the last. When he got through the final door, he found that half of Angelio had arrived before him. Supplicants waited around the room like so many living statues. A nun with a couple of charity girls huddled under the folds of her cloak. A stocking-maker with a selection of stockings over one arm. A mask-maker holding a fabulous creation like half a forest with birds and butterflies nesting in it. A lawyer's clerk with a leather wallet. A matronly woman whose business Tammo couldn't guess. And a sour-faced rail of a fop that Tammo took for some cash-strapped relative. All struggled not to yawn or fidget in a room whose shutters were barely open, although it was past the tenth hour. All turned and scowled, as a footman whose self-importance touched imperial heights, announced:

"Citizen Tammo Capell. The bird charmer."

"Ah, Citizen Capell. Come closer, if you please. The early morning light irritates my eyes. Florian, a little privacy for the citizen."

The voice that came from the toilette table at the far

end of the room didn't so much speak, as breathe out. A sensation of lazy summer afternoons, and cornucopias overflowing with ripe fruit. As Tammo drew nearer, a wave of gardenia perfume flooded him. He made several futile attempts to gulp his Adam's apple down.

"Marchesa della Pamina." He swept off his hat and bowed in what was supposed to be a gallant gesture, cursing the frog-like sound his voice had become. "At your service, my lady."

The Marchesa laughed. A languid, throaty sound, like she had just woken up in a luxurious bed. A shaft of dusty light from the half-opened shutters illuminated her face. She was a striking woman, with green eyes that could pierce your soul, and curling auburn hair. And a great deal of white breast. Tammo's scalp prickled under his wig. He fought hard against the urge to scratch.

"At my service?" Her smiling lips were the pink of cherry blossom. "I sincerely hope so. Pray, put your birdcage on the table and let me see your wares. Thank you, Florian."

The footman placed a screen between Tammo and the roomful of hangers-on. It was bright blue and depicted a number of golden foreigners going in and out of golden tea houses. Tammo would not have called the resulting arrangement privacy. The Marchesa was attended at her toilette by a maid on the left, who was just now passing a string of pearls from her own warm neck to the Marchesa's; and a maid on the right, who was putting the finishing touches to the fontange that towered on the Marchesa's head like a lace rampart. A brown-faced page boy in a turban offered the Marchesa chocolate in a blue bowl.

Tammo took deep breaths and attempted to find a place for the birdcage amid a bewildering array of female accoutrements. What could be the purpose of raw egg white, unless high-born ladies had very strange tastes in breakfast? Did Celestina need this amount of paraphernalia to begin her day? Surely not! The Marchesa was, what, thirty? Five-and-thirty? Young girls like Celestina needed nothing but the blush of youth to achieve... No, he'd better not go down that route. It was hard enough to concentrate with all that gardenia and décolletage. Five-and-thirty and looking damned good on it! Tammo cleared his throat and tried to swallow again.

"Just a small sample of my craft, my lady." He bowed again, just in case. "A rosefinch, caught in Angel's Wood just this morning, to match my lady Pamina's household crest. It hasn't yet been trained to any particular behaviour. But if my lady Pamina would care to suggest something..." Tammo's sweating fingers fumbled to unclasp the flute case.

"Ah now, this is what they say is unique about you, Citizen Capell." The Marchesa dismissed the hair-combing maid with a snap of her fingers. "You can make birds answer to your will. Is this so?"

"Yes, my lady." That wasn't quite how it worked, but you didn't argue with a Marchesa.

The Marchesa took a bowl of chocolate from the page boy and sipped it. Her green eyes narrowed. "So, if I told you that I wished this bird to go and shit upon the head of the Nobile Faramondo…?"

Tammo gave an explosive cough. "I…er…" He cleared his throat. "Anything your ladyship wishes."

"I do wish it." The Marchesa's voice had lost its bedchamber allure and became as calculating as that of a court minister. This wasn't a lady to be crossed. "Florian, move the screen and let the citizen see. That useless macaroni in the silver coat. Yes, I know you can hear me, Amadigi. If you think you're getting another centesimo of my money, you're an even greater lackwit than you've proved so far. If that were possible!"

Florian looked irritated at having to remove a screen he'd just put up, but Tammo didn't feel sorry for him. Stuck up prig! He followed the line of the Marchesa's pointing finger toward the sour-faced fop. Tammo couldn't say he felt sorry for him, either. He looked like he deserved to be covered in bird droppings.

He undid the latch to the birdcage and put the flute to his lips. *Fly on. Lighten your load.* His breath and fingers echoed the rosefinch's own call, recalling forest and freedom. *Right on that silver birch. And see how the sour-faced fop enjoys tha*t!

For a moment, he felt a slight thickness in the atmosphere, as if something wanted to push the notes back. But the next moment, the rosefinch exploded from the cage and deposited its waste on the fop's head. The man's expression became even sourer than before. He took out a large handkerchief and slowly began to wipe. One of the charity girls nudged her friend behind the nun's back and giggled into her shawl.

"Excellent," said the Marchesa. "That disposes of that. Your skill pleases me, Citizen Capell. Call again next week at the same time. God save you."

Tammo stopped halfway through shutting the rosefinch back into its cage again.

"I beg your pardon, lady Marchesa? Do you not want this bird?"

The Marchesa was already beckoning the nun over to her toilette table. One of the maids curtseyed and removed the raw egg.

"I have no need of a bird, citizen." The Marchesa was no longer looking at him. Please remove it. And you needn't bring one next time you come either." She looked at the nun. "Now, Sister, I see you wish to appeal to my charity again."

Tammo backed out of the room, bowing, past the waiting petitioners. As he passed the shit-covered fop, the man cursed under his breath and spat on the floor. It's his own fault for wasting money, Tammo thought. That's the trouble with the idle rich. Always spending coin they haven't got.

He made his way down the stairs, along a corridor and out of the tradesmen's entrance. Tammo stood under the loggia of Piazza Saint Seraphiel, surrounded by walls of soft saffron. The bell was chiming a quarter past the hour.

"Well, that was odd," Tammo said to the rosefinch. "What am I going to do with you now?"

The rosefinch twittered at him in a shrill voice. It was probably hungry now it had more room in its belly. Tammo supposed he could keep it for another patron, but a better thought was growing in his mind. A bird for a lady. Something to prove his worth. He could give the rosefinch to Celestina.

"That's it. That's how I'll woo her." He made little kissing noises at the cage. "You shall be my ambassador."

His shoulder dipped as Coronis landed with a loud *caw*. He turned to look the crow in the eye. She cocked her head, as though asking him a question.

"What's it to you? Ill-omened bird."

He scowled. But Coronis had a point. If the Marchesa didn't want his birds, what *did* she want him for?

4

Twin Souls

Maestro Sarastro banged his folio down on the harpsichord. "No! No! No! It's: *Scorn not, proud Octavian, the fire of a goddess' love.* Are you listening to me, Bellina? Sweet Michael! Will someone take those bloody dogs away?"

"How dare you? No one touches my darlings." La Bellina clutched the struggling pugs to her breast, so their heads bore an unfortunate resemblance to an extra pair of bosoms.

"Oh, lah! Here she goes again." Il Cupide leaned back against the window seat and took a pinch of snuff. He held out the open box to Carlo. "Seraphini?"

"Thank you, I don't." Carlo waved the offending box away. His stomach was beginning to tighten. This was the worst part of rehearsals. The inevitable clash of personalities. He took a deep breath and let it out. With La Bellina playing Venus, it would be a miracle if anyone fell in love.

It was the first rehearsal of the season, for an opera called *Venus, Slayer of Hearts,* and the soloists were gathered in Maestro Sarastro's rehearsal room. It had not started well. The maestro had waited until everyone arrived, scores in hand, to make the announcement that Carlo would be replacing Morestelli as primo castrato and singing the role of Prince Octavian.

"No Morestelli?" La Bellina had looked aghast, fanning herself rapidly, while the pugs yapped around her ankles. "But I always sing opposite Morestelli. He is my twin soul, the torch to my flame. Without him, how can I make the divine music my public adores?" She turned toward Carlo, dark eyes flashing in her angular face. "He is a mere infant! How can he convey the emotion of a primo's aria? Surely Il Cupide should be promoted, if anyone."

Maestro Sarastro's hands tightened on the music desk of the harpsichord. "The role of Octavian was written for a sopranist. Il Cupide, as you well know, is a contralto. Do you expect me to rewrite my entire score for the sake of your preferences, Signora?"

Il Cupide flushed puce and raked a fingernail down the spine of his music book.

La Bellina gave an affected sniff. "I still don't understand why my dear Morestelli can't be here. It is extremely vexing."

Carlo exchanged glances with Giovanni and the bass, Scipione. They were both young and new to the Teatro. He wondered if they felt as awkward as he did. In a corner behind the harpsichord, a young contralto, L'Amoricana, took a sudden interest in the texture of her fingernails.

"I beg your pardon, Signora, but these orders come

from the Duke himself." Maestro Sarastro's voice was soft and contained, but Carlo knew from experience that it would not be wise to push him further. "If you have any complaints, I suggest you take them up with His Grace."

"Indeed I will, maestro!" La Bellina had never been wise.

At this point, the pugs had seen a bee and gone into a barking frenzy, which broke the atmosphere and allowed Maestro Sarastro to begin the rehearsal. But now it was starting all over again. Carlo sighed. In his life, music had always been an antidote to violence and confrontation. So, why were those who made music so quarrelsome?

Carlo placed a hand on La Bellina's arm. "Hard of heart is he who would scorn your heavenly pugs," he sang.

Several people burst into laughter behind him. The tension was broken. For now.

A whiff of vanilla crept around his cheek, followed by a brush of soft curls. "Still playing the peacemaker, Nightingale? I don't fancy your chances with her, la!"

"I don't fancy anyone's chances with her," muttered Scipione. "Although, I'll wager you eunuchs can throw tantrums to rival hers, if you wish."

Giovanni blushed and fanned himself. Carlo looked over his shoulder. "You're her son in this opera, Giovanni. Can't you go around with your Cupid's darts and create some loving-kindness?"

"Speaking of Cupid's darts…" Giovanni lowered his voice. "That snuff box of Il Cupide's. Gift from the

Noblesse Argante. It's said they keep tryst every night. In the Cavalier Argante's carriage."

"And from where, exactly, do you get your priceless vanilla scent?" Carlo raised an eyebrow.

Giovanni opened the fan to its full extent and snapped it shut, signifying *you are cruel*. "A generous lady patron, if you must know. She adores me, but I am quite, quite chaste with her."

"But not with her husband," Scipione whispered in Carlo's ear.

And there was the other down side to rehearsals! It was inevitable certain conversations would arise during an opera called *Venus, Slayer of Hearts*. But the gossip that passed among singers made love sound a frivolous and bawdy thing.

Love should be like an aria, Carlo thought. All gentle sighs and sweet caresses. Not rough tumbling in a carriage. What had body parts to do with love, anyway? If there was a true organ of love, it was the voice. That was where true feeling, true sensibility lay. Music was what hailed men's spirits from their bodies. That was why they sang on stage each night, wasn't it? To invoke ecstasy. He couldn't understand why a singer, especially a eunuch, would speak as if any other ecstasy were possible.

The pugs struggled free of La Bellina's arms and ran in circles round her skirts. One of them made a little puddle on the floorboards. L'Amoricana squealed and gathered her own skirts about her ankles. Maestro Sarastro's jowls began to quiver and his face turned puce. Any moment now…

With a speed that took her breath, Carlo lifted La Bellina by the waist and spun her around in a circle. The veteran diva was a tiny woman by anyone's standards; to someone of Carlo's height she had the proportions of a doll. Her skirts swung out, as her feet flew past at the level of Giovanni's knee garters. Her screech became a glissando that rose beyond the upper stave.

"Oh, my beloved, Venus! I go mad for love! I die for the goddess in my arms!" Carlo lowered La Bellina to the floor and went down on one knee, taking her by both hands. "Send from my sight these jealous satyrs"—he nodded toward the pugs—"that you and I might love unmolested. Just for the length of Act Two, divine lady! Let our sweet whispers be heard above their uncouth barks." He kissed each of La Bellina's hands twice. Then he glanced up and winked at L'Amoricana. "Forgive me, dear betrothed. I will love you again in Act Three."

The entire room burst into applause. Maestro Sarastro's manservant took advantage of the opportunity to extract the pugs and wipe up the puddle. The maestro flared his nostrils and thumped out an imposing chord on the harpsichord.

"Act Two, Scene One. *Scorn not, proud Octavian, the fire of a goddess' love.*"

The music room of the Pageno mansion was much as it had been seven years ago, when Celestina had taken Carlo there to warm himself during his all-night vigil at her brother's coffin. Afternoon sunlight lit up the soft greens and golds of its furniture, and glanced off the mirrors and chandelier. The gods, Pan, Apollo and Orpheus, danced around the walls in painted form. Celestina's harpsichord stood under the arched window; its lid open to display that marvellous scene of a castle by the sea that had always excited Carlo's imagination. The sopha where Carlo and Celestina had conversed so often stood in its usual place before the fireplace. The only thing that had changed significantly over the years was standing behind the music stand, next to the countess' harp: a sullen-faced boy with a violin rammed under his chin as if he meant to asphyxiate himself with it.

"I don't care," he said, as Pompey—one of the Pagenos' statuesque Oyoan footmen—showed Carlo into the room. "D minor shouldn't have a B-flat in it. It's stupid."

"Those are the laws of music, Nobile Rinaldo. They govern us all. Is that not so, Signor Seraphini?"

The weary-eyed tutor on the other side of the music stand turned to Carlo with a look approaching desperation. Carlo smiled. He recognised the man from his days at the conservatorio. The poor fellow looked as if he would prefer a class full of boisterous choristers to this one pupil. Carlo couldn't say he blamed him.

"Quite correct, Maestro Loreto," he said. "How is D minor to get down the stairs without B-flat to lend a helping hand? A most obliging little note, I've always found. And ever so friendly."

Rinaldo threw the violin down on the floor, causing his

maestro to wince. It must have cost at least three hundred soldi.

"I'm not taking lessons from him! He's a capon."

He pushed past Carlo and ran out of the room, violin bow in hand.

"Nobile Rinaldo! Come back this instant and apologise."

The maestro gave Carlo a look somewhere between apology, frustration and panic, before hurrying after his charge. He had barely passed Pompey before Carlo heard a familiar cranking, whirring, carriage-wheel-turning sound, and a gentle voice said:

"Rinaldo. What have I told you about minding your maestri? Poor Maestro Loreto is quite worn out."

"I'm perfectly well, noblesse, I assure you. Everything is under control," Loreto mumbled.

"Your capon friend was spying on my lesson." Rinaldo's voice rose. "I don't take instruction from man-seemers."

"Rinaldo! Wherever did you learn such language? Signor Seraphini is Papa's protégé. You must treat him with respect."

"No, I mustn't. I will be master here one day, and then you must do as I say, Celestina. And I shall tell Mama that you are meeting Papa's prot—whatever you said—alone, without telling her. And we'll see what she has to say about that."

There was a sudden silence, and then Celestina's voice again, a fierce whisper:

"Don't you dare do anything of the sort. Be good,

Rinaldo, and I shall let you drive my little carriage in the park."

More whispers and mutters that Carlo couldn't decipher. The cranking and whirring began again, and the gilt and lacquered house carriage appeared in the doorway, with Celestina sitting inside it.

"I hate to bribe him like that. Mama spoils him enough as it is." She gave a sad smile. Then her look transformed to one of joy, like a scene changing in the theatre.

"But let us not think of that now. Carlo, it's so good to have you home."

She held out both her hands. Carlo knelt by the house carriage and kissed them, one by one. How small they were, how dainty! Her skin was pale and flawless as that of a waxen doll, although there were rough spots on the palms, from constantly turning the carriage handles. Dear Celestina had always been independent, even as a child. It had always given Carlo heart to have a friend who understood what it was to be diminished in body, yet strong in soul. She was the gift the Archangel had granted him, in response to Tammo's prayer. A soul friend among the rich and powerful. He felt the need for that today.

Celestina turned to the footman at the door.

"Pompey, will you lift me onto the sopha?"

She turned the brass handles on either side of the carriage and propelled herself toward the fireplace. Carlo watched in silence as Pompey came forward to take his young mistress in his arms. The dexterity with which Celestina manoeuvred her box-chair on wheels never failed to impress, nor did the dignity with which she allowed herself to be lifted by Pompey. Her white arm encircled the footman's neck, and she looked out from her perch on his forearms with the bearing of a benevolent empress. She had been reliant on both carriage and footman since the age of seven, when a fever had left her paralysed from the waist down, much the same age Carlo had been when he'd submitted to the cut and the bath of ice. It was one of the bonds that had brought them together as children.

Celestina smoothed down her skirts and whispered for Pompey to bring some wine and cinnamon water. She was looking radiant today. Her dove-grey skirt was covered with tiny peach roses; peach ruffles on her bodice matched the bow at her neck and the peach shoes peeping from underneath her hem. As an eighteen-year-old, she was little changed from her childhood self, Carlo thought. The same doll-like figure, the same arched brows, the same soft brown hair. Only there was something about her expression today that he had never seen before. An air of mystery, or of hidden knowledge. He couldn't quite place it.

"I do apologise for my brother," Celestina said, with a final flap of silk. "If Papa doesn't take him in hand soon, I fear he will run positively wild. And it is ungentlemanly of him to speak of you as he did. I won't allow it, Carlo."

Carlo delicately took her hand in his.

"Nobile Rinaldo is still young. He will have every chance to mature as he grows, with such a sister to help him."

Carlo feigned a smile. Somehow, he doubted his own

words. The young heir to the Pageno title gave Carlo the shudders, despite his small size. Of course, it was understandable that the Countess should dote on him as she did. Rinaldo's birth had followed the tragic death of his elder brother, Orlando. A bereaved mother relieved to have produced a live heir may well be tempted to spoil the child. But there was something in Rinaldo's eyes that reminded Carlo of the school bully, Paolo Agresto. He would never say as much to Celestina, though. Rinaldo was her baby brother, after all.

He decided to change the subject.

"I saw the Mother Superior leaving as I arrived today. I had no idea you were still taking lessons from her."

Tiny furrows appeared between Celestina's eyebrows.

"I'm not." One hand tightened around a silk rose on her skirt, crushing it to a bud. "Mama has been meeting her behind my back again. The nuns want my dowry for the convent. Since I can't get married, they think I should become a bride of Christ."

"What?"

Pompey chose that moment to reappear with refreshments. Celestina sat rigid, smoothing out the creases in her skirt. Carlo poured hot cinnamon water from the kettle, biting his lip as he replaced it on a silver trivet. Pompey bowed and retreated into the hallway. Celestina glanced around, then poured herself a small glass of tokay wine before she spoke.

"Ever since I came of age, Mama and Papa have been arguing about me. As if I don't have a mind of my own!"

She knocked back a mouthful of wine and banged the glass down. Glasses and bowls clinked together. Carlo steadied the table. "Where I will live, who will support me when they're gone."

"But the Count and Countess have years in them yet," said Carlo. This conversation unsettled him. The loss of Morestelli was enough of a shock; he wasn't about to contemplate life without his patron.

"I know, but that's the way it is with parents." Celestina swallowed the remaining wine in her glass and started on the cinnamon water. "It's all alliances and settlements and the family name. All our relatives and acquaintances are marrying their sons and daughters to one another."

"Yes, I suppose they are."

Carlo sipped his cinnamon water, allowing the comforting spice to warm his throat. His own family were peasants in the Angelian countryside. He had not seen them since he left to study at the conservatorio, aged ten. His father in particular, he never wished to see again. Perhaps his many brothers and sisters had wives and husbands of their own now. It was not a subject he concerned himself with. Castrati did not marry. That order came from the Apostolic Father himself. Marriage and its rites were for the begetting of children. It was not for the infertile. Looking at Celestina, Carlo suspected that fact bothered her more than it did him. All her childhood acquaintances were marrying one another. Had she a secret love among them?

"But you do not wish to take the veil? What does your father say?"

A queasy feeling began in Carlo's stomach. He needed Celestina now, more than ever. If she went to a convent, he would never see her again. Never have a friend in high society who saw him as more than a voice and a character on a stage.

Celestina let out a breath and calmed herself.

"In some ways, a contemplative life makes sense. At least I would have a use in this world and be no man's burden." She sighed. "But I can't... And Papa insists it is Rinaldo's responsibility to take care of me." She stirred the bowl with a spoon, round and round, a spiral of brown speckles turning on the surface of the water. Then she looked up at Carlo, her hazel eyes serious. "Papa seems so troubled lately. Have you noticed, Angel-boy? He's at the palace every day, late into the night sometimes. He never was before."

Her voice wavered. Carlo reached along the sopha and took her by the hand. The fact that she had slipped back into her childhood name for him made her seem all the more vulnerable. She drew in a sudden breath and let it out. Carlo stroked the back of her hand with a thumb.

"Is it because of the Duke and Nobilissimo's quarrel, do you think?" he said softly.

Celestina shook her head, so that stray curls bounced against her temples.

"There's more to it than that. They never tell me anything, so I don't know what. But I think, I think..." She held Carlo's hand tighter and lowered her voice. "...I think the Duke may be in danger."

Carlo pressed his lips together. There was something going on in Angelio. But it wouldn't be wise to jump to conclusions. Not if there was danger involved. He looked into Celestina's face. There was such trust in those soft-lashed eyes. As though she believed Carlo could solve all her difficulties. He supposed that, over the years, he had become an older brother to her. And she, his little sister. Certainly, she was much dearer to him than those sisters whose names he had now forgotten. He lifted her hand to his lips and kissed it.

"Whatever troubles he bears for the Duke, your father will not forget you," he said. "He loves you more than his own life; I know that."

A pretty blush spread over Celestina's cheeks, peaches to match the peach in her dress.

"The love we carry from our earliest days never leaves us."

"Indeed, noblesse." Carlo smiled. "And trust me, my lady, you are no man's burden."

He kissed her hand again, tenderness welling in his heart. Celestina understood, he knew she did. He should confide in her about Tammo. He should do it now.

Celestina parted her lips to speak.

There was a scuffle at the door and a swish of skirts. Carlo turned his head to see Teresa, Celestina's former governess, hurry into the room, her cheeks red with exertion, the familiar work basket on her arm. The poor woman was constantly at her needlework. Carlo imagined her bedchamber to be stuffed full of handkerchiefs and embroidered pockets no one ever needed. Her main duty, however, was as Celestina's body servant and chaperone. A job she took very seriously.

"Oh, Noblesse Celestina!" Teresa's skirts brushed against upholstered chairs as she bustled into the room. "How could you deceive me so? What would your mama say if she saw you sitting alone with the young…singer?" Teresa considered the word *castrato* to be indelicate.

Celestina tossed her head.

"Sweet Michael, Teresa! It's only Carlo. What do you imagine a castrato and a cripple could possibly do together? We are neither of us capable."

Teresa gave a cry of horror. "Noblesse Celestina! May God forgive you!"

Carlo took the opportunity to refill his and Celestina's bowls, disguising his blushes in clouds of cinnamon-scented steam.

"We were discussing the religious life, if you must know." Celestina folded her hands in her lap, as demure as Teresa could wish. "Do you find the Carmelite spirituality preferable to the Benedictine? Being named for the saint of Avila, I assured Carlo that you would, but he thought you might incline away from the mystical toward a more communal practice. Your thoughts, Teresa?"

"I…er…your…young ladyship is no doubt correct in these…er…matters. With your leave, I will take up my embroidery if you have no further…er…questions."

Celestina giggled into her bowl of cinnamon water.

"Did you know, I used to sing at the convent?" Carlo

said. "Back when I was at the conservatorio. Tammo used to say I was singing to a room of invisible skeletons."

Celestina's eyes danced. "Skeletons! They probably are. A load of mouldy old black-clad skeletons!" A laugh like a puff of air escaped her. She drew the bowl toward her lips and smirked. "Now tell me all about *Venus, Slayer of Hearts*. Papa tells me you are to sing primo."

<h1 style="text-align:center">5</h1>

The Language of Birds

Tammo stood in the grand entrance hall, shining his shoe on the back of his stocking. He had done this three times already, and the shoe was unlikely to get any cleaner, but Tammo had to do *something*. The hall's arches of coloured marble stretched upward as if they wanted to entice something down from the sky. It made him feel like a tiny figurine inside some vast automaton, waiting for someone to come and wind the mechanism before he was permitted to move. The chequered squares of floor tiles resembled a giant chessboard. A chessman, that's what he was. Standing in place while the other side made its move. But was he still a pawn, or would Celestina finally permit him to be a knight?

The rosefinch twittered in its cage. Tammo glanced to the right, at the decorated staircase leading to Count Pageno's reception room; then to the left, in the direction of the ascending platform by which Celestina travelled from floor to floor. Surely someone would come soon?

He had decided this time to knock on the front door,

in his persona as Bird Charmer to the Nobility. After all, he would have to do the same thing at the Marchesa della Pamina's house this afternoon. He was already regretting it. Coronis had stubbornly refused to leave his shoulder, and the wrinkling of Caesar's nose as he looked down from his godlike height was enough to let Tammo know what the footman thought of her presence.

"I have a delivery for Noblesse Celestina."

Tammo had hefted the cage for Caesar to inspect. He bit the inside of his cheek, concealing the strain its weight put on his shoulder. He could have brought the rosefinch in a different cage, one that he carried on his shoulder like a satchel, but that made him look too much like a street hawker. This one was a special purchase, crafted to resemble a fairy-tale house, with a front door and two turrets. For a lady, for Celestina, he must bring the most elegant cage he could, however much it made his arm ache.

"I will inform the family of your request."

Caesar's voice managed to convey the manners of a guide to etiquette with the warmth of a vault. Tammo scowled as the footman strode away on his long legs, Saint Maurice the Legionary in maroon livery. From whom did Caesar and Pompey inherit such resonant bass voices? Had he such a voice, Tammo thought, conversation with Celestina would be a different thing entirely.

Footsteps on the stairs caused Tammo's heart to leap, and then sink in the same breath. He had been hoping for the whirr of the house carriage. His heart sunk even lower when he saw Caesar approaching, from a completely different direction to that in which he had left. The footman held out a gloved hand.

"I will take the birdcage now, if you please."

Coronis gave a caw of outrage. Tammo tried to keep the same emotion from showing on his face. He had hoped, at the very least, for a few words with Teresa, if not with Celestina herself. How was she to understand the intention of the gift if Ceasar just plonked it on a table?

"Was there no message?" He looked at Caesar, hopefully.

"No message." Caesar opened the front door to show that Tammo's visit was over.

Tammo made a strangled sound in the back of his throat. "You did say who the gift was from, though? You did give my name?" Despite the breeze from the open door, Tammo's head was sweating.

"Oh, I know who you are all right, Citizen Capell." Caesar gave an ironic smile, as though Tammo's identity was a joke. "God save you, citizen."

The door closed. Tammo stamped down every one of the portico steps. He didn't know when he'd last been shown out of a door with such insulting politeness. Self-righteous footman! If he was not twice Tammo's size and built like Achilles, Tammo would have taken him outside and shown him what Angelian citizens were made of. He kicked the bottom step with his heel, no longer caring about the appearance of his shoes.

"Damn it all to Hell! I was that close!" he said to

Coronis, who ignored him and flew up to sit on a balcony. "And he took my blasted cage, too!"

A guffaw from nearby made him glance round. Fenice was coming out of the passageway at the side of the mansion in a bonnet and shawl, a basket over her arm. She shook her head at Tammo and gave a sigh that had more than a pinch of laughter still in it.

"Oh, you are one for entertaining a maid!" She gave him a nudge with her hip. It touched his leg just above the kneecap. "I step out to visit the haberdasher and what's the first thing I see, but Tammo Capell giving the front step a piece of his mind?" Her eyes twinkled. "I hope it deserved it."

Tammo found his innards leaping about in all sorts of ways he had hoped to reserve for Celestina. To compensate, he tried to assume a lordly air he'd learned from Carlo.

"Excuse me, Fenice, but I have a great deal to do." He dipped his head and turned on his heels, intending to stride off down the street. Fenice's footsteps kept pace with him at double time.

"Well, since you can't go anywhere without crossing the river, you can escort me to the ferry," she said. "There are a lot of ne'er-do-wells out there. A maid could be set upon."

She gave a shudder and pressed closer to Tammo's side. Tammo couldn't help feeling that being set upon was something that Fenice would rather relish than otherwise.

"So..." Tammo made a note in a memorandum book with

the stub of a pencil. "…Four swans, two dozen doves and two dozen sparrows. The swans to pull Venus' celestial carriage. The doves and sparrows to be released into the auditorium in Act Three during the Hymn to Love, and fly gracefully back to the stage. No. Droppings." He scored lines with his pencil under the last two words. "And are the swans required to fly?"

He looked into the eyes of the lean-faced man sitting on the other side of the desk. The man looked down his nose at Tammo; rather difficult to do since it bent noticeably to the left-hand side.

"Swans? Fly?" The tone of voice implied that Tammo had suggested the swans might perform the *intermezzo* ballet. "The swans are to pull Venus' carriage. Which will contain La Bellina. Can you contrive to make her fly, too, Citizen Capell?"

The theatre manager's voice had a nasal edge to it, making him sound as though he had a permanent cold. But since Tammo's ruined vocal cords made him sound as though he had a permanent sore throat, he could hardly mock the man for that. His dullness of wit was another matter.

"No, I cannot do that," he said. "But will the carriage move along the ground, Signor Contarini, or will it fall and rise by means of some machine? I need to know that much."

"I don't see why. That is a matter for Signor Verdi, the artistic designer. It has nothing to do with your contract to supply His Grace's theatre with birds for the opera season."

Signor Contarini waved a hand, as if about to dismiss Tammo from his presence.

Tammo pressed the pencil point into his palm in an attempt to keep his temper. "It matters, Signor, because if the carriage rises and falls, the swans must rise and fall with it. The audience will not wish to see them hanged by their necks on golden chains."

And if you think I would let that happen to any one of my birds, you've got another thing coming, Tammo thought. The Teatro di Palazzo might have been one of his major patrons but he wasn't going to take any cock-and-bull from them. Citizen Capell's birds came highly trained and were to be treated as the virtuosi they were. That was the deal. It was what made Tammo much more expensive than the average bird catcher, but also much more desirable.

"Very well." Signor Contarini gave a sigh heavy enough to suggest that he had much better things to do, and waved a hand in the direction of the door. "Speak to Verdi, if you can get any sense out of him. You know the way to the stage."

Tammo's chair scraped the floor as he stood up.

"This will affect the price." He hovered by the desk to make sure the manager understood.

Signor Contarini didn't look up. "The Duke's money, not mine. I only balance the books." He picked up a piece of paper, sighed, and moved it to another pile. "Just come back and give me the quote when you're done."

He was still squinting over the papers as Tammo closed the door and made his way through the dim corridors and up the narrow stairs that led to the stage. Coronis rode on his shoulder, making tiny movements with her claws to balance herself. As he drew nearer the stage, he was met with a mixture of tallow smoke and sawdust. Sawing and hammering started and stopped at intervals, interspersed with curses and bawdy comments.

Tammo emerged stage-right, and found himself treading on a paint-splattered cloth. He stepped around paper sketches, between trestles, and over abandoned tools.

Signor Verdi and his men were hard at work preparing a woodland scene. The artist himself was suspended on a cradle, sketching leaves and birds onto a cloth backdrop. On other cradles, his apprentices copied sections of outline from sheets of white paper, square by square. This was probably one of the scenes Carlo would stand in front of when he sang his arias as Prince Octavian. The eyes of all Angelio would be upon him. Tammo had never fully understood Carlo's desire to place himself in the glare of the footlights. Standing on a stage lit by a hundred candles was the stuff of Tammo's nightmares.

The hammering started again. Tammo looked round to see a gang of carpenters producing what would be the flats, wooden pieces of scenery to be slid into place on either side of the stage by means of grooves, to create a sense of perspective. Although these had not yet been touched by Signor Verdi, Tammo could detect the outlines of trees and bushes in the shapes the carpenters had cut.

"Those flats are like me," he thought. "Shuffling

around in the side-lines. Pushed away as soon as I'm done with."

It was hard not to let bitterness about Celestina colour his view of everything. What had he thought would happen with the rosefinch? That Celestina would fly into his arms with gratitude? That she would whisper protestations of love beneath the portrait of Orlando? He scowled and chewed his lip.

"At least my doves will get the reception they deserve," he thought.

He liked the idea of doves he had trained sharing a stage with Carlo. It was one of the reasons he had taken the job. There was a sort of balance to it, like the painted scene and the flats. Singer and bird-charmer, each playing his own part.

Balance ran through his friendship with Carlo, like a seam of gold through a rock. Back at the beginning, in the crypt of the Sancti Michaelis, the Archangel had taken a sacrifice from each of them, in order to grant the other's wishes. Health and strength from Carlo to give Tammo his gift with the flute; satisfaction in love from Tammo in order that Carlo and Celestina be friends. The balance must be maintained. They had found that out as boys, when their selfish actions at Carnival had almost broken their friendship. Tammo had sworn to Michael that he would protect Carlo; he must always do so. He may well lurk in the wings as far as high society was concerned, but his role was every bit as vital as Carlo's.

His eyes narrowed as he looked again at the painted

backdrop. He knew that tree. And that rock. And that little clearing.

"It is, isn't it?" he said to Coronis as much as to anyone. "It's Angel's Wood."

Signor Verdi stopped his work and looked around. He wore a soft cap to cover his head in the absence of a wig, and his fingers were black with charcoal.

"You recognise it?" A smile tweaked the corners of the artist's lips.

Tammo shrugged and scratched the back of his neck. "Lived there for five years, haven't I? Not much of the place I wouldn't recognise."

A look of recollection came over Signor Verdi's face. "You're the bird charmer, aren't you? Forgive me. I become so absorbed when I draw that I wouldn't know my own mama." He waved his hand over the backdrop with a sheepish look. "Hardly my best work. What do you expect with nothing but tallow to draw by? It's meant to be Venus' enchanted grove on the Isle of Cythera, but I thought to honour His Grace with a depiction of his own woodland. Doubtless as a woodsman you see a thousand errors. And the courtiers will be far too distracted by fireworks and ascending platforms and each other's outfits to even notice what I've done…"

His voice trailed off. Tammo recognised only too well the needy tone of an artist seeking affirmation. He'd heard it from Carlo's lips enough. "It's a fine piece of work," he told Signor Verdi.

The painter blushed. "A mere trifle. I can only hope it's

a fit setting to display your birds. I assure you, the ladies of Angelio anticipate them almost as keenly as they do Signor Seraphini."

"Really?" It was Tammo's turn to blush. Coronis gave an impatient caw. "Yes. Well. While we're on that subject, I must ask about Venus' carriage…"

Caffe Armide was abuzz with custom as Tammo slid into his customary seat beneath the Annunciation. Every table in the booth was full. The air was thick with the smell of roasting coffee, dense smoke from the pipe of a bow-legged man by the window, and the general aroma of over a dozen men crowded into a small room. Tammo was forced to share his table with two priests, who were avidly debating the merits of a tapered pen-nib versus a square one. One of them had a greyhound, which sat under the table chewing a bone, but occasionally decided that Tammo's shoe might be more nutritious to chew on instead.

Through the clouds of smoke and steam, Tammo spotted the same three merchants he had seen before, gravely sampling roasts and blends on the other side of the room. The one with the queue and the almond eyes turned toward Tammo and briefly nodded his head in greeting. Tammo answered with a stiff jerk of the neck. He had enough on his mind right now; he didn't need merchants vexing him.

"Ah, have you heard the news, Citizen Capell?" Armide came bustling over to Tammo's table, a coffee in each hand. Through the smoke, his red wig looked like the flame of a candle. "A dreadful business, to be sure." He leaned closer to Tammo, as if passing confidential information, although his whisper was pitched to ensure it carried around the room. "The Nobilissimo has set up a secret police, to spy upon his father."

"No, you buffoon!" One of the priests broke off halfway through praise of a certain penknife he'd had from his father, which had never failed him in fifteen years. He waved a news sheet in Armide's face. "Someone wrote to the editor of the *Fount of Knowledge*, under the name of Signor Oscurita, informing him that there was a secret society abroad, intent on bringing the Duke down. Load of mischievous nonsense," he added, before returning to the subject of his father's penknife.

"I heard he's hired an assassin from Lysfleur in the guise of a harlequin," said a pock-faced man at Armide's back.

"In the guise of a priest was what I heard," said his neighbour, staring hard at the two priests.

The younger of the priests leapt up, and his dog with him, the hackles standing up on its back. He began to say something about the antiquity of his family, but it was drowned out by the pock-marked man also standing and saying something about insulting a priest. Whether he was denouncing or advocating it would have been hard to say, however, as by this point almost every man in the coffee booth was weighing in with his opinion.

Armide danced between the customers like a ballerina,

saying, "Gentlemen, citizens, pray calm yourselves. Another pipe of tobacco, perhaps?" and other helpful things of that sort. Poor little Michelangelo, who had that moment come into the room with a tray of hot shellfish, blanched and shrank back into the passage.

From the corner of his eye, Tammo saw the Mingguo merchant rise from his seat. His face was as impassive as that of a plaster saint in a church; Tammo wondered if he even understood what the argument was about. At that moment, the pock-faced man bumped into the merchant, and something fell from the pock-faced man's pocket. No one else seemed to notice, which was just as well, thought Tammo, as the priests would be scandalised. It was a playing card, of the sort known as Angel Cards. There were certain games you could play with them, but they were more commonly used for telling fortunes.

Tammo stared at the card, now being trodden into the sawdust by numerous pairs of heels. He bit his lip hard. The picture was something he saw every day, in the silver hand of the Archangel on the dome of the Sancti Michaelis.

A pair of scales.

This time when he called on the Marchesa, Tammo was shown to a room of more intimate proportions. A green and gold brocade curtain was drawn aside to reveal a room decorated entirely in cream and gold. It made Tammo feel as if he had stepped inside an enormous wedding cake. Every panel of the wall was painted with a different scene.

Shepherds dancing with maidens, fauns playing syrinxes, a family flying a kite. In each of the four corners were bookcases, beneath female representations of the four winds. These were surrounded by leaves of gold, which appeared to grow up pillars and trail across arches. The shelves heaved with calf-bound volumes in blue, russet, chestnut, tan. Tammo knew that, were Carlo with him, he would not be able to resist browsing the shelves. Tammo was much more interested in the room's owner.

The Marchesa sat on a pale gold sopha before the fire, which was blazing strongly despite the sunshine outdoors. It had a sweet scent; rose petals and maybe a hint of cinnamon. Tammo fought the urge to rub his nose. When Florian announced his name, the Marchesa looked up from the journal she was reading. Her emerald eyes scoured his soul.

"That will be all, Florian."

She dismissed the footman with a wave of the hand. He gave a supercilious smile and vanished. Tammo swallowed hard. Her voice had that same smoke-and-velvet quality as the other day. A pendant hanging from a green ribbon seemed to be placed for the exact purpose of showing where her bosom might be found. Tammo felt it was cowardly of Florian to deny him moral support.

"Welcome to my private library, Citizen Capell." The Marchesa gave a leg-melting smile and tucked one auburn curl behind her ear. "Usually, I invite only the most exclusive selection of guests here, but I'm prepared to make an exception for a man who is willing to provide…shall I say an exclusive service?"

"I trust my skills will be equal to your ladyship's requirements."

Tammo felt all the blood rush to his head as he bowed. What was the Marchesa hinting at? She'd made it quite clear last time she didn't want a songbird. And now here he was in a private room, without even a footman to witness the meeting. He remembered all the tales he'd ever heard in coffee shops about noblesses who seduced common men into being their lovers, exacting from them terrible vows of secrecy and leaving them in constant fear of their husbands' revenge. He wished he had not persuaded Coronis to wait for him outside.

The Marchesa gave a delicious laugh. "Pray, don't look so frightened, citizen! I'm not asking for anything indecent. Tell me, have you heard of my weekly salon?"

"I've heard rumours, your ladyship."

The Marchesa della Pamina's salon was exactly the sort of thing Armide liked to gossip about. Allegedly, only the brightest minds in Angelio received an invitation. Poets, philosophers, mathematicians, astronomers. Armide said two nobiles had once fought a duel over the right to a seat in the Marchesa's salon, although knowing Armide, it might have really been settled over a game of backgammon.

The Marchesa inclined her head, as if to acknowledge that any and all rumours were true.

"It is an institution of which I am very proud. A centre of reason and enlightenment, on which I may dare to say the future of Angelio depends." She smiled, a smile full of secrets and fascination. "Just the other week, we were discussing the language of birds. A fascinating subject, as I'm sure you'll agree, Citizen Capell. Some say it is a mystical tongue, akin to the language of angels; others, that it may be transcribed mathematically in order to reveal secrets about the workings of the universe. Personally, I find such theories old-fashioned and superstitious, although I know the conservatorio sets great store in the copying of birdsong."

"It does indeed, my lady." Tammo felt on safer ground here. When he had first met Carlo, the eunuch had spent a great deal of time nightingalising, as he called it, singing the songs of birds back to them, and writing out their songs as musical notation. Tammo had done something of the sort himself, when he first started using the dark flute.

"Personally, I am more interested in the practical applications of such a language. Which is why I am so very interested in you, Citizen Capell." The Marchesa leaned forward on her sopha. "Would you say that you speak the language of birds? How do you charm them with that delightful flute of yours?"

"I…er…it's difficult to say."

Tammo's head grew hotter. How could he possibly describe what happened when he played the dark flute? The oneness he felt with the birds and with the whole of nature. The way Coronis seemed to know his feelings. The Archangel was in there somewhere, too; he was sure of that. But he had no idea what the Marchesa meant when she spoke of a mystical language of angels. The Archangel had always spoken to him in plain Angelian. As for the workings of the universe, he would rather leave that to someone else.

"I sort of copy their song and, well, talk to them in my head, I suppose. They seem to know what I want."

"Indeed. Indeed." The Marchesa's emerald eyes glittered in the firelight. "And could you make men and women know what you want, do you think, by playing that same flute?"

Sweat poured down the back of Tammo's neck. The scent of rose and cinnamon swirled in his sinuses. What sort of a question was that? He was a bird charmer, not a…what? A magician? A sorcerer?

"That's an interesting question, my lady…" His voice growled and squeaked worse than ever.

To his shame, the Marchesa burst into peals of laughter. "Oh dear! I appear to have put you in a panic, citizen." She ran a finger along her neck ribbon. She wore a large enamel and diamond ring, depicting a wreath with flowers. "Shall we consider a simpler question? If I were to tell you a fable of two birds, say, a quail and a pheasant, would you be able to express their story and characters in music? With your dark flute and your copied birdsong? For the benefit of our philosophical discussions, you understand? You would play from behind a curtain. No one would see your face."

So, this was the assignment the Marchesa wished to engage him for? Nobles had some strange ways of passing the time! As for whether he could actually do it, Tammo couldn't say he'd ever tried, but it sounded possible. And he could hardly refuse the Marchesa della Pamina!

"At your service, your ladyship." He made a bow.

"Excellent!" The Marchesa's voice purred like a cat. She took the journal from a low table and held it out. "You will find the fable here, set in verse. I trust you are capable of memorising it. God save you."

She left in a waft of rose scent before Tammo had time to draw breath.

6

Venus, Slayer of Hearts

Carlo took a deep breath and filled his lungs with the scent. Incense and white lilies; a smell as familiar as breathing itself. The smell of worship, of purity, and above all, the smell of Homecoming Mass. He opened his mouth and sung:

"*Canite Domino canti cum novum.*" Sing to the Lord a new song.

The voices of violin and viola wove around each other. Flute and oboe lilted. Carlo's voice soared above them all, a sound from heaven itself.

"*Canite Domino omnis terra.*" Sing to the Lord all the earth.

He filled his lungs again, feeling the ribs expand against his embroidered waistcoat, his salmon pink coat.

"*Gloria et decor ante vultum eius.*" Praise and beauty are before him.

It was the song heard every year in the Sancti Michaelis Archangeli. The song of the returning singers, come to offer their thanks before God and Saint Michael the Archangel for a safe return to the birthplace of song, and to ask a blessing on the forthcoming opera season. Only the greatest of the castrati soloists were ever chosen to sing these words. Only those whom the Archangel had blessed with both voice and fame. Carlo still couldn't believe he was the chosen one. This was where it all began; his career as primo castrato.

"*Adorate Dominum in decore sanctuarii.*" Adore the Lord in his holy court.

Behind Carlo, the altarpiece of the song chapel was a vision in marble and painted fresco. Sculpted seraphim spread their wings to form a graceful archway. Nine angels—each with a different musical instrument in hand—represented the nine heavenly songs. At the apex, Michael soared among the morning stars, as they sang for joy at the dawn of creation. Everything was pure white and gold, tinged with the rosy pink of daybreak. The cathedral was a lily, opening to the first warmth of sunlight, rejoicing in the wonder of new birth.

"*Tunc laudabunt universa ligna saltus.*" Then shall all the trees of the wood rejoice.

Everyone was here. Il Cupide. La Bellina (minus the pugs, thankfully). Giovanni, dressed in forest green velvet, looking almost pious. L'Amoricana wore a lace veil, giving her the look of a painted Madonna. Was it ironic, Carlo thought, that this morning they praised God and Saint Michael, and this afternoon they disported themselves as pagan gods and goddesses? Such was the life of a singer.

"*In fida sua.*" Carlo held onto the high note, paying out

his breath, letting it shimmer in the air before coming to rest with a graceful cadence. "Amen. Amen. A-men."

"Seraphini! Viva Seraphini! Long live the blessed knife!"

Carlo let his gaze stray for a moment to the wrought iron gates of the song chapel. Homecoming Mass was a private service for singers and musicians only, but that didn't stop crowds of admirers gathering in the cathedral body, eager to show support for their favourite soloists, and to hear them sing for the first time this season. The spiritual elders of the cathedral, far from discouraging the practice, were as keen for it as anyone else. In music-loving Angelio, piety was rarely expressed in silence. Carlo was certain he could see two priests and a knot of nuns among the lively crowd.

"Viva Seraphini!"

They knew his name already. Carlo could remember when it had been Morestelli singing in this chapel, and he had been a conservatorio pupil, filled with frustrated longing to stand where that crowd stood now and hear the great man's voice.

As if Carlo's thoughts had created him, he noticed a man in the crowd with the proportions of an adult eunuch. Tall, portly, with long arms and legs. He was dressed in dark blue with silver embroidery. Most interesting of all, he was already wearing a plain black carnival mask, although Carnival didn't officially begin until the Feast of Seraphim. Perhaps the man had made a mistake with his almanack.

There was something about his figure, the way he

stood, that looked familiar. Could it be Morestelli? If so, then he was in Angelio after all. Not ill or absent. But what was he doing?

Maestro Sarastro raised his hand for silence. Reluctantly, Carlo looked away from the man in the crowd. He waited for the shouts to die down, took a breath, and began the second movement.

"O Glorious Prince of the heavenly host, Saint Michael the Archangel."

Carlo had wondered if the Teatro di Palazzo would be as magnificent and as chaotic as he remembered. It was both. As he arrived for what the Kapellmeister of Festeburg would have called a *sitzprobe*—a seated rehearsal by orchestra and singers alone—he was met with a glorious mixture of gilded ceilings and open machinery, of candle smoke, sawdust, sweat, perfume and horse manure.

While the soloists took their seats at the front of the stage, and the musicians tuned up in a fenced-off pit at their feet, carpenters were busy hammering the crests of noble families to the boxes engaged for the season. Signor Verdi and his painters were frantically trying to make some old scene flats of rocks look more like ocean waves. A young boy in a brown waistcoat was desperately counting candles, and having to start over every time the hammering made him lose count. La Bellina's pugs ran rampant around the stage. One of them cocked its leg against a wooden tree.

Thankfully Signor Verdi was too busy with the rocks to notice.

Maestro Sarastro swaggered in through a side door, his ball-topped cane tapping on the floor in syncopation with the hammers. The young boy dropped all his candles and swore.

"You lot had better have warmed up your voices. Why is it so bloody cold in here?" He scowled at the carpenters, as if they were personally responsible for the temperature. "And you can stop that infernal hammering. We are practising the art musical."

"I lit the fire behind the stage, maestro," a voice spoke from the wings.

"Well, that's no use to my singers when the curtains are closed. Get some candles lit, man!" Sarastro roared. There was a hasty scuffle of feet. The candle boy trembled.

It *was* cold. Carlo had kept his cloak on, as had most of the other singers. It was unusual, so early in the season. Was this a foretaste of the bad winter everyone said was coming? He took from his pocket a little flask that Casale had given him and took a few sips of warm rosehip water with honey.

"From the top, please!" Maestro Sarastro beat on the floorboards with his cane.

The opera they were rehearsing had been written especially to celebrate the betrothal of the Duke's youngest daughter to the Dauphin of Lysfleur. It was the usual concoction of frustrated love, mistaken identity, solos, scenery, trapdoors, ballets and performing animals. As primo castrato, Carlo played the young lover, Prince

Octavian, who was seduced in the first act by Venus, masquerading as his bride. The real bride was then abducted by Venus' jealous husband, Vulcan, god of fire. Naturally, everything worked out for the best by the time each principal singer had sung four or five solos in different styles. Fashionable Angelio only cared for happy endings.

With a flourish, the strings and woodwind launched into a lively overture. La Bellina gargled with something and spat on the floor. L'Amoricana gave a little cry of disgust and inched her chair away from Bellina's. There was a horrible squeak as it scratched the stage. The pugs came round, stumpy tails wagging, and licked at the mess.

Carlo turned the page to his first solo, the song of Prince Octavian when he first arrives on Venus' island of love:

"On the shores of Cythera
I wait in expectation
For she whom I love, she whom my heart adores."

If there was a true irony to his singing life, Carlo thought, it was that he should play a man so easily seduced. Whether it was due to his surgery or not, Carlo had never once felt lust in his life. He wasn't even sure he knew what it was. Love, on the other hand, love often filled his chest to bursting. However renowned his lung capacity, there wasn't room sometimes to contain the strength of his emotion.

Since Tammo had come back, Carlo had found himself feeling lonely for him, even when they were in the same room. There was a new urgency to his love, that left him no longer content with cheerful banter and a comradely arm around the shoulder. Carlo wanted more. Only he didn't know what. Were Tammo to fling Carlo upon a silken couch and smother his face with kisses, Carlo believed he would run for his life. Yet when they were together, the air between them crackled with the magnetism of a lodestone. It was all but impossible not to touch.

If only he could express his feelings with the ease of a Prince Octavian! He would beg Tamino for the right to love him. Just to be near him.

"In agitation, my heart beats
As I listen for her steps."

It was funny, but Carlo found himself thinking back to his conversation with Celestina. There had been something different about her, the other day. A new confidence. Something that made her seem more…womanly. Carlo shook his head. He supposed she was growing up. He couldn't expect her to stay a little girl forever.

Ah, but Carlo had missed his chance that day! He had been about to broach the subject of Tammo. Before Teresa came in, he and Celestina had been speaking of love. She had said the love of one's earlier days never leaves us. And she had blushed so prettily.

Carlo's fingers twitched as he turned the next page of the score. Was Celestina in love? She had spoken with such regret about acquaintances getting betrothed. And like a selfish fool he had asked her nothing. He had said it himself; she was no longer a child. Was there some young nobile she had known since nursery, now passing her over for a girl with able legs and an able womb? Poor girl! She really was his twin soul, if she was stuck in an impossible love. He must try and get her to speak of it next time they met.

La Bellina had begun to sing the recitative that opened the opera. Venus was upset by her recent failed love affair with the mortal Adonis. She vowed to make mischief for the next mortals who set foot on her island.

"So that their hearts will bleed for love," La Bellina sang.

"They will grow pale and weak, utterly in my power."

It was true, Carlo thought. Venus was a slayer of hearts. But, like Prince Octavian, he would not allow her to defeat him. Tamino was coming to stay at his apartment tonight. Carlo would make the most of every precious moment they had together. He would be bold.

Casale had turned down the beds and put in the warming pans by the time Carlo and Tammo had drunk a posset and made bedtime devotions at Carlo's pretty little prie-dieu.

The first time he'd been introduced to this arrangement, Carlo's manservant had been confused to learn that Citizen Capell was to have a bed in a curtained alcove of Carlo's bedchamber. It didn't fit with any received ideas of hospitality. Two men sharing a bed, a manservant could turn a blind eye. An honoured guest being given his own room was fitting. But, a guest in an alcove, like another servant?

"It isn't seemly, signor," he had tried to argue.

"It is my wish," Carlo had replied. "And the wish of Citizen Capell."

Now, after two years in Carlo's employ, Casale took his master's odd wish as a matter of course. This had been the sleeping arrangement the first time the friends shared a chamber, in the Apricot Room of the Pageno Mansion, and this was how they liked it. Carlo in the luxurious four-poster and Tammo in the homely alcove. It suited the tastes of each.

"He's learning." Tammo grinned, when Casale put his head round the door to ask what the crow would like for breakfast. "Do you remember the first time he saw me with Coronis on my shoulder? I think he thought she was going to eat him!"

"Leave the poor man alone, Tamino." Carlo slipped a blue and red embroidered dressing gown from his shoulders and climbed the three stairs up to his bed. A soft feather bed had been one of the first things Carlo had bought with his wages as a sopranist. He loved the feel of smooth sheets against his skin. The purity of it. The sensation of floating among clouds. "Casale does a good job. I couldn't manage without him when I travel abroad. It's not his fault you try to steal his job when I'm in Angelio."

"I do not." Tammo pulled on a pair of bed socks and rammed a night cap over his bristles. "I just make it clear that protecting you is my job. Always has been."

Carlo pulled the blankets up to his chin. They were warm with the retained heat of coals and hot metal.

"And you do a wonderful job, dear twin. Just like you

did with the Marchesa della Pamina. The most fashionable woman in Angelio! A veritable triumph for your business. What is it she has engaged you to do, precisely?"

There was a moment of quiet, broken only by Tammo rustling and creaking on his bed. Soft candlelight played over Carlo's bed curtains, a suit hanging on the back of an upholstered chair, the tapestry on his wall. Tammo gave a wide yawn.

"Oh, just the usual sort of thing." He stretched stiffly like a cat, his hands and feet pressing against the wall of the alcove.

"What? Become her lover?" Carlo lowered his eyelashes, a sly smile on his lips.

"Carlo!"

A shoe came flying across the room. It fell short of Carlo's bed and hit the floor with a bang. Coronis opened her eyes and cawed. Carlo giggled and wriggled under the blankets.

"Anyway, isn't it sopranists who are supposed to have aristocratic lovers?" Tammo propped himself up on one elbow and looked Carlo in the eye. Scowl marks appeared between his eyebrows. He suddenly looked more serious. "Have you ever, you know, done it? I mean, I know castrati can't marry, but everyone has to let it out somehow."

Carlo drew his knees up to his chest and hugged them under the blankets. He felt as if someone had pushed a cold brick into his stomach. His twin was well-meaning but he was wrong, all wrong. When Carlo looked at himself in the mirror, the desire reflected back at him was of a different nature entirely.

He sighed. "You're right, castrati can't marry, and some of us are glad to escape a duty we cannot perform." He emerged from the sheets again and turned onto his side. "I have everything I need and more. Why seek elsewhere when the one I love is with me already?"

He turned his head away quickly, glad that the shadows hid his blush. Had he said too much? Tamino was dear to him, so dear. The last thing he wanted to do was hurt his friend with feelings he couldn't return.

As boys they'd been affectionate and close, although Carlo had always had to be careful not to aggravate Tammo's dislike of "girly" sentiment and physical touch. But now that they only met for half the year, during opera season, Carlo was less certain how his friend regarded matters of the heart. It was not something he would ever mention in a letter.

As Tamino had said, other people treated the escapades of Venus as a matter of course. They "did it". They had to "let it out", whatever that meant. Had Tammo…? Was there someone he went to, when Carlo wasn't around to see? He didn't want to think of it, yet he needed to know.

He took a breath. "Have you never thought of marriage yourself?" He put on the light tone he used when singing flirtatious duets. "With Fenice, perhaps? She always seems very willing."

"And risk having my head cracked open by Pompey? No thanks!"

Carlo twitched a smile. "I hear that Pompey is courting the new under-maid these days. You'd be quite safe." He waited just long enough to hear the rumblings of Tammo's latent temper before adding seriously: "I wouldn't want you to be lonely, dear twin, for the sake of protecting me."

Tammo made a noise in the back of his throat that reminded Carlo of an impatient mastiff. "Marriage! Who needs to be spliced and have some harpy torment him for the rest of his life? Freedom. The flute and the forest. That's what I need Carlo. If it's good enough for Grimaldi, it's good enough for me. Besides, Coronis is enough of a wife to me." He glanced to where the crow perched on the post of Carlo's bed, her head tucked under her wing. "I don't need another female giving me superior looks all the time."

He flopped onto the pillow and was silent for so long that Carlo thought he had gone to sleep. But then he yawned and said: "Like you said, Carlo, why seek elsewhere? When the most tantalising love of all is hanging right in front of your face?"

Carlo hugged himself under the blankets and smiled. The glow in his heart warmed him all the way down to his toes.

He woke to the sound of Casale cleaning out the fireplace.

"Sorry to disturb you, signor." Casale hunched his shoulders and brushed furiously at the ashes. "Citizen Capell left early. He said to tell you he's at Angel's Wood tonight, but he'll be in Caffe Armide this afternoon if you want to meet him."

"Thank you, Casale."

Carlo stretched his toes down the length of the bed before turning the blankets aside. Sunlight was coming in through the slats of the shutters; it lit the room enough to see by, but not enough to warm it. He reached for his dressing gown and yawned.

"Bring Orpheus in, would you? I want to feed him myself this morning." Having Orpheus close would help Carlo feel Tammo was still near him.

He glanced at the alcove bed. The sheets were still rumpled, the pillows lying askew. A single black feather, a memento of Coronis, lay on the floor between the two beds. Carlo fought the urge to fling himself upon the bed where his twin had lain, to press the pillow to his cheek, and breathe in the scent. His twin loved him! He had as good as said it. Perhaps Carlo could be even bolder next time. Perhaps it was not just princes in operas who were able to express their true feelings.

The sound of birdsong made him look up. Casale was carrying Orpheus' cage into the room, an expression of concentration on his face. Carlo smiled. Orpheus! The bird Tammo had caught for him in the lime tree outside Carlo's dorm at the conservatorio. The first gift of their friendship. Carlo couldn't help but feel that a little of Tammo had got into Orpheus that day. The song thrush seemed to understand him so well. To willingly offer him companionship. To love him.

"Come on, beautiful boy." Carlo held out a hand as Casale opened the cage door. "Come to Carlo."

Orpheus took to the air with a whirr of wings and flew to Carlo's outstretched finger. Carlo lifted up his other hand to stroke Orpheus' back.

Suddenly he flinched. "Ow!"

He looked down at his hand, where Orpheus now sat, trilling merrily. Then he looked back at Casale, whose face was a study in confusion.

"He pecked me." Carlo was incredulous. "But he never pecks me."

"Let me look, signor." Casale shooed Orpheus away from his master's finger and took Carlo's pale hand in his brown one. "Shall I fetch a handkerchief, signor?" Casale asked.

"What?"

Carlo lifted his finger to catch one of the shafts of sunlight, and turned it over.

It was bleeding.

7

The Marchesa's Salon

Tammo tilted the journal, first left, then right, trying to catch the shaft of sunlight that slanted toward the box bed. The mattress creaked and rustled as he twisted himself about. Bits of straw prickled him. He swore under his breath. What was he expecting to see in the wretched thing that he hadn't read a hundred times? He was going to have to come up with a musical interpretation today. The Marchesa expected him to play at her salon this afternoon. He squinted over the delicate handwriting and read the words again:

The Quail and the Pheasant
That plucky little fighting bird, the Quail,
Seeks water from the Well, to no avail.
An arrogant gold Pheasant guards the way,
And never leaves his post by night or day.
Too small to fight the Guard, the Quail despairs,
Until a Rose, in whispers sweet, declares:
"The spoils belong not always to the strong.

With my advice, you'll feast where you belong.
Go stir the Courtyard dust into the air.
Make dull the feathers of that Pheasant there.
When once he sees his golden Gleam is gone,
He soon will lose the Seat he's perched upon."
The Quail does as she bids. The Pheasant yells
To see his dull Reflection in the Well,
And flees away post-haste to take a bath.
At his departure, Rose and Quail both laugh.
For now that there is none to guard the way,
The Quail can drink the Water when he may.

It was a beast fable. The sort they'd had to translate in literature classes at the conservatorio. Usually, they had a moral lesson. *Look before you leap. One good turn deserves another. If at first you don't succeed, try again.* The trouble with this one was that Tammo couldn't work out for the life of him what the moral was meant to be.

Pride goes before a fall. That might work if the pheasant was the main character. But it seemed to Tammo that the story was about the quail. On the whole, he would rather take the quail's part than the pheasant's. A *plucky little fighting bird.* That was him, wasn't it? He'd spent all his life standing up to bullies like Paolo Agresto at school, who had picked on him for his small size, his scars and crow's voice. Now he was fighting for respect as a businessman, among aristocratic clients who were all too ready to put the honest working man down. And he meant to prove wrong anyone who said he would fail.

He who laughs last, laughs loudest. That could be it. But there was something cruel about the quail's laughter with the rose at the end of the story. Perhaps the pheasant was the hero, after all?

He should have asked Carlo. Carlo was good at that kind of stuff. Poetry. Literature. But that would mean telling him about the Marchesa and…Tammo bit his lip and thumped the pillow. Why had he clammed up as soon as Carlo mentioned her name? It wasn't as if he'd done anything indecent with her. All she'd asked him to do was play the flute. That was his business, wasn't it? The flute. Birdsong. So why did he feel so guilty about it all?

Why couldn't he tell Carlo? They were best friends. They used to tell one another everything. Now all Tammo seemed to do was collect secrets Carlo could never know.

"What are you doing in there, lad?"

"Nothing."

Tammo stuffed the book under the mattress and rolled out of the box bed before Grimaldi could open the doors. "I have to go and prepare something for this afternoon." He strapped on the flute case and put on a moss green coat.

Grimaldi scratched his beard and nodded, his bright eyes narrowing. "Does it involve shifting those swans and those four crates of doves that are cluttering up the place? I'm having to walk an extra furlong a day to get around them." He tapped his bad leg. "But don't mind me. Fit as a fiddle, I am."

Tammo breathed out heavily. "They're up against the wall. Not in the way of anything. And I told you, they're going to the Teatro tomorrow." He took a leather cap from a hook on the wall, and pulled it down hard over his ears. "And don't start splitting those logs. I'll do it later."

"Don't blame me if there's an accident while you're gone," Grimaldi grunted. "Those swans get out; they'll break someone's arm."

"No, they won't." Tammo swung out of the door.

Grimaldi looked at his back. "Two centesimi says they will."

Tammo shuffled his feet on the red-and-white tiled floor. He didn't feel prepared for this at all. He had spent a good hour in the woods, with Coronis flapping back and forth in the canopy above him, trying out every call of quail and pheasant he knew. He'd even thrown in a few grouse and woodcock calls for good measure. He still wasn't sure what the Marchesa wanted from him. He'd tried imitating the sound of water, playing fluid scales that bubbled up and down, to represent the well. Coronis had liked that. Well, all creatures longed for water, didn't they?

Maybe that's what it was all about. Longing. Michael only knew, Tammo understood that feeling! He'd woken from another dream of Celestina last night, sweating and ashamed of his body. Why hadn't that lackwit Caesar let him speak to her the other day? Tammo tried to picture her with the rosefinch, cooing and singing to it, while it twittered and piped back at her. He'd wanted her to picture that bird as him, loyal and devoted. Now he wasn't even sure she knew it was a gift from him. It was meaningless.

He'd run out of time to practise in the end. Had to hurry back to the cottage to change, his fingers numb, his nose sniffling from the chill in the air.

Why was it cold already? It wasn't even October yet. He'd seen larks congregating in groups on his way down the hill into the city. That was a bad sign. It looked like a bleak winter was coming, before autumn had properly started. Tammo had exchanged frowns with the clouds. It was unnatural. Un-Angelian. And it was bad for Carlo's health. If he wasn't careful, that toothless, red-haired house mother would lock him in the singers' apartments and only let him out to sing. Tammo and Carlo had big plans for Duke's Day this year. They would come to nothing if Carlo was confined to quarters because of the stupid weather.

Tammo breathed into the dark flute to calm himself. His fingers ran over the familiar carvings of birds and foliage that trailed along its ebony length. A footman with only moderate self-importance had moved him to the gallery some time ago, with instructions to wait behind the curtain until it was time to start playing.

Tammo looked over his shoulder. No one was coming. He took hold of the curtain covering the doorway. It was pale gold with forest green and gold embroidery, and made of some heavy material, brocade or baldacchino. He pulled it back, just enough to peep into the wedding-cake library.

So that's where that narcissist Florian was today! Tammo could see him going around in spotless livery and white gloves, serving drinks and sugared almonds to the Marchesa's guests. A pleasant hum of conversation arose from among the lace cravats and pomaded hairstyles.

Tammo's eyes narrowed. That was interesting. The guests were already wearing their Carnival masks. The Marchesa, in her chair by the scented fire, had a magnificent creation like an owl's face. Bird of Minerva, goddess of wisdom. Tammo remembered that from school. That figured. Someone like the Marchesa would enjoy being seen as the goddess at the head of the gathering.

But none of the guests were wearing such fabulous creations. They were dressed, one and all, in plain black masks. It made the gathering look like a secret vote in the Council of Nine. Tammo wondered if this uniform was *de rigueur* for all meetings of the salon. It was typical of the games nobles liked to play. They were always dressing up as shepherds or gods, or anything other than what they were. If only the average citizen could change his identity so easily! If Tammo could become a nobile for a day, he could pay a call on Celestina in his own right, and Caesar could do nothing to stop him.

Tammo inched closer. From here, he could catch fragments of conversation.

"...dismissed me out of hand," one nobleman was saying. "After five years dancing at his heels. Naturally, one of You-Know-Who's cronies got the post."

"Naturally." That was the man beside him, whose wig curled down his back in a fork shape. "And we all know who controls the marble trade."

There was a great deal of murmuring and fluttering of fans. Someone passed a snuff box around. Tammo heard a stifled sneeze.

"I still say we look to Lysfleur," said someone. A woman, he thought.

There were several cries of, "Hush!" One person exclaimed loudly, "Lysfleur? Michael smite it! Where was Lysfleur when we lost the coastal hamlets? An enemy once, an enemy forever."

"Hear, hear!" said several voices.

Tammo chewed his lip. What in Michael's bootstraps was this all about? He thought they were supposed to be talking about bird language.

"And I say we look to the bud, my lords. A hand to the bud and a rose to our lips."

That was the Marchesa's voice. Tammo gripped the curtain tighter and stumbled, making the curtain rings clank together. One of the guests turned his head toward the doorway. Tammo dropped the curtain and backed away. Better leave off that game. The Marchesa sounded as commanding as a general. If he was caught ear-wigging, he was likely to lose more than just his commission, and he didn't have the voice to join Carlo's profession.

He went back to pacing the chequered floor, stepping on only the red tiles as if he were a child. There was an upholstered chair on one side of the doorway, a polished table on the other. Tammo didn't need to be told that neither were to be touched. Crazy, wasn't it? Chairs that weren't for sitting on. Tables that were just for looking at.

His mind went back to Grimaldi's cottage and the old settle made from every kind of wood in the forest. What would Grimaldi say if he could see this place? Only he would never see it, would he? He never left Angel's Wood. Hated the city with a passion. Yet it was the city that supplied him with a living. Silly, stubborn old goat!

A cabinet with glass-fronted doors was built into the wall, beside the pointless table. Tammo had seen cabinets like this in most of his patrons' houses. Cabinets of curiosities. This one was modest compared to some; the Pagenos had one the size of a small room.

It was the colour of new milk, elaborately decorated. An arched pediment at the top was crowned with a small pair of antlers. Behind greenish glass, looking like artefacts from Atlantis, were shells, coral, skulls, chessmen, wax saints...

And birds! Linnets and firecrests and bullfinches. Mounted to look as if they were flying still. Tammo scratched his neck and chewed on his lip. These poor creatures would not hear his music. Should he feel upset that they had lost their lives to furnish a rich woman's cabinet? Or be happy that their existence was extended beyond the lifespan they would have had in the wild?

As an Angelian, you couldn't afford to be too sentimental. Everyone ate songbirds. It was an important part of the winter diet, keeping families out of starvation. Feathers, too, were important for warmth, as well as status. Where would Carlo and the other singers be without their three-foot feather headdresses? Yet there was something that made Tammo queasy, to think that he was about to bring the language of birds to life in front of this dumb choir, condemned to a rigid mimicry of life until they fell apart.

To distract himself, he turned his attention to a pair of ivory figurines, squashed between an albatross egg and an amethyst crystal. A woman with beads dangling from her headdress, and a man with a conical hat and long queue. Natives of Mingguo. A shiver went down Tammo's back. No, this was worse. It reminded him of that eerie foreigner at Armide's. Did the man have nowhere better to be? Mingguo, for example! Why was he always staring at Tammo? And what was that uncanny thing that had happened the other day with the Angel card? The Scales, of all things! Right when Tammo was thinking about Michael keeping the balance.

"You stay out of it!" He made the sign of the horns at the little ivory figure. Then, feeling foolish, he fingered the linnets and orioles on his flute again.

"Citizen Capell?" Florian had appeared on this side of the curtain, in that silent way footmen had. The way he looked at Tammo suggested he had found something unpleasant on his shoe. "Her ladyship asks that you begin playing in your own time. The discussion is about to begin."

He disappeared behind the curtain, somehow managing to leave it hanging perfectly, as though it had never been touched. Tammo considered making horns at him as well, but knowing his luck, the curse would backfire.

He edged as close to the curtain as he could, and

breathed into the dark flute to warm it. The familiar scent of rosewood filled his nostrils. Inside the library, the noise level had dropped to the sound of one voice. He couldn't tell whose.

So, that other conversation had just been chit-chat. Now was the time that they discussed the secret language of angels, or whatever it was. It was time to think about the quail and the pheasant. Time to send out thoughts of triumph over the odds.

He began with an overblown trill, curling his tongue as he blew. That was the pheasant, crowing from his perch on the well. How proud he was, how haughty!

Tammo trilled again, lower, harsher. This wasn't as hard as he had expected. The pheasant was a coxcomb, a fop. An image of Florian flashed across Tammo's mind. Yes, the pheasant was like that. Arrogant pillicock! And what about that lackwit dandy the Marchesa had wanted the rosefinch to shit upon? He would throw in a bit of him, too. The dark flute *crarked*, repeating the call.

Tammo was beginning to feel he could see that arrogant pheasant. He deserved to be pushed down the well, never mind lose his plumage!

"That's very well, but you know he has eyes everywhere," someone in the salon said.

Tammo's throat tightened, mid-breath. What was that?

A picture flashed across his mind. A glimpse of wings, enormous wings of a shimmering kind of blue Tammo had never seen before. The surface of the wings was covered with eyes, actual eyes with lashes and lids that blinked. And the worst part was, all the eyes were looking at him. Not glancing, but staring, as if they could see right through his skin and into his soul.

His arms dropped limply to his sides. Was he about to faint? That had never happened before. He pulled off his wig, and ran a hand over his bristles. Easy, Tammo told himself. Don't forget to breathe, hey? He gave a half-smile to himself. Lackwit.

"What happened to the music?" said someone.

In haste, Tammo put the flute back to his lips. He didn't want Florian coming back again. Just get on with it. No eyes. No wings. No fainting. No distractions. He gave a lingering trill, feeling the warmth of the holes under his fingers. The quail. The plucky little hero. That's who he should focus on.

He spat out three grace notes in the upper register, mimicking the *whip, wh-whip* call of the quail. His head was still fuzzy, like someone had plunged it underwater. He gave it a shake. That was better.

He could picture the little bird now. They had quail at the cock-fighting ring sometimes. Fierce little things for their size, with spurs on their heels. The question-mark crests on their heads reminded Tammo of the plumes knights used to wear on their helmets. Now, that was the image he needed. A fighting quail. *Whip, wh-whip. Whip, wh-whip.* The quail may be small, but he was wily. He would dirty the feathers of the pheasant and remove him from his post. Then let Angelio see who was the greatest!

Tammo pushed his grace notes higher, shriller. The sound of the dark flute swelled, filling the gallery, caressing the green and gold curtains, and dripping like honey into the salon.

"And dirty his feathers? Lah! What a notion!" Had Tammo imagined that? One of the guests in the salon had repeated his thoughts.

But that would mean…Tammo let the flute drop and wiped sweat from his upper lip. The Marchesa's questions returned to his mind.

Would you say that you speak the language of birds? Could you make men and women know what you want by playing that flute?

The chequered floor swayed under Tammo's feet. What exactly had he got himself into? Influencing men and women. Putting words into their heads. Tammo's fingers trembled over the flute's carven leaves.

Don't be afraid. Deep breath. Keep playing.

He couldn't go back to Angel's Wood with his head like this. He had to keep walking. It didn't matter where.

The dark flute beat against his leg; the Marchesa's coin weighed heavily in his pocket. His neck was still clammy with sweat, his mouth dry, but he'd be damned if he showed his face in Armide's.

The cloth of his breeches *wheeked* as he strode on, faster, faster. Mind that handcart. Don't tread on that cat. Just keep walking. Left, right, left, right. A church bell chimed. He flinched and kept going. Uphill, that should do the trick. More strain on the calves; get the heart pumping; rid his brain of these crazy thoughts.

Ought he to tell Carlo? It had been Carlo's wish that Tammo be given the ability to charm birds. Should Carlo be told that, insane as it sounded, he could now charm people?

But if he did that, then Tammo would have to tell Carlo *how* he knew. He would have to describe the Marchesa and her…charms. And admit that he'd entered into a contract without fully understanding the terms.

Then, what would his twin say? "Oh, Tamino, how could you?" Or, "So, she is your paramour. And what does the Marquis say to that?" Or even worse, "Tell me more about the eyes." No, no, that would never do.

Besides, Carlo had enough to think about. The opera. His début as primo. He might swagger like a god onstage and blow kisses to admirers in the piazza, but Tammo knew how vulnerable he was. This bad winter everyone said was coming. The disappearance of Morestelli. These things affected his friend, and he couldn't expect that pious manservant Casale to watch out for him. There were some things only a sworn twin could do.

"Where the hell is Coronis?" he muttered.

He had crossed the river and was powering through the building site that was the expansion of the Mansion Quarter. Men swung from scaffolding like monkeys. Stonemasons chipped away at enormous sandstone blocks. Tammo coughed as the dust caught in his throat. He ought to be taking better care of his good clothes, but he couldn't bring himself to care.

A left here. A right there. He was going nowhere in particular, just upward. It was a lie. It wouldn't have convinced Michelangelo. But he could keep telling himself that, until the burnt umber façade loomed closer, and his footsteps slowed, and he found himself gazing up at the East Loggia. Gazed until his eyes burned with it.

A familiar black shape flapped down from the maple. Tammo grunted and shrugged his shoulders. His gaze never moved from the arches and rondels on the second floor.

"Up there is her chamber," he said to himself. "The curtains of her bed, her dressing mirror…"

He sighed. Coronis cocked her head. "Celestina! Why don't you speak? Don't you know I'm going crazy for you?"

His left hand lingered over the flute case, playing with the clasp. He chewed on his lower lip, stroking the leather tube, thinking.

8

A Kiss in the Dark

Carlo had never seen so many cherubs coming from one piece of marble. They tumbled over one another, looking up, looking down, embracing one another like children. The cherub at the front of the cloud held a trumpet to its lips with one hand, while stretching out the opposite wing.

When Carlo had stood vigil in this chapel seven years ago, there had only been one cherub. Him. These marble brethren were even more scantily clad than he had been that night, but at least they wouldn't feel the cold during their chilly vigil.

The tomb was enormous. It filled at least as much space as the altar, which Carlo always thought of as standing at three by the clock. The tomb stood at six. South-facing. The direction of summer. That was some comfort.

Beneath the cloud of cherubim, the tomb widened into a sort of shelf, flanked by four adolescent angels with long curls and tactfully placed banners. To Carlo's eyes, they looked as though they were lolling against the school wall, waiting for their maestri to call them to lessons. But they were merely lending glory to the central figure, a boy of less than ten summers, who was dressed as magnificently as a general. Every detail of the sculpture was perfect, from the embroidery on his stockings to the curls of his wig. In his right hand he held a lily; his left rested on his sword hilt. He looked confident and carefree, as though no sorrow could touch him. If only that were true.

"You finished it, my lord," Carlo dared to say.

Count Pageno stood beside him, one hand covering his mouth. His eyes had not left the marble figures for what felt like hours. Carlo had not even seen him blink.

"During the summer." The Count cleared his throat. "A fine piece of work, is it not?" He continued to stare at the tomb.

"Very fine," Carlo agreed.

It was best not to say more. The Pageno household had just held its annual mass in remembrance of Orlando's passing. Carlo had been commissioned to sing, as he had every year since Orlando lay in the glass coffin. Of course, Count Pageno had the monks at Michael di Giustizia say mass for Orlando's soul every week. But that was not the same as remembering, as grieving for the life Orlando had barely had time to taste.

"Are you prepared for Opening Night?" the Count asked.

"As I'll ever be." Carlo smiled.

The Count nodded. He rubbed at his chin; the mourning ring he always wore glinted in the light.

"It is your destiny, Carlo. Your rightful place. When

you stand on the stage of the Teatro on Friday night, you will bring great glory to the House of Pageno."

Carlo made a half-bow. The Count looked at the marble Orlando again and took a deep breath.

"I am proud of you, Carlo. Not only of your talent, but of the man you are becoming. If I may call you a man." He made a dismissive gesture with his fingers.

If, indeed, Carlo thought. There was a poem circulating the coffee houses at present. No one knew the author. Its title was: *A Castrato's Love.*

You ask me who I am: what will I say?
I cannot answer "man" or I will lie,
And "woman" is still further from the truth,
The mask of gender but a part I play.

Such was the truth of a castrato's life. One was always less than a man, even when one was more than a boy. One fell between the cracks of social distinction. Man and wife. Father and son. Master and servant. Orlando might be an eternal boy, immortalised in marble, but Carlo was not much different. A figure of artifice, chiselled by the hand of man. At once beautiful and grotesque.

The Count began to pace, one arm behind his back. Carlo fell in step beside him.

"Do you remember, Carlo, what I told you of a young castrato I patronised once? How I feared you would follow him into dissolute ways?"

"I do, my lord."

The boy in question had fallen victim to the disease of

Venus and died in pain. Slayer of Hearts, indeed! And of other parts beside.

The Count smiled for the first time this morning. "I never spoke a more foolish word in my life." He shook his head. "How can it be that one day should bring me both the greatest sorrow and the greatest joy of my life? The day that you, Carlo, entered our lives."

Carlo said nothing. He was wondering if he dared ask Count Pageno whether the masked man in the Sancti Michaelis was really Morestelli. Why was the great castrato walking the streets of Angelio in disguise? Spying? But spying for whom? Had the Duke recruited him as an agent, or had he gone over to the Nobilissimo's party?

Carlo tripped over one heel, trying to regulate his pace to the Count's shorter stride. He righted himself and walked on, circling back toward the tomb.

Morestelli could never be disloyal to the Duke. He owed His Grace everything. But then, so did the Nobilissimo. It hadn't stopped him from rebelling. Gathering a rebellious faction around him. A whole tribe of echoes to reflect his narcissistic self. Carlo's stomach squirmed. Why was the world made up of feuds and plots? Orlando was better off out of it.

Count Pageno was looking at the tomb again. This was not the time to ask. Carlo made his excuses and quietly walked away.

"I miss him every day, Angel-boy." Celestina was hugging

the monkey Giacomo, who was now elderly, his fur dull and patchy. In Carlo's opinion, this made him more bad-tempered than ever. He was glad Celestina had such a firm hold on the creature.

"As is only right, noblesse. Your sisterly love does you proud." Carlo poured more chocolate.

He looked around the room for something to lift the mood. A birdcage in the shape of a palace, with onion-domed turrets and a red-roofed balcony, had been placed on a half-moon table. Inside it, a rosefinch flew from perch to perch, twittering and pecking at seed. Hadn't Tammo charmed a rosefinch for the Marchesa della Pamina?

"Did Citizen Capell bring you that bird, noblesse?"

The wistful look vanished from Celestina's face. She leaned over the arm of the sopha and waved at Pompey to bring the cage closer. "You are such a tease, Carlo! But only see how much he loves me. Here, Pompey, take Giacomo. He'll only get jealous."

Pompey's face revealed nothing as he extracted the screeching Giacomo from his mistress' arms. Quite possibly, a footman's training prepared you for the occasion on which you had to manhandle a rebellious monkey. Carlo silently thanked Michael he had been trained as a singer instead.

Celestina opened the door to the birdcage. A few downy feathers fluttered out. "Come to me, Carlino. Come and kiss me."

"You named him Carlino?" Carlo raised his hand to

cover a giggle. "I must say, noblesse, what you lack in originality, you make up for in consistency."

As a girl, Celestina had named twin goldfinches Carlino and Carlotta. Carlo had never known whether to be flattered or embarrassed.

"Insolence!" Celestina rapped his knuckles with her fan. "You know full well I named him after his benefactor."

"Ah, so I'm a benefactor to a rosefinch, am I now? I do apologise for being so remiss in my duties. Next time I shall bring a bag of sunflower seeds and a silver spoon for the christening."

Celestina tossed her head. "Take no notice, Carlino. You love me, don't you?"

The rosefinch whirred its wings and flew about Celestina's head, alighting on first one shoulder, then the other. Every time it landed, it leaned its head against Celestina's neck and made little kissing motions with its beak.

"Be careful he doesn't peck you, noblesse," Carlo said.

"Silly." Celestina stroked the scarlet feathers with a finger. "He would never do that. He loves me."

So I thought of Orpheus. There was a scab on the back of Carlo's hand, like a crimson bead. All these years, he had loved the song thrush like a child. Now he couldn't take Orpheus from his cage without wondering if he would peck again. What could have made him do that? Maybe Orpheus was getting old. Carlino was a young bird, but those kisses made Carlo uneasy.

"Put him away, noblesse," he said.

For a moment, he thought Celestina was going to refuse outright. Then she cupped Carlino in her hands and kissed the crest on his head. "Until later, my little Carlo."

The door of the room banged open.

"He's not your little Carlo." A shrill voice, with the arrogance of an emperor. "He's just a silly bird. When Papa gives me a gun, I'm going to shoot him and put him in the Cabinet of Curiosities. And stupid Giacomo as well."

There was a screech that would have frozen blood in Hell, and the skittering of claws on marble flooring. Rinaldo laughed.

"Giacomo! Come here, signor!" Pompey's attempt at a whisper sounded like granite slabs rubbing together. He hurled himself in the direction of the harpsichord. Giacomo dodged him and leapt into Teresa's work basket.

Carlo stood up and made a bow. "God be with you, Nobile Rinaldo, on this solemn day."

Teresa was now screeching as loudly as the monkey. She was standing and flapping her skirts about. Giacomo vaulted over Celestina's house carriage, just as Pompey made a grab for his tail.

"This what?" Rinaldo scowled.

"Your brother's memorial day, you naughty boy!" Teresa's attempt at chastisement was rather spoiled by her leaping upon a chair.

"Oh, that. Well, mourning is fine for women, I suppose." Rinaldo swaggered across the room with the air of a man at least forty. "I'm telling on you, Celestina. For seeing Seraphini alone, again. And then you'll go to the convent."

"Hardly alone, nobile." Carlo nodded toward the circus going on behind them.

"You should be saying your prayers, Rinaldo. For dear Orlando's soul." Celestina fastened the cage door shut on Carlino and held out her arms. "Come, Giacomo." The monkey leapt onto her bosom and was instantly silent. Pompey hissed an oath.

"I've said my boring prayers. Now I want my mask for Carnival."

"Rinaldo!" Celestina shot him her sternest look.

"You should do penance for such wicked words, nobile!" Teresa folded her arms across her chest as the best way of recovering her dignity.

"Silence! You're my sister's servant, not mine." Rinaldo's baby features twisted into a sneer.

"Pompey, will you fetch Signor Sirio?" Celestina said.

Carlo privately wondered what a tutor could do that would make any difference. If he was whipping the boy, it was having no effect.

"I shan't do as he says." Rinaldo pouted. "And I'm still telling. You promised me I could drive your carriage in the park, but I haven't done it."

"Shall I leave, noblesse?" Carlo said.

Celestina put her hand firmly over Carlo's. "You shall drive it, Rinaldo. We shall all go. A week from today. What do you say, Signor Seraphini?"

"An excellent plan, noblesse." Carlo made a bow.

That mysterious look was in her eyes again. That look full of untold stories.

It was only later, as he was leaving the mansion, that Carlo realised he had never asked about her secret love.

"Bravo! Bravissimo! Viva Seraphini!"

Carlo bowed for the third time and exchanged a glance with Maestro Sarastro. The maestro stood up at the harpsichord and made a particular turn of his wrist. Carlo filled his lungs for another repeat of the final stanza:

Dearest heart, beloved bride,
Stay! oh, stay with me!
You, my perfect happiness.
You, my twin soul.

The music of the strings and woodwind was nearly drowned out by cheers and the stamping of feet. On the left-hand side of the pit, a gentleman in a batua mask tapped on the box above him with a brass stick. At this signal, the occupants of the fifth tier boxes released hundreds of sheets of paper. People in the boxes below leapt to catch them as they fluttered past. Carlo saw one enthusiastic youth almost tumble right out, before he was dragged back to safety by two friends. The youth bowed and received an applause all of his own as Carlo sung on:

You, my perfect happiness,
My perfect, perfect happiness.

The pieces of paper were sonnets in praise of him, Carlo knew. Only the third night and already he had his own sonnets! It was like a dream, like every dream he had ever dreamt as a child, all coming true at once. People in the nearer boxes began to pelt the stage with roses. Their scent, bruised out of them by the heat of a thousand candles, swirled around Carlo's pearl-encrusted buskins. He glanced up at box forty-three. A blur of rosy wings caught the corner of his eye. Surely Celestina hadn't brought the rosefinch to the opera?

He planted his feet in a heroic stance to draw breath for the final *messa di voce*.

You, my twin—

Carlo held onto the word *twin*, making the note swell and fade, swell and fade, as Maestro Sarastro had taught him in the conservatorio. There was a collective sigh from ladies across the auditorium. In the pit, someone swayed and went down like a tree into the arms of her friends.

Twin—soul.

Now for the surprise, added especially for this evening. Carlo opened his cloak wide, and on the last word, let it fall. Three of Tammo's doves exploded from behind him in a flash of blue powder and soared to the ceiling to touch wings with gods and angels.

The Teatro erupted into louder applause. Carlo bowed again, making sure to give special attention to the ducal box. It looked as if the Duke was present for the third night in a row. *Venus* was proving to be the most popular opera Maestro Sarastro had written. Carlo was sure his old tutor would be making the most of the favour it afforded him.

He tipped a bow and a playful wink to the maestro

before striding to the wings, pulling the plumed helmet from his head. He ran a hand through his damp hair. Now he could rest until Act Three.

On the way downstairs to the tiring rooms, he passed Scipione the bass, making ready to rise through the trapdoor as Vulcan, Venus' jealous husband.

"In the mouth of the wolf," Carlo grinned. Scipione had told him yesterday that the motion made him queasy, and that the fireworks that went off at either side of him were singeing his eyebrows smaller every night.

"May the wolf choke," Scipione rumbled, and went to take his place in the machinery.

The tiring room was empty when Carlo got there. Casale had left him a carafe of honeyed rosehip water, and returned to the apartment to prepare supper. The dressers were probably trying to repair Giovanni's Cupid outfit, which he had accidentally torn with his arrow in the last act.

Carlo sank into the chair before the mirror and peeled off his cloak, letting its velvet folds drape over the back of the chair. He would need to change into the red outfit with bleeding hearts on for Act Three, but there was time yet. He gargled the rosehip water in the back of his throat before swallowing, then leaned closer to the mirror to see if his make-up had run. A little. He dipped his fingers in the pot of crushed pearls and massaged his cheeks.

You ask me who I am: what will I say?

It was all a masquerade, really. Carnival and the opera. The masks and make-up and tricks of the light. And a castrato was the greatest masquerader of all. Neither female nor truly male. Singing of passion and making women swoon. (He hoped that woman in the pit hadn't hurt herself.) Yet Carlo was as chaste as the Virgin Mother. The thought of what Count Pageno's former protégé had done made him sick. Rutting with one person after another, until his body filled with sores and he writhed in madness.

Did you have to want to lie with someone to truly love them? Love was beauty and purity, like Narcissus by his pool or Diana hunting under the moon. Love was a friend sitting beside you on the bough of an ash tree as the sun set. Love was…

"The four seasons are warming up for the ballet. Want a hand getting into the tomato costume?"

Carlo looked up. His twin was standing in the doorway, waistcoat open to his knees, hair ruffled until it stood vertically on his head. He was grinning at his own joke, that sly half-grin that brought his pinched features to life.

Of course. He had almost forgotten Tamino was in the theatre tonight. There was no other way the doves could have done their trick onstage at such short notice. Carlo felt something pluck at his breast. The three words he longed to say swelled in his throat. His lips parted.

"Tomato costume, indeed! One more quip against the seamstress' art from you, dear twin, and I shall leave you to the mercy of mistress Fenice and a limitless amount of pins." He picked a flower from a vase on the toilette table and flicked it at Tammo's head.

Tammo plucked it from his shoulder and shoved it

down the back of Carlo's neck. Anything else that might have been said was swallowed up in stifled giggles.

The fire had died down to an amber glow. A perfect match for the apricot brandy Count Pageno had sent, now diminished to puddles in the bottom of two crystal glasses with golden rims. The glasses were a gift from a bishop in Vulcanetta. Or was it a baroness in Festeburg? Carlo stretched his long legs toward the embers. An invisible hive buzzed in his chest, warm and tasting of harvest.

"So, then she said: And what am I supposed to do about the mess in my wig, Citizen Capell? And I said: Signora Bellina, the poor creatures have been holding their bowels in these two arias. If you wish to avoid accidents, I suggest you leave the stage by the other staircase."

"Oh, you never did!" Carlo nuzzled his twin's shoulder with his temple. It smelt of charcoal and the acrid tang of caged birds. He moved a little higher, touching Tamino's scar with the tip of his nose. So smooth, so shiny. Like ice between the cobbles on a winter's day.

"Carlo!" Tammo gave a shudder. "That tickles." He stuck a finger in Carlo's ribs. "See how you like it."

Carlo gave a scream of laughter and slid onto the tiles. He sat in a heap of arms and legs, giggling, then clapped a hand over his mouth to silence himself.

"You're drunk, Carlo," his twin's voice rasped in his ear.

"So are you." Carlo twisted around to look at Tammo's

face, close to his own. "Your nose is all red. Like a little cherry." He tickled it with the ends of his hair.

"Stop it, Carlo. You're going to make me sneeze."

"Long life to you!"

Carlo wrapped his arms around his knees and looked at the distorted reflection of himself in the fire irons. He felt as if his mirror self had swapped places with his bodily self, and he was now watching himself from a pleasant distance. He felt alive and so full of love. Bursting with love.

Tammo gave a huge yawn. "I need to go. I'll get a bed at Armide's."

"No. Stay." Carlo pawed at his twin's sleeve. "Stay, Tamino. I'm going to the park with Celestina tomorrow. You can come, too. She won't mind. She has a carriage with…with…"

He'd lost his train of thought. The lattice in the centre of the shovel looked like a cage. A little, little cage. For a little, little bird.

Had he already asked Tamino about Celestina's rosefinch? He recalled saying something about it. Sometime after the second glass. Then he'd asked about the Marchesa della Pamina. Or had he? He'd poured a third glass and Tamino had used the chamber pot. And then he had asked Carlo… Yes, Tamino had asked him; that was it. Asked him what?

He hiccupped. "I fear I may have drunk too much." He touched his fingers to his eyelashes. There were tears there. Where had the tears come from? A sudden panic rose in his breast. "You won't leave me, will you, Tamino? You love me, don't you?"

"Let's get you to bed." Tammo's voice had a gruff gentleness Carlo seldom heard. He squatted down and hooked his arms under Carlo's armpits. "Come on. One. Two. Three."

There was a brief tug-of-war, Carlo's size against Tammo's determination. He was up. He was down. They were losing balance.

In a burst of giggles, they tripped over each other and tumbled onto the sopha.

Tammo's face was level with Carlo's. The pinched features, flushed with brandy. The darting eyes. The lips parted, gasping for breath. Carlo closed his eyes…

…and pressed his lips against Tamino's. They were softer than he had imagined. Damper. Like cold pasta. Was that a disappointment? He softened his mouth, turned one kiss into many, a chain. A bird fluttered in his chest. He reached out a hand to cup Tammo's cheek.

The shove Tammo dealt him sent him flying across the room.

"What the hell are you doing?" Tammo scrubbed his mouth with the back of his hand. "Sweet Michael, Carlo!" He spat into the fireplace. Embers hissed.

"Sweet Michael!" Tammo swore again. He worked his mouth as if he had tasted rotten food. "I'll see you when you've sobered up. I'm going to Armide's. Goodnight."

Coronis swooped after him, a shadow in the darkness.

Carlo touched his own lips, tentative. Warm petals. He

tugged a bolster from the sopha and hugged it to his chest, staring into the fire with burning eyes.

He was still sitting there when Casale came in.

9

A Drive in the Park

Tammo had a headache. His tongue felt as though someone had tried to carpet it. Carlo's silver tongue scraper didn't seem such a bad idea. He scratched his neck, staring from chair to washstand to embroidered Madonna.

Hadn't he started off at Carlo's last night? What was he doing at Armide's? He tugged on a stocking, wishing it was cleaner. His head told him he'd been drinking last night. With Carlo? Why would he leave the eunuch on his own? He stumbled across the chamber to his shoes, tripping over one in the half-dark. And where the hell was Coronis? The crow was always in his chamber when he awoke. Always.

"Coffee and rolls, Citizen Capell." Michelangelo crashed into the room, causing an anvil blow to Tammo's head. A tray went down with a second crash.

"Another nippy day out there. People are saying it's a judgement on the Nobilissimo. Do you think it is? Because my mother says I should come back to the village if that's so. She says that when the Archangel swings his sword…"

"It's just weather," Tammo growled, more harshly than he intended. Michelangelo was banging the shutters open. Tammo's eyes streamed with the sunlight. He sniffed. Something in the sensation kindled a memory of last night. Something about Carlo tickling his nose. That old gesture from when they were boys. Why did the thought of it make his stomach churn? Was it just the hangover?

"Are you… Oh, where's your crow?" Michelangelo turned in circles, as if expecting Coronis to appear like a magic lantern picture. "I brought her a biscuit."

"Well, you can take it back to the kitchen." Tammo balled his fists to stop himself from losing his temper completely. It wasn't the boy's fault he had drunk too much and misplaced his friends. But if Michelangelo stayed in the room much longer, Tammo couldn't vouch for the soundness of his bones.

He heaved a sigh as the door closed, and looked at his breakfast. Coffee. Good. He needed that. The rolls made him feel like retching, but years of childhood hunger made him reluctant to leave any food untouched. He squared his shoulders and began to tackle it. Sip. Chew. Swallow. Force it down.

Holy Michael! He remembered now. Carlo had kissed him. Not a boyish kiss or the sort an uncle gave you at a wedding. On the lips, lingering, tender. Like a woman.

Or a lover.

He steadied himself, willing his breakfast to stay down. They had both been very drunk. He remembered that. Perhaps it had been a game? Carlo larking about, as always.

Only it hadn't felt like a game. It had felt like how he dreamt of kissing Celestina.

Tammo dug his fingernails into the edges of the table as his gut jerked. Maybe it had been a dream? A bizarre dream, like the one about the Carnival mask. Michael's dregs! If only his head didn't ache so much.

Oh, sweet Michael! He remembered something else now. Carlo and Celestina were going to be in the park this morning. Riding in Celestina's carriage.

Tammo took deep breaths, sweat soaking his collar. Right now, Carlo was the last person Tammo wanted to see. He wouldn't be able to look his twin in the eye after a dream like that. Even the thought of it made him blush hot enough to strike a horseshoe on. But to see Celestina. In a public place, away from closed doors and appointments and Caesar's slights…

It was too much to resist. He had to get close, to share a word with her. He had to know if her hints at love were true memories or dreams, too. He had to be there.

He bolted the rest of his breakfast. Washed. Dressed. Scowled in the mirror at the bleary-eyed, unshaven gargoyle that looked back. It would have to do.

He strapped on the dark flute and hurried down Armide's staircase. He would go out the back way and settle his bill later. At this point, the last thing he needed was to be waylaid by Michelangelo, Armide or that infernal foreign merchant.

There was a scent of musk on the air from the perfumers' shops as he wound his way toward the ferry point. He would be in that park. And he would make Celestina notice him.

The park gave a display of autumn colour to rival the glories of the opera. The trees were small but made up for it in vibrancy. Gold, russet, orange, red. In the last week, the season had advanced noticeably. Berries clustered, scarlet and black. Seed cases bristled. There was even a touch of mist in the air.

Tammo chewed his lip. Grimaldi had only heard of such a cold autumn from old men in his youth. If his tales of terror were to be believed, winter would be horrendous. Carlo should be taking better care of himself, not gadding about in a public riding park. Another shudder of embarrassment ran through Tammo. On second thought, Carlo could manage fine without him.

The riding park was a new addition to the Mansion Quarter. In Tammo's boyhood, nobles had been content to take exercise in Angel's Wood or wait for an invitation to the Ducal gardens. Now the hour of the evening stroll saw hordes of well-dressed Angelians going up and down the chalk paths like a flock of silken sheep. Walking, riding, driving open carriages. And most importantly, greeting and admiring each other.

At this hour, the drives and avenues were relatively empty, but there was still the odd nursemaid with children trailing wheeled toys, or pairs of young men putting blood mares through their paces.

Tammo paced between the stands of rowan trees, his shoes leaving footprints in the damp chalk. The trouble with his abrupt separation from Carlo was that he now had no idea where in the park Celestina would be. Should he head for the east gate, the one closest to the Pageno Mansion? Or would they be further into the park by now?

A child began to wail close by. A wheel had come off its wooden horse. The nursemaid picked the child up and tried to soothe it. Tammo hunched his shoulders in an attempt to dampen the sound. Why did the smallest children make the loudest noise?

The infant's sobs drove nails into Tammo's skull. At this rate, he was going to lose his breakfast rolls. Why didn't the nurse just shut the child up? Couldn't she see that other people had important business in this park?

His hand twitched over the clasp of the flute case. Without thinking, he unfastened it and pulled out the dark flute. Its vines and finches were comforting under his fingers. He raised it to his lips, blew, and trilled.

Be quiet. He directed his thoughts at the child. *Be quiet and stop crying.*

He envisaged a wooden horse, its wheels intact and turning perfectly. *See. It's all mended.* His imaginary self showed the horse to the child.

For a moment, the visionary horse quivered and began to fade. Behind it, Tammo could see the faintest outline of a blue wing, covered in eyes that blinked and stared. His heart raced.

No way am I falling for that again. Tammo flared his

nostrils. He closed his eyes, breathing deeply, playing slowly. The wooden horse became more substantial; the vision of wings faded.

"That's my brave boy," he heard the nurse say.

Tammo opened his eyes and stared at the flute in his hand. The child was calm, clinging to the nursemaid's hand, two drips under its nose.

He'd done it again. He'd charmed a person. This was incredible. The power, the thrill. If only the effort hadn't left him feeling so queasy and fuzzy-headed. But that was doubtless down to the brandy. Next time he'd be sober.

A violent cawing from the rowan trees almost made him drop the flute. His head snapped round. Coronis was perched in a forked bough, tail upward, head downward. Her obsidian eyes were filled with scorn.

Tammo swore. "Ill-omened bird! You scared the breeches off me. And where have you been all night?" He gave a sharp whistle. "To me, girl!"

With the deliberation of a priest at mass, Coronis lifted her tail and let a splat of white-and-black guano drop inches from Tammo's shoulder.

"Sweet Michael!" Tammo spat.

Coronis gave an even louder caw and flew across the park, out of sight.

He was still giving chase when he saw the carriage. A phaeton, open and lightly sprung, pulled by a single bay mare.

Carlo was unmistakable in the passenger seat. Even seated, he was head and shoulders above the average citizen, and broad in the back. He was wearing a caped greatcoat, like a coachman, and a felt cocked hat with a veil over it. Celestina was holding the reins. Plumes bobbed on her tricorn hat, which held down the lace mantilla shawl that covered her shoulders.

Two ponies trotted in the phaeton's wake. One carried the ever-present Teresa, veiled in her own mantilla. The other bore a cocksure lad of five or six, in a red riding coat. He had a riding crop in his hand and was whipping the pony every few minutes, with loud whoops. Tammo felt tempted to take the riding crop to the boy's backside. But, of course, no commoner could strike Nobile Rinaldo.

Celestina, Rinaldo and Teresa were wearing matching harlequin masks, black with maroon trim. Tammo slowed his pace, feeling naked about the face. He'd forgotten about Carnival. Even barefoot boys had masks of orange peel or salad leaves. Compared to the Pageno party he would look uncouth. Un-Angelian.

He slipped behind one of the taller trees, thankful for his wiry stature. He needed to think about this carefully. Make the best approach. Without thinking, his left hand went to the flute case again.

"You said I could drive the carriage." Rinaldo's voice rang out, harsh and shrill. He lashed the air with his riding crop. "You promised, Celestina. I will tell Mama that you don't keep your promises."

"In a little while, Rinaldo. Wait until we get to the cypress avenue. It's safer there."

Tammo fought to calm the waves that surged through his blood at the sound of Celestina's voice. Should he make a bow? That would be both gallant and respectful. Or should he saunter casually by and pretend he hadn't noticed them until the last moment?

"You said to wait until we got to the circle drive. And we're at the circle drive. So, tell the eunuch to get out and hold my horse. It's my turn now."

Sweet Michael, how that child's voice went through his head! Celestina reined the mare in and drew breath to say something, but Teresa interrupted. "Oh, let the little lord have his drive and give us all some peace."

Celestina began whispering apologies to Carlo, who whispered something back, and climbed out of the phaeton. Even with the veil, Tammo could see how pale and queasy he looked. He must be more hungover than Tammo.

Tammo cursed to himself as Carlo took the pony's head and Rinaldo scrambled down, jogging the eunuch's elbow as he ran to the carriage. Step out now and he'd be face-to-face with Carlo. How would it be if he withered with embarrassment, right in front of Celestina?

"Now then. Hold the reins gently and say: *Canella, walk*. Canella is good. You don't need to drive her hard." Celestina placed the reins into her brother's hands.

When he thought of this day later, Tammo wondered if there had been a moment when they truly believed the nobile would do as he was told. If so, it was short-lived.

Rinaldo flicked the reins so hard, Tammo heard the leather crack. Teresa's horse shied, and the pony Carlo was holding whinnied and tossed free of his grasp.

"Vai! Vai, Canella!" the young nobile shrieked at the top of his lungs.

Celestina made a grasp for his wrist. "Rinaldo, no!"

It was too late. Canella's ears had flattened to her head. The poor mare shot off at a tremendous pace, causing the seat of the phaeton to bounce violently.

"Rinaldo!"

"Noblesse Celestina!"

Teresa's horse was turning in circles. Carlo was still fighting a battle with the skittish pony. But Tammo saw none of it. He was already running. The phaeton was bouncing on its springs. On this circular path, it could be on two wheels at any moment. He had to get hold of the reins. He had to stop Canella's flight before Celestina and her brother were flung from the carriage.

Michael, give me strength, he prayed.

His lungs felt near to bursting. Chalk flew up from his heels. He was close to the shaft now. If Canella chose to kick out, he could break a rib and say goodbye to playing the flute. Celestina was gripping her brother's shoulder. Her face was ice pale. Without working leg muscles, she had no way of bracing herself against the phaeton's swaying.

"Rinaldo, give me the reins. Give me the reins." Her voice shook.

Tammo pushed his body harder, faster. He had to get ahead of the carriage. He stretched out his hand. The billowing ends of Canella's mane brushed his knuckles. Nearly there. If he could just get hold of the harness…

"Hey! What do you do there, sirrah?" Rinaldo had noticed him. The little nobile turned to stare down from his seat, disdain on his face. The temporary distraction caused the reins to slacken, the galloping hooves to slow ever so slightly.

"Got you!" His hand closed around the brass ring on Canella's bridle. "Whoa, Canella! Easy, now. Easy. There's a good girl."

For a moment, Tammo thought Canella was going to toss free of his grasp. He was almost tripping over his feet, trying to keep up, hold the bridle and calm the horse all at once. But Rinaldo's moment of distraction had given Celestina the chance to take the reins.

Her voice rang out, clear and strong despite the shaking. "Canella, stand!"

Canella snorted and drew to a halt, tossing and blowing. In one movement, Tammo dropped the bridle, clambered up the chassis, and caught the swaying Celestina in his arms.

"It's all right, noblesse. I've got you. You're safe now." She was so small, so soft. He could feel her heart pounding against his. Instinctively, she had grasped the back of his coat and clung to him, trembling and gasping. "You're safe," he said again.

Oh, God! Oh, sweet angels above! She was in his arms. Him. Tammo Capell. Her cheek smelled of honeysuckle. He breathed deeply, his head reeling.

"Unhand my sister, shabbaroon!" Rinaldo prickled with indignation.

Celestina sat back, as if released from a dream, and readjusted her mantilla. Tammo hastily jumped from the carriage onto the path. He blinked rapidly, trying to catch his breath. Celestina stared.

"But it's Citizen Capell, is it not? Rinaldo, it's Citizen Capell who brought my sweet Carlino and your whistling bullfinches. He's a friend of Signor Seraphini."

Rinaldo pouted, clearly vexed at being denied the chance to exercise his feudal rights.

Celestina leaned over the side of the phaeton and lowered her voice. "I cannot thank you enough, Citizen Capell. You are my knight in shining armour."

Tammo cleared his throat and stared at the chalk, hoping she couldn't see his burning cheeks. "I would do anything for you, Noblesse Celestina." He coughed again and scratched his neck. "Surely you must know…"

"Oh, my sweet darlings! You're safe." Teresa and Carlo had finally managed to control the ponies and catch up with the phaeton. Teresa had dismounted, shawl askew, and was trying to fuss her way into the carriage. "If anything had happened to you…… Oh, holy Michael, your mama and papa!"

"All is well, Teresa. We're quite safe. Citizen Capell acted swiftly." Whatever else Celestina might have said was obliterated by a torrent of country dialect and half-remembered prayers.

Tammo felt his spine stiffen as he became aware of

Carlo standing close by him, holding the ponies' heads. Tammo had never seen him so pale. He looked as if he was about to vomit.

"Sweet Michael, Tamino!" His soft soprano voice shook with emotion. "I thought I'd lost you. If the horse had kicked out. Or you'd fallen under the wheels." He gave a sharp sniffle. "My dear, dear twin!" He took a step toward Tammo, his free arm stretched wide.

It was obvious how shaken Carlo was. Tammo was feeling pretty shaky himself. It would have been a small enough courtesy to open his arms, to let his friend take comfort in the warmth of his embrace. But last night's shame burned too strongly. He didn't want Carlo there, reminding him of what he'd allowed to happen.

He made a sound of annoyance and looked away. "Oh, don't be such a girl, Carlo! I'm all right now, aren't I?"

He didn't look to see the effect of his words on Carlo's face.

He had no idea how he ended up in the stable yard. There had been a general cavalcade of confusion, of snorting horses and Teresa's prayers. Tammo found himself carried along in the mêlée.

He now stood amid a maelstrom of horse blankets and buckets of hot mash. Grooms and stable boys hurried about on predetermined paths that no one but themselves could see, all of which placed Tammo in the way of wherever they needed to go. He'd lost sight of Carlo. And of Celestina.

Sweet Michael, his pulse still quivered when he thought of her in his arms! *Her knight.* That's what she had said. Not some pawn on the edge of the chessboard.

And she knew it was he who brought the rosefinch. She knew! Of course, she did. He was much more to her than a messenger. *I cannot thank you enough, Citizen Capell.* There had been admiration in her voice, he was sure of it. Dare he go so far as to say desire?

"Tammo Capell!" Fenice was running toward him, cap strings a-flutter. There was a light in her eyes that somehow matched the song in his heart.

Let her come. Let her tease him all she wished. Nothing could dim the light inside him right now.

"They said you were here." Fenice's words came in bursts, her short steps making her sprint across the courtyard an Amazonian feat. "They said, Tammo Capell is a hero. He saved the young mistress' life. I said, he's been doing that since he was a boy."

She flung herself at him, a bulldog in petticoats. He lifted her off the ground and swung her round, not caring who saw. He was a giant today. A Titan. A demigod. He planted a kiss on the side of Fenice's neck.

"You can put that in the bank," he said. "Count it as largesse."

"Large?" Fenice raised her eyebrows as Tammo placed her back on solid ground. "In your dreams, Tammo Capell!"

She looked over her shoulder and winked as she walked away.

He didn't care.

10
Shame

"Ha! Horse of clubs takes the two of swords and the *settebello*." Scipione swept the cards toward himself with his meaty hands.

"May your teeth fall out, Scipione!" Giovanni looked in despair at his cards. "I have the worst hand ever."

"You dealt it yourself," Scipione rumbled.

The young man at Giovanni's side, still dressed in the brown stockings and leaf-festooned tunic of a dancing faun, leaned close until his lips brushed the famous ringlets. "That doesn't stop him from cheating. Never trust a bass, I say."

"Never trust a nimble-footed fox like you, rather!" Scipione took a swig of claret. "Seraphini, it's your turn. Wake up, man!"

Carlo stared at the cards in his hand. Swords. Cups. Coins. Batons. What did it matter? He pushed the five of coins across the table with a sigh.

"La! What sort of play is that?" Giovanni shook open a masquerade fan, the sort with eye holes you could peep through. "You have a match in your hand; I can see it from here."

"Forgive me." Carlo fumbled to amend his move and accidentally knocked Scipione's pile of captures to the floor.

"Seraphini!" Several voices cried out together.

"Forgive me," Carlo muttered again.

He hadn't wanted to join the card party in Giovanni's apartment. What he had really wanted to do was to climb into bed, pull the curtains around him and shut out the world forever.

But Scipione had ambushed him on his way up the staircase. "You can't go creeping off to your chamber every night. We need a fourth at scopa. Come and save me from Parnasso and his pirouetting paramour. Straight from his Baroness to that!" Scipione rolled his eyes. "Where does he find the stamina?"

"Some market I don't frequent, sadly." Carlo covered a yawn. "Forgive me, Scipione, but a full performance, plus receiving admirers, plus rehearsals for the new Duke's Day opera…"

The bass singer placed a hand on Carlo's velvet sleeve. It was surprisingly gentle for a man of his build. "Look, I know your friend hasn't been around these past few days. It's not my place to pry, but for sweet Michael's sake, come out and enjoy yourself instead of moping in your chamber. If anything, to keep certain tongues from wagging." He nodded toward Giovanni's door.

He had tried to feign jollity at first. Giovanni's apartment was more lavish than his own. The card table had been set up in an alcove before a high balcony window, hung about with gold-coloured curtains. The shutters were open, and the moon hung low and misty in the sky.

Carlo shivered and dabbed at his nose with a handkerchief. The seasons were turning far too quickly this year. Could it be that Michael had turned his back? Carlo had always maintained that the Archangel did nothing of the sort, that he loved his Angelian children unconditionally. But at this hour of night, it was all too easy to believe in omens.

Usually, he enjoyed scopa. It was a good Angelian game that took him back to nights in the Conservatorio dormitories. Celestina and the other nobles played with the cards of Lysfleur, at games like piquet and quadrille. And in Festeburg they had used strange cards with acorns and hawk bells as suits. But now the game reminded him too strongly of Tamino. Tamino who had rejected his kiss with oaths and violence. Tamino, who had turned aside from him in the park. Tamino, his beloved twin…

"Now then, my sweetlings. Who's for lampreys?"

One by one, the players glanced up. Citizeness Aldo bustled into the apartment, a tray on one arm. She gave a smile that would have benefitted from more teeth. "I cooked them especially for my little songbirds. And for my dancing butterflies."

She ruffled the dancer's hair. He exchanged glances with Giovanni, who let the fan slide along his alabaster cheek. In the language of the fan, that meant, I want you.

Carlo's stomach clenched. Had Tammo believed Carlo

had *wanted* him? Bodily? How could he? Tammo had known him from boyhood. They were twin souls. How could he believe Carlo to be so…so…?

"Lampreys, Signor Seraphini? Fresh from the river today." Citizeness Aldo wafted the tray under his nose.

He waved it away before he retched. "No. I thank you."

"Oh, go on. Just a little one. I know you singers; you think you can survive on…" The housekeeper's chatter ceased mid-flow as she caught sight of Carlo's face. She cupped a hand to his cheek. It smelled of fish. "Oh, my poor little sugared almond! Are you sickening for something? You're white as Michael's wings."

She turned to Giovanni, her rouged lips pursed. "Oh, Signor Parnasso! You're a wicked being to keep your friend from his bed, and him so pale. I'll fetch you a tonic, Signor Seraphini. Citizen Aldo swears by it. Coughs, toothache, ringworm, the flux: it chases them all away. If you'll just give me a minute…"

Carlo forced himself to take the fishy hand in his and kiss it. "Thank you for your concern, Citizeness, but I assure you, I am quite well." Michael alone knew what might be in any tonic the Aldos used. "Quite well," he said again, playing his hand to prove the point.

He felt as though he had swallowed cold rocks.

When he and Tammo had first made their bargain with the Archangel, Carlo had been the first to speak. He had begged Michael, beyond hope, to take some of his natural gifting and use it to give Tammo a gift for bird charming. He had asked with barely a second thought, knowing the strength of his friend's desire. The Archangel had warned him that he would be weakened by the bargain, that his health would suffer, but Carlo had refused to be swayed. As a eunuch, he had always been delicate, feeling the cold easily and lacking the muscular strength of uncut boys. If he had considered the consequences at all, he had merely imagined more of the same.

What he hadn't imagined was the bone-weariness that followed him, day in and out. The life of a singer required stamina. And that was hard to sustain. Carlo relied on his twin to lend him strength. That had been part of the bargain, too. The Archangel had told them, "Your friendship must hold fast. For the sake of friendship these gifts have been granted, and only through friendship shall any good come of them."

Tammo had not visited Carlo for nearly five days. There had been no knock at the door, no hasty message from Armide's. Even at the Teatro, his twin had managed to avoid him. The doves had flown every night, but there had been no sign of their master.

Is he really so ashamed of me? Carlo thought.

He had written letter after letter, then burned them, unsent. How could he explain? He barely understood the feelings himself. He needed his twin in front of him, so he could look him in the eye and show him the purity of his love.

But what if Tammo pushed him away a third time? It

would be the bath of ice all over again: the barber-surgeon's knife, and the smack of his father's belt. The mere thought of such things made Carlo want to curl up small and hide beneath the table, as he had done in his mother's kitchen. If Tammo rejected him, it wouldn't matter how many roses and sonnets they threw at him onstage. He wouldn't be able to stand there in the first place.

A shaft of pale sunlight illuminated Michael's image, as Carlo knelt in prayer.

"…and place myself, my loved ones, and all I possess under your powerful protection. Oh, most noble Prince of the Angelic Hierarchies, valorous warrior of Almighty God, my beloved Archangel Saint Michael. *In nomine Patris, et Filii, et Spiritus Sancti.* Amen."

Carlo kissed the hand of the painted archangel, and rose from his prie-dieu. He still prayed, without fail, morning and night. Eight years at the conservatorio had fixed the habit in him. But there was more than just habit to Carlo's prayers. Carlo had seen the Archangel with his own eyes. Twice. Until now, he had been certain that, when he prayed, Saint Michael's wings of love surrounded him. Now he wondered if there was a good reason why he had not seen the Archangel in so long. Some sin or failure that was making everything fall apart.

He glanced at Orpheus, darting to and fro in his cage. The song thrush's sudden movements had started to make him flinch, in a way they hadn't before. Casale had been the one to feed Carlo's pet these last two weeks. The scab on the back of Carlo's hand had faded to a pale pink, but he no longer felt safe with Orpheus on his wrist. Nor did he wish to hold his other birds, in case they treated him in like fashion.

He sighed deeply as he fastened his cloak at the clasp. It shouldn't be this way. His own beloved birds had become spectres of the cut.

He would go to Armide's and seek out Tammo. There was just about time before rehearsal. This was all a misunderstanding; they could clear it up. They were best friends, sworn twins. They never fell out. He and Tamino would be laughing and joking together again in no time.

"Make up both beds for tonight," he told Casale on his way out.

"As you say, signor." Casale tugged his springy forelock.

Carnivale displayed its colours everywhere. Even in the sombre streets of the financiers, which ran between the cockpit, south of the river, and Piazza Giustizia where Caffe Armide stood. The faces of bankers and their clerks were hidden behind batua masks, while above the doors, the crest of more than one banking family was surmounted with a golden horn of plenty.

Carlo had covered his own features with a simple black-and-silver eye mask, but had taken the extra precaution of hiring a chair. "Signor Seraphini" was gaining popularity with each performance, and Carlo did not intend to face his twin surrounded by swooning admirers with porcelain miniatures of him pinned to their hats.

He quietly dropped a handful of centesimi in the hat of the chairman, and stepped out into the piazza. The smell of roasting coffee met his nostrils, along with a whiff of starch and lavender from the wig-makers, and something that smelled like dishwater.

Coffee shops were not places Carlo frequented very often. Signor Contarini liked to keep his singers indoors whenever possible, safe from damp and miasmas. Carlo covered his mouth with his cloak against the pipe smoke of the outdoor chocolate drinkers, and walked along the tiled portico, past each numbered door in turn. All of them had Tammo's trade card in their windows: *Purveyor of Fine Singing Birds*. Which booth was his twin more likely to take? This one? The next? One of the outdoor drinkers lowered his pipe and stared. Carlo blushed. This was hardly inconspicuous behaviour. He needed to be decisive.

He opened the door of the nearest booth. It was occupied by just one man, sitting alone with a small dish of coffee and a news sheet. Like Carlo, he had his collar up and his eyes masked. Carlo settled at an oblong table beneath a mirror.

The doorbell rang, and in came two foppish young men whose masks were masses of feathers. They flopped onto the red velvet benches. One of them put his feet on the table and crossed his silk-stockinged ankles.

"Michelangelo!" he yelled. "Michelangelo, you useless jackanapes! Get in here now. We're parched, sirrah!" He turned to his companion. "And my aunt told him to make the filthy bird shit upon me. It was a world of work to have that suit of clothes cleaned. It's quite a favourite. I would not wish to replace it."

"Have not the funds to replace it, you mean," his companion said.

The first fop sniffed. "As to that, my funds were tied up. I only wished my aunt to tide me over. I've had awful bad luck at cards recently."

"And the banks are in the hands of the…ahem… golden pheasants."

"Too true, cousin." The first fop sniffed again and touched a lace handkerchief to his nose. "But now it seems the old lady has had a change of heart. Not before time!"

He took a silk purse from his belt and waved it in his companion's face. The clank of coins could be heard from Carlo's seat. "For services rendered." He flung the purse on the table and stretched out again, his arms folded behind his head.

The second fop sniggered. "Services? You? My Lady P must be turning senile."

The first fop shrugged. "Stranger things have happened." He lowered his voice, but not enough to prevent Carlo hearing his words. "Have you heard the latest on this so-called secret society of the Nobilissimo's? I heard from the Noblesse Argente, who had it from Baroness Flavio, who heard it in the confessional, that a certain chamber in the Bishop's Palace…well, let's just say it's not just the Dean and Chapter that meet there…"

Carlo noticed the man by the door take out a pencil and write something in a memorandum pad. As he did so, a ring winked on his finger. Three rubies and a Sacred Heart.

Carlo's eyes widened. That was Morestelli's ring. Morestelli was a spy; there was no longer any doubt. That was why Carlo had replaced him on stage. The Duke was using his former primo castrato to gather intelligence about his son's plot. Carlo should tell this to Tammo.

If he could get Tammo to speak to him again.

"Sorry to keep you waiting, signors." A skinny boy in an apron too big for him appeared through the back door. He bowed to the fops in a jerky manner, like a marionette.

"About time, Michelangelo," said the second fop. "We ought to have you horsewhipped."

As the boy took their orders, Carlo noticed that Morestelli carefully placed some coins on the table, rose from his seat and left the caffe without so much as a sound. Away to the Duke, Carlo thought. Was the Bishop really conspiring against him? The idea brought bile to Carlo's throat.

He turned back and gestured to the boy. "Pardon me, but is Citizen Capell hereabouts? A very dear friend wishes to speak with him."

"Oh no, signora." The lad had evidently decided from his voice that Carlo was female. "He hasn't spent no time here for days. Just collects his letters and goes. Citizen Armide is sore put out, I can tell you."

"And where does he go, my boy?" Carlo took a copper denaro from his purse.

The boy threw his hands in the air. "To the wind! Who can say? No one tells such things to the likes of me."

Carlo had tried consulting Armide, but the red-wigged caffe owner had been rushed off his feet and was no more forthcoming than his pot-boy. By then, the hour of rehearsal had arrived and Carlo was forced to take his leave. Closing the door behind him, he drew his cloak tighter, shivering although the sun was high. He felt sick at heart.

A caw from one of the outdoor tables drew his attention. A crow had landed and was pecking at its reflection in a copper chocolate pot. Carlo drew a breath.

"Coronis?"

The Archangel had smiled on him. Tammo's bird would seek him out, and carry a token from Carlo, as she had done in the past.

He turned his steps toward the table. "Coronis, I..."

The bird gave another caw and flew off toward the bell tower of Piazza Giustizia without a backward glance. Carlo stepped back and plucked at his lip. He must have been mistaken. This bird was not Coronis; it was only his longing that had made him think so. But it looked just like her.

"A friend may desert another unintentionally. But that friend must take care. The balance is precarious. Many more false moves and the scales will tip."

Carlo looked around, frowning. A foreigner in a full-length robe decorated with dragons, his hair dressed in a queue, scraped back from his bald forehead, had come out from another booth. He gave a half-smile as Carlo met his eye.

Carlo blinked. "I…God save you, signor. You are very kind." The stranger's words had taken Carlo by surprise. He supposed they were some kind of Ming proverb, but they were strangely apt. "Have you been in Angelio long? You will find Carnival most diverting."

The stranger's eyes flickered with amusement. "Long enough, signor. May the wolf choke this evening." He made a deep bow and returned to the caffe.

"What is it this time, Bianci?" Maestro Sarastro banged out a chord mid-phrase and stood up at the harpsichord. His jowls shook as he exchanged a glance with Herr Wilhelm, the stage director.

"Is there a problem, Signor Seraphini?" Wilhelm's Festeburg accent had more than a touch of weariness in it.

"The helmet is too heavy." Carlo took it from his head. Damp curls clung to his forehead. "I can barely hold my neck straight in it, let alone sing."

Herr Wilhelm gave a tense cough. "It is the same helmet you wore in *Venus*. You never complained before."

"Forgive me, but it now has a plaster dragon and three extra plumes on it. And I must wear this great chain about my neck." He tugged at the offending item.

"The dragon is to signify Saint Michael's defeat of our ancient enemy. This is a Duke's Day opera…" Herr

Wilhelm prepared to repeat himself for the third time that day, but Maestro Sarastro had no such patience.

"What the hell has got into you today, Bianci? Are you sickening for something? By Michael, if I hear so much as a sneeze out of you, I'll make sure you don't set foot outside this opera house until Lent! Not even for Count Pageno, do you hear me? The voice comes first. Always.

"Now mark through that recitative again and let's have no more of this behaviour. I expect it from La Bellina but not from you. Not from you, sir!"

Carlo swallowed his tears and replaced the helmet. "Yes, maestro."

"Carlo!" Celestina opened her arms. "What a lovely surprise! I wasn't expecting you today."

"How could I stay away, noblesse?"

He kissed her softly on the cheek, then knelt by the house carriage to receive her embrace. She smelled of honeysuckle, of silk and sunshine. He drew her closer and leaned his head against her girlish bosom. It felt maternal, protective. Carlo found himself blinking back tears as sudden memories of his mother's arms flooded his senses. How he needed female comfort right now!

There had been so much he had thought about saying to Celestina on the way over to the mansion: about Morestelli and the plot, the eligible young nobles who wouldn't marry her, Coronis, Orpheus, his fruitless search for Tammo, the horrible helmet at the Teatro... But now that he was here, he couldn't be bothered with the effort of conversation. He just wanted to feel the closeness of a friend, the warmth of her touch, the sympathy of her smile.

Celestina twirled one of Carlo's curls around her finger. "Oh, Carlo! Do you really mean it?"

Carlo said nothing, only held her closer. She drew in a ragged breath and let it out slowly. Something hard pressed against Carlo's ear as she did so. Something hidden beneath her bodice.

He looked up at her, his eyelashes damp. Celestina was beaming. She leaned in, the scent of honeysuckle growing stronger, and kissed the top of his head. "I knew you would!"

Carlo sat back on his heels, feeling in his pocket for a handkerchief to blow his nose. He tried to clear his head of the smell of his mother's baking, and the beat of a human heart against his face. There was a dusting of powder on Celestina's bodice, he noticed, and on the indigo ribbon that disappeared beneath it. Some of his maquillage had come off. He hoped she didn't mind.

"The day Carlino arrived, I knew you would," Celestina said.

Carlo felt as though he had missed part of a conversation. He had no idea why Celestina was talking about the rosefinch. He dabbed the corners of his eyes. "Where would I be without you, dear noblesse? If you should choose the religious life…"

Celestina looked scandalised. "Why would I do that?" She took his face between her hands. "You're my Angel Boy and I, I…"

"Celestina!"

The voice that spoke from the doorway was like frozen crystal. Countess Pageno's figure cast a shadow across the marble tiles. Her bouffant hair and silver gown were outlined by the sun at her back; her lips were tight. "The Mother Superior is waiting in my salon. She expected to find you there."

Carlo scrambled to his feet and made a hasty bow. Despite his best efforts, he had never managed to win the heart of the Countess, and he hated to cross her.

Celestina straightened herself in her chair. Her tone was every bit as clipped as her mother's. "Tell her I have company."

The Countess' lip twitched. "I see no company. Only one of your father's sopranists, who ought to be at the Teatro."

"Countess." Carlo inclined his head once more and made to leave.

Celestina seized hold of his wrist. "Signor Seraphini has a name, Mama. The whole of Angelio seems to know it. I fail to see why we may not use it in his presence."

Both women had stiffened. Were the beams from their eyes made visible, Carlo thought, they would be duelling, rapier against rapier. His stomach clenched.

"Countess Pageno is right," he said. "I have a performance tonight."

He tried to disengage his wrist, but Celestina kept hold. The air in the room virtually crackled, the overture to a storm.

"Very well, Mama." Celestina's voice was so brittle it could have smashed. "I will attend the Mother Superior. She is, after all, a woman of God and it's hardly her fault you keep summoning her up like the Ghost of Samuel. But only when I have taken respectful leave of my guest."

Her emphasis on the last word was unmistakable. Carlo could see the Countess fighting an inner battle between the desire to reprimand her daughter upon the instant, and the need for exemplary behaviour before her social inferiors. The latter won by a hair's breadth. Countess Pageno glided from the room like a swan moving over a lake, the hush of her silver skirts the only sound.

Celestina dropped Carlo's wrist and clenched both hands. "Hateful woman! She won't keep us apart, Carlo. I won't let her."

Carlo looked over his shoulder, to where he was certain the Countess was waiting, out of sight. "You should not speak like that, Celestina. Not of your own mother."

"Yes, I should. Do you know, she wants me to decide by Duke's Day whether or not to join the sisters?"

"And what will you say?" Carlo's gut twisted.

She took both his hands and gave him a fathomless look, her hazel eyes brimming with emotion. "Find out with me. Come to me on Duke's Day, after the festivities. Please. I shall be alone then. Mama and Papa will be at court. We can make our own feast. Please. Just for a short while. I shan't keep you from the opera."

"Of course, I shall come." He squeezed Celestina's

hands gently. It seemed to him that she was a little girl again, in need of his brotherly support.

Celestina's lower lip trembled. "Oh, Carlo! They call us cripples, but what do they know? What do they know?"

She kissed his hands, one by one, and turned the handles of the house carriage.

11

The Salon Again

Tammo reluctantly withdrew his lips from the paper. If he kissed the signature many more times, he would wear it to holes. He held the letter at arm's length, grasping to stop it fluttering in the wind. He already knew the words by heart, but he had to look once more. To ensure his imagination had not deceived him.

Citizen Capell,

I write this to express my heartfelt thanks for your heroic action in the Riding Park. I find myself a trifle indisposed today, following yesterday's adventures, but it is nothing worse than that which I bear in the everyday course of my palsy. Were it not for your quickness of thought, my very life might now hang in the balance, for which I thank Our Mother and the Blessed Archangel Michael.

Please accept the enclosed scapular as a token of my gratitude and esteem. I remain forever in your debt, Citizen Capell, and will pray daily for your soul.

Your grateful friend,

Celestina, Noblesse of the House of Pageno

The scapular's two silken panels were decorated about the edges with beads and silver stitching. At the centre of each was an image of the Archangel, his wings spread wide.

Tammo wore it now beneath his chemise, his skin pleasantly quivering at the touch of something Celestina had stitched with her own fingers. (He had dismissed in the first few minutes the possibility that the scapular was the fruit of Teresa's ceaseless embroidery.) He pressed the signature to his lips again, the scent of honeysuckle on the paper now more of a memory than an actual smell.

Your grateful friend. Did that mean what he thought it meant? She could have said *patroness* or *acquaintance*, or even stopped at *grateful.* But *friend.* That was an intimate word. A word of—dare he say it?—love. And it was addressed to him. Not to *dear Carlo,* or *beloved Angel-boy,* but to Citizen Tammo Capell. Tammo. Him.

Tammo clutched both letter and scapular to his breast. He must speak with Celestina. He must see her privately. Hear the words from her own lips.

He blushed the colour of beetroot. Celestina's lips. His thighs turned to water.

He stuffed the letter deep into his waistcoat and began chopping Grimaldi's firewood like a man with a vendetta against logs.

How could he contrive to see her? Could he bear to wait until Duke's Day?

Celestina was certain to attend Ducal Mass at the

Sancti Michaelis. Her father was the Duke's right-hand man, after all. Tammo could wait outside the cathedral. After Mass came the Water Ceremony at the Morningstar Fountain. Angelians queued to drink from the holy spring that was shown to the First Duke by the Archangel Michael as the place where he should build a pure and pious city. Half of Angelio would be there. He would be sure to *see* her there, but how could he draw her aside in order to speak with her?

Tammo scowled. He had planned to be with Carlo on Duke's Day, but that was before…

He gave a particularly savage chop. Woodchips flew in his face. He had enough on his mind; he was back at the Marchesa's salon this afternoon. His instructions were in the pocket of his best velvet coat, currently hanging up in Grimaldi's cottage. The old blacksmith would never go through his pockets, but Tammo felt grateful Grimaldi's reading skills were basic at best.

"Easy there, lad! You'll put your back out that way. Oh, you can look at me like that," Grimaldi said as Tammo stood back and wiped his brow. "You come back to me in twenty years' time and say I didn't warn you. 'Course I'll be cold in my grave by then. Not that you'll stop to give me a thought. The young never do."

"No, I'll have flattened this place to make way for an aviary." Tammo laced his voice with sarcasm, knowing Grimaldi didn't mean the words any more than he did. He hefted the axe again, but Grimaldi placed a hand on his forearm.

"Take a rest, boy. No need to rush." He sat heavily on the edge of the water trough, took out a piece of cheese and a knife and began peeling off the rind. "Plenty here for two," he said, gesturing at Tammo with the knife.

Tammo flopped beside him and took the piece of cheese Grimaldi offered him. It crumbled in his mouth, sweet and nutty. A bit soft for his taste, but Grimaldi's teeth weren't as strong as they had once been.

Droplets clung to cobwebs and moss on the side of the forge. The fogs would be here soon. And it was not yet Duke's Day. The year turned too quickly. A wood pigeon began to coo from the russet branches. Deeper in the woods, a second pigeon answered.

"Where's that bird of yours been these past few days?" Grimaldi said between smacks of the lips.

"Don't know." Tammo looked at his feet. He had spent two hours hunting Coronis in Angel's Wood yesterday, time that should have been spent procuring more flamecrests for patrons. Coronis had always done her own thing; she wasn't a pet bird. But she usually stayed close by. Could she have found a mate? It seemed a little late in her life for that.

Grimaldi chewed stolidly on the cheese and picked something from his beard. "And what about the other songbird? Your nightingale friend? Weren't you stopping over at his place tonight?"

"He's...busy." Tammo's voice lowered to a growl. "Duke's Day. Singing. The usual fol-de-lols."

"You should invite him here," Grimaldi went on. "Get some forest air into his lungs. Better for his health than that pox-ridden Teatro."

Tammo fidgeted, his eyes on the axe. Grimaldi's tone suggested idle conversation, but Tammo wasn't so sure. He wished he'd taken his room at Armide's now. He didn't need Grimaldi's opinion on his friendships. Carlo was fine. Tammo just… needed a break from him. What did the old man know of friendship anyway? If it wasn't for Tammo, he'd be a hermit.

"But you hate visitors." He scowled at Grimaldi.

Grimaldi chewed the last bit of cheese with maddening slowness. "Your visitor, not mine. Last visitor I had was more trouble than he was worth. He was only going to stay for a bowl of soup."

Tammo snorted and shook his head. He hadn't forgotten his first days with Grimaldi. Every day it had been: *Just one more day, until I get back on my feet.* That was five years ago.

Grimaldi heaved himself to his feet with a groan. The lame leg dragged a little heavier these days. Tammo thought he was going to limp back to his anvil in silence, but the blacksmith paused and turned his head.

"Funny what brings one man and another together. Aye, and what drives them apart." He rubbed his bad leg, grumbling in the back of his throat. "Once a thing's broken, it's mighty hard to meld it back together."

Tammo stared at the empty cheese rind in his hand.

He drew a deep breath, filling out his ribs. Then he drew back his arm and tossed it deep into the woods.

Tammo scratched his chest again, trying to do it in such a way that Florian wouldn't notice. The scapular was itching him. The silver stitching, probably. Or the nervous sweat he was in, waiting outside the Marchesa's salon once more. The itch moved to the back of his neck. He tugged at his collar, desperate to rake his fingernails into the skin, knowing he couldn't. If he kept on like this, Florian would think he had fleas. Tammo wasn't going to give him the satisfaction.

Play as before until Florian comes to you. Then wait outside the salon for further instruction.

The Marchesa's note had come to him at Armide's. Tammo had registered the disappointment on Armide's face when he had not opened the letter over a leisurely dish of coffee, but paid the fee in silence and pocketed the note.

"Will you be wanting your room, citizen?" Armide had wanted to know. "Only Duke's Day will soon be upon us and that window commands a splendid view..." He wrung his hands.

"Let it out to whoever you like." Tammo's cheek twitched. He wanted to be away. "It's your caffe."

He had turned on his heels before Armide could frame a reply. Gone back to Angel's Wood. The cold blue of an autumn sky illuminated his instructions, while he sat on a fallen log and read. Beetles scurried between the decaying leaves. The Marchesa called for him to play once more.

He tucked his feelings of guilt inside his breast pocket with the folded letter. So what if his music gave him power over human minds? They were just a load of pampered fops, sitting about in masks, playing their pointless games. If the honest citizen got the upper hand for once, it was about time!

Well, he had done the playing part. Though he said it himself, he was becoming quite good at quail and pheasant song. Without putting it into words, he felt that the beast fable made sense now. It felt right; that was it. Perhaps he had managed to charm himself, along with the nobles in the Marchesa's salon? The thought made him want to laugh. *You lackwit, Tammo.*

But now he was bored. He had already been standing here for two quarter-strikes of the clock. Behind the brocade curtain, he could hear the hum of voices, rising to an occasional oath or guffaw. The Marchesa's guests seemed to be making their own entertainment, without the aid of a musician. So, why keep him waiting indefinitely?

He shifted his weight from one foot to the other, trying to ease the pinch of his best shoes on his feet. The itch had moved from his chest to his back.

To distract himself, he exchanged grimaces with the Ming statues in the cabinet of curiosities. He had come to dislike them, irrationally and intensely. Their stare was piercing, their carven eyes too knowing.

A flash of sapphire wings seared Tammo's mind.

He scratched his chest savagely. Damn the Marchesa! He could be in the woods now, seeking out birds for other patrons.

"Should I play again?" he asked Florian. He had much rather not speak to the footman but this forced inactivity was making him nervous.

Florian let out an irritated breath through his nose. "Her ladyship will be with you shortly."

His voice was as smooth as ever, but the tap of one finger against the gold button of his knee breeches told Tammo that Florian was also impatient. With a practised movement, Florian lifted the edge of the curtain, enough to allow a bright stripe of the salon to show.

The black-masked guests relaxed in a variety of poses: sitting, standing, leaning on the backs of each other's chairs. Some were chatting together, others silent. One nobile had taken a book from the shelf and was leafing through it.

In her customary place on the pale gold sopha sat the Marchesa. A folded fan tapped against her lips beneath the owl mask; her gaze was fixed on a portly lord in the centre of the room, who was examining the contents of two drawers he had removed from a miniature chest. Tammo saw the gleam of what looked like marbles dropping through his fingers one by one. A drawer of black marbles and a drawer of white.

A ballot. Was that what he was waiting on? He chewed his lip. What were they voting on, he wondered?

The portly nobleman stood up and clapped his hands. "Signors, signoras. The whites have it!"

There was a smattering of applause and a loud *Deo Gratias* from somewhere in the room. The Marchesa gave a sigh which, had Tammo heard it in other circumstances, he would have thought signified sensual pleasure.

She curtseyed to the black masks. "If you will excuse me for a moment."

She was coming their way. Florian let the curtain drop and backed against the wall. Tammo licked his dry lips and rehearsed courtesies in his head.

"Citizen Capell." The honey and cinnamon of the Marchesa's voice set Tammo's pulse fluttering. Had she no way of turning off the allure? It messed with his thinking.

He dropped into a formal bow. "Marchesa della Pamina."

"Rise." The Marchesa dismissed Florian with a gesture. She took a breath, causing a good deal of lace to rise and fall, and a pearl in the hollow of her throat to quiver. Tammo bit the inside of his cheek. "Walk with me."

The Marchesa's skirt hushed over the red-and-white tiles. Tammo followed, a pace behind. On either side of them, gilt leaves and hunting scenes in bas-relief scrolled past. Tammo avoided looking at the cabinet of curiosities. Those damned ivory figurines! He could swear they were haunting him.

"You have served me well, citizen," the Marchesa said. "You will be amply rewarded. However, there is one more service that I know a loyal Angelian like you would not refuse."

Tammo nodded, unsure whether to bow again. What

did she want from him now? She already had him charming people's minds, for sweet Michael's sake!

The Marchesa stopped and turned to face him. Below her mask, her mouth was a rosebud of rouge, with a beauty spot in the "coquette" position at its right-hand corner. There was chalk powder on her lower teeth.

"You have heard of the unfortunate situation between the Duke and the Nobilissimo?"

Tammo nodded, barely a blink.

"A tragic state of affairs for our city." The Marchesa shook her head. "A son turning against his own father. Hostile factions at court. Spies everywhere." She shuddered and glanced over her shoulder, as though she expected spies to drop from the chandeliers. Her voice lowered to a throbbing whisper. "I'm afraid it might come to bloodshed."

The feathers on the Marchesa's mask trembled. For a moment, Tammo had a vision of himself heroically clasping the Marchesa's heaving bosom to his own as he fought off armed traitors. He blinked hard to dispel it.

"My friends and I…" The Marchesa looked toward the salon. "My friends and I are deeply concerned for the future of Angelio. We have between us certain information that could help the Duke. But if we were seen handing it over…"

She stepped closer, just a fraction past the modest distance required by etiquette. Gardenia perfume breathed in Tammo's face. "Citizen Capell, if you could deliver certain letters to Count Pageno, we would ensure you were amply rewarded for your trouble."

"Give letters to the Count?"

An image of the front portico of the Pageno Mansion with its golden pheasant and marble steps reared up in Tammo's mind, along with a vision of Caesar's impassive face. He hadn't been permitted to make a delivery to Celestina, let alone to the master of the house, the Duke's right-hand man. "Your ladyship, I don't think he would see me."

A smile came to the Marchesa's lips, making the beauty spot rise. "Ah, no. You would not deliver the letters face-to-face. Much too dangerous! We thought that, with that charming flute of yours, you could find a more subtle means of entry."

"Find a way with my flute?"

For a heartbeat, a flicker of irritation appeared in the Marchesa's eyes. Then it was smoothed away. "Citizen Capell, I'm sure a man of your...ah...comeliness, has certain friends in the Pageno household. Friends who, with a little musical encouragement, might be persuaded to let you in by a quieter route and ensure you reached the Count's study undisturbed."

The bigger part of Tammo wanted to laugh the Marchesa's words to scorn. His comeliness! Had she seen his scars? Heard his crow's voice? But another part of him was still overwhelmed by her ladyship's gardenia perfume and the quivering pearl at her throat. Some ladies liked a bit of rough, didn't they? Maybe the Marchesa was one of them.

And she wasn't alone. Your grateful friend, Celestina had said. My knight in shining armour. He pushed the thought away. Celestina was pure, perfect. He wouldn't bring her into this.

But there was another friend. Someone who was sure to do anything for him, who could barely keep her roving hands off him, even without the flute's charm. Fenice. She would let him in for the right enticement, as she had since he was a schoolboy.

And once he was in the mansion, once he had finished the Marchesa's business, then he would find Celestina. And declare his love.

"I think I know someone who would oblige, my lady," he said.

The Marchesa smiled. "Good man. I knew I could rely on you. This is what will happen. A messenger in a fox mask will meet you in Piazza Saint Seraphiel tomorrow at the hour of the evening stroll. He will give you a package of letters to deliver to the Pageno mansion. You will show these to no one, nor will you open them. Their content is a matter of utmost security and for Count Pageno's eyes only. Do you understand?"

Tammo nodded. What did she think he was, a traitor? Of course, he wouldn't open the Count's letters.

"You will convey these letters to the Pageno mansion and secrete them in Count Pageno's private library. Choose a time when there are few people in the house. During the Duke's Day festivities, for example. You will speak of your actions to no one." She leaned closer until Tammo could taste gardenia. "Lives may be at stake."

He dropped into a deep bow. "I will not fail you, Marchesa. I swear on Michael's sword."

The Marchesa's emerald eyes sparkled. "I know you will not, Citizen Capell. You have been most helpful. The house of Pamina will not forget you. Florian!" The footman appeared at her side with silent grace. "Escort Citizen Capell to my agent to collect his payment. Citizen, Angelio thanks you for your service."

She turned and walked toward the open curtain of the salon, the silken train of her gown whispering over the tiles.

12
Cold Cupid

The leading chairman tripped on a cobble. The sedan chair lurched and swayed to the left. Carlo's head bumped against the padded interior, jerking him out of a yawn. He sniffed and tried to rub his eyes, forgetting for a moment the velvet mask he wore. Sweet Michael, he had almost nodded off there!

He drew aside the curtain and looked out. The air was grey with mist and the wet cobbles shone. No wonder the poor man had slipped. If things kept up like this, Duke's Day would be a miserable affair. Thankfully, he would be indoors for most of it, first with Celestina and then at the Teatro, singing the part of Tancredi in that dreadful helmet.

The Teatro. Carlo cupped his hands to his mouth and yawned again. Sweet Michael, but this Duke's Day opera was hard work! All that sword-swinging and drawn-out death scenes. He couldn't stop yawning. Thank God for eye masks; at least they hid the purple shadows that seemed to grow darker each day.

Somewhere in the pit of his stomach, a feeling nagged

at Carlo that this bone-weariness was more than the exhaustion of hard work. More than the melancholy that made it harder to get out of bed every morning. Something was seriously out of balance: with him, with Tamino, with Angelio itself. But he was too tired to think it through.

He had seen Tammo twice since the incident with Coronis, both times in the Teatro's crowded backstage. Both times his twin had given no more than a curt nod over the crates of doves he carried. The second time, Carlo had tried to force a way through, waving frantically at the stagehands. He'd moved L'Amoricana to one side with a hand on her shoulders.

"Tamino!" He had raised his voice as much as he dared. Il Cupide was singing a solo at the time. "I need to speak with you."

"Busy, Carlo." Tammo had shouldered the crate and disappeared toward the stables, quickly obscured by men rushing forward to lower scenery and trim candles.

"You're standing on my hem, Seraphini." L'Amoricana had looked up with a wry smile.

"A thousand apologies, bella." L'Amoricana was a sweet girl. There was no need for her to suffer because Carlo was miserable.

And now he was miserable again, sitting in a damp sedan chair in… Where was he now? He leaned out of the window, pulling up the muffler he wore, to cover his mouth and nose. Ah, Piazza Saint Seraphiel. He could see the clock of Saint Seraphiel's church, and the sign of the Mask-maker's Guild hanging above a row of shop fronts. He had ordered a new mask for Duke's Day, an ivory creation with a lyre of Apollo at the crown. Perhaps he should stop to check on its progress? The creation of beauty always soothed his soul. Although he really ought to stay out of the damp. He had sneezed three times this morning.

Wait. There, outside the mask shop. Talking to that man in a fox mask. He knew the hat, the moss green coat. The flute case that hung in place of a sword. Even the ridiculous Pulcinella mask couldn't disguise the familiar gestures. The thrust of that chin said, *You dare criticise me. Just try it.*

"Tamino!" The muffler smothered his voice. He pulled it down, banged on the roof of the sedan chair. "Stop the chair! Stop the chair!"

The chair swayed to a halt. Carlo clambered out without waiting for the man to open the door. "Stay there." He pressed a coin into the man's hand. "Just…wait."

His voice caught in the back of his throat. He cleared it and began running across the piazza, heedless of the wet cobbles. He must catch up to Tammo. Tell him he was sorry. That he loved him. That he didn't love him. Tell him anything at all, so long as it would make Tamino talk to him again.

"Tamino!"

Tammo's head jerked up. Carlo was near enough to see the eyes widen, the shoulders hunch over the ears. Not still ashamed of him, surely?

A pang shot through Carlo's heart. "Tamino, please!"

Tammo lowered his head and exchanged furtive words

with Fox Face. The man took a package from under his cloak and handed it to Tammo. Carlo watched as Tammo opened his cloak, tucked the package inside…

A cold grip seized the back of his neck.

Blood rushed to his head, throbbing, throbbing. His legs became liquid. An eerie music sang in his ears. It was like someone had taken a chorale, transposed it up three octaves and sung it back-to-front. The discord was painful.

Carlo gasped hard. He could feel himself being cut by the barber-surgeon all over again. The voices in his head were all the little castrati screaming, screaming. Helpless against cold steel and ice. And behind it all was the throb-throb-throb of his own pulse. He wanted to block it out, but his body was ice-water. Blinding lights pierced his eyes.

Then he saw.

Enormous wings, an impossible shade of blue. They were covered with eyes—fathomless and fiery as the depths of the sun—that looked into his soul with condemnation and pity. The eyes were as large as the whole world. He couldn't move. He couldn't breathe. There were needles in his head. The eyes were about to swallow him.

A reek of garlic and cheap liquor breathed over him. Rough hands patted his cheeks. Carlo opened his eyes to see the two chairmen crouched over him, surrounded by a growing crowd.

"Am I awake or asleep?" he murmured.

"Signor Seraphini?" The fumes grew worse as the leading chairman brought his face level with Carlo's. His chin was covered with brown and grey stubble, and there was a stye on his lower eyelid. "Did you slip? Sweet Michael, you're sheet white! Ludo, let's have that rag-water."

His thick-necked companion handed him a goatskin bottle, and he proceeded to tip the contents down Carlo's throat. It was liquor of the roughest kind. Carlo spluttered and coughed. The chairman heaved him into a sitting posture. Pains roiled in Carlo's stomach. His head swam.

"Signor Seraphini? Stay with us now." The chairman shook him.

"It's Signor Seraphini!"

An excited buzz ran through the crowd.

"Seraphini. It's really him."

"I love you, Seraphini!"

"Sing for us, won't you? I'd love to hear a tune."

"What? All that shrieking and wailing?" said another voice. "Give me a fiddle over a warbling capon any day."

"A capon flat on his back," someone giggled. "Hey, Seraphini! Have you lost something?"

"That's enough!" the chairman roared. "Give the man some air."

"The man-seemer, you mean," the giggler said.

But he was already being shouted down by other voices, telling him to, "Pipe down," and, "Show some respect." One particularly strident female voice began praising Carlo's talents and achievements in detail Carlo himself would struggle to recall.

"Come on then. Let's be having you," said the chairman in a softer voice.

He nodded to his companion, and the two of them

raised Carlo by the armpits and walked him through the crowd, back to the sedan chair. Carlo blinked and swayed as the red roofs and balconies of the piazza resolved themselves from watery impressions back into solid realities.

What had happened? Had he fainted? There had been eyes and… No. No more of that. It was a dream, nothing more. But why had he got out of the sedan chair? It was damp and drizzly outside. He hated the damp.

Tamino!

Carlo gripped the chairman's arm, so hard he could feel the pressure of his signet ring against the man's bicep. He twisted his head round, trying to look.

"What's the matter, Signor?" said the chairman. "This way to the chair."

"I have to… There's someone I need to…" Carlo craned his neck, trying to see past the crowd. Its various factions were still shoving each other and trying to shout each other down.

There was the guild sign. The shopfront. The window with its green shutters and thick glass. The shopkeeper was standing in the doorway, no doubt attracted by the commotion in the piazza. There was no sign of Fox Mask. He had gone.

And so had Tammo.

Duke's Day was every bit as grey as Carlo had expected. And then some.

As the day wore on, the heavy mist became colder and

colder, until people swore they could feel sleet in it. The crowds that gathered at the Morningstar Fountain to see the first families of Angelio emerge from Ducal Mass had their tricorns pulled down and their tabarro cloaks drawn tightly around their necks.

Those with houses on Saint Michael's Square had made a tidy sum by renting out their upper rooms to those with enough coin and forward planning to pay for a cosy viewing spot, sheltered from the mist and drizzle. The truly enterprising laid on food and drink too, and invited some of the street entertainers indoors, to provide a little lively music for their guests to eat by.

"My cousin had fifteen in his front chamber this morning. And a Slavonikan band with a hurdy gurdy," the cab driver told Carlo, as he handed him in. "Had to move all the furniture into his daughter's' room. He and his wife were rushed off their feet, running up and down stairs with wine jugs and plates of tripe-and-Parmesan. Made a pretty penny, though. Almost three whole ducats, if you can believe that! That'll see them all into the pit tonight. So, you'd better sing your best for them, Signor Seraphini."

"As if they were my own family," Carlo promised, with a forced smile.

As if he gave more than a passing thought to his own family! Count Pageno and Celestina were his family now. And Tamino. His twin, Tamino... Carlo pressed his Cupid's lips together. He would not weep before the cab driver.

Carlo adjusted the brass hand-warmers inside his

gloves, as the cab man made the door fast and climbed up onto the driving seat. The cab had no foot-warming box and only waxed paper for windows. A pity. The journey from the Teatro to the Pageno mansion was not a long one, but it was crucial that Carlo keep his voice intact for tonight's performance. Really, he should have been at home, breathing in steam and resting with a muffler around his throat. Maestro Sarastro would spontaneously combust if he knew his primo castrato was driving around in a cab in mist like this. But he needed to see Celestina. And he was sure she needed him.

Today was the day of her final decision about the convent. He prayed to Michael she decided to stay as she was. But if she felt she had a vocation, he would understand. He, too, felt the force of chastity running through his veins. Only his vocation was song. And instead of wedding Holy Mother Church, he longed to be joined to Tamino in the spiritual love between friends, which the maestri called Platonic.

Now that future was slipping away from him. He had to get it back. Celestina would help him. Celestina would know what to do.

The Duke's banners flew high from boats and barges on the river: blue and silver with the Ducal fountain-and-crown insignia. Like the day itself, the banners commemorated the First Duke, who had received Angelio as a gift from the Archangel.

Aristocracy and citizens alike would party hard today, despite the weather. Carlo blanched to think of the money that would be lost in games of chance, and the blood that would be shed by man and beast in fights both organised and otherwise. Within the confines of the Teatro, the only fighting Carlo hoped to see was the stylised swordplay of the opera. It was true that fights sometimes broke out in the pit. He had once seen two rival orders of nuns come to blows over the respective talents of Il Cupide and Figliolo. But hopefully there would be enough action onstage tonight, to keep the audience's bloodlust in check.

Carlo wedged himself as far into the corner of the cab as he could. He was forced to bend his neck a little; like most things in Angelio, the cab had been designed with shorter passengers in mind. He held his pomander to his nose, in the tiny space between mask and muffler, hoping the scent of jasmine would eclipse whatever dank odour was lurking in the upholstery.

At least there was no dust from the building site today. The stonemasons and sculptors' apprentices would be in the piazzas, laying bets on dog fights, and drinking one another under the table. It was strange to drive past half-finished arches and columns, stone vines ending abruptly mid-leaf, a hand or buttock emerging from rough rock. Seen through the mist, it resembled an enchanter's garden, where nature was slowly being turned to stone. Carlo shuddered and drew his cloak tighter as the cab-horse trotted on.

He had expected to find Celestina in the music room. Instead, he was met by a footman he didn't know and escorted through the grand entrance hall to the ascending platform on its left. It worked in a similar way to stage machinery at the Teatro, by means of weights and pulleys, operated by the turning of a brass wheel. The Count had had it built for Celestina, so she could travel from one floor to the next in her house carriage.

Would it still be used, Carlo wondered, if Celestina went to the convent? It was an odd thought: the idea of the house without Celestina. Would the gilt house carriage be left behind too, or go to Michaelis Curationum with her? Those in holy orders took a vow to renounce possessions, but surely the nuns would leave Celestina some means by which to get around.

The ascending platform juddered to a halt on the first floor. The sweating footman strained to secure the brass wheel, and slid back the Ming-styled screen to reveal a Ming-styled bedchamber beyond. Without a word, he indicated to Carlo that he was to follow, past hangings adorned with cranes and pagodas, then under the benevolent gaze of the Virgin Mother, who was standing conveniently in an alcove.

In the salon beyond, the walls were pale blue, with scenes of shepherdesses painted onto gilt-edged lozenges. A fire was burning in the grate, and before it sat Celestina, in the gown of a female Harlequin. Pheasant's tail-feathers sprung jauntily from one side of her head; a soft brown ringlet curled about her neck. The indigo ribbon at her throat dipped below the patchwork neckline.

"Signor Seraphini, noblesse." The footman bowed.

Celestina glared frost at the man. "Why haven't you taken his hat and cloak, Giulio? He's wet through. Come, Carlo." She moved her skirts aside and patted the pale blue sopha. "Sit before this fire immediately and have some almond liqueur before you catch cold. You may leave us when you're done, Giulio. Wait, just poke the fire a little. It's dreadfully cold for Duke's Day, is it not? Yes, yes, that's enough, Giulio. I do believe the dread winter everyone spoke of has arrived already. Sweet Michael, Carlo! Your lips are cold," she said as Carlo kissed her hand. "We must do what we can to warm them up."

Carlo murmured a few standard courtesies as the hapless Giulio looked around for a suitable place to hang his outer garments. As soon as the footman left, he leaned close to Celestina, his voice a nervous whisper. "Aren't these your mother's apartments?" He glanced over his shoulder. "I mean, does she know you're entertaining in her private salon?"

Celestina patted his knee in a way that made him wonder if she'd started on the almond liqueur before him. "Fie, Carlo! Mama is at court with Papa. I am the lady of the house in her absence. Now, drink up. You haven't touched a drop." She put a hand to her mouth with a giggle. "Teresa had ever so many once I got her started. She's snoring away on her bed like a bulldog."

Carlo raised a hand to the liqueur glass, as if fending it off. "I shouldn't before a performance. Perhaps a little wine and hot water?"

Celestina pouted. Carlo was reminded of her as a little

girl. "It's ill luck not to toast the Duke on Duke's Day. And you can't toast with watered wine." She smiled like a cherub in a painting. "Just the one. For me, Carlo? I shan't get you drunk. And it is a special day." She buoyed out her skirts. "Do you like my carnival dress?"

"It is as lovely as its wearer, noblesse." Carlo gently teased Celestina's ringlet with a finger. "Is this to be a grand farewell to Carnival, or have you decided to remain in society?" He plucked at his lip, his pulse growing faster. "I must confess, I had hoped…"

"I am staying." Celestina folded her hands in her lap. "I spoke with Mama and Papa this morning and it is all decided." She lowered her eyelashes. "There was a time when I was tempted, sorely tempted, to go along with Mama's plan. The life of a nun did make a certain sense, given my circumstances. But since the start of this season, I have had reason to hope…"

"Heaven be praised!" Carlo could not prevent the exclamation bursting out. He took both of Celestina's hands in his and kissed them fervently. She was staying. His soulmate remained. Now, at last, he could unburden his heart to her. All the hurt, all the confusion he had felt since that kiss with Tammo. Her feminine compassion would guide him back into the light.

"Noblesse…" he began.

"Celestina. Call me Celestina."

"Are you sure that's quite…?" His objection was cut off by the flash of Celestina's eyes. "Celestina. Of course."

He licked his lips and stared into the fireplace, as if

inspiration was to be found among sparks and crackling logs. A drop of water fell from his hair onto his eyelashes. He blinked it away. "Celestina." Her face was so expectant, so eager. Of course she would understand. "I've been wanting to speak with you for so long."

"So have I." Celestina's voice trembled.

"What? I…" Really? Did she already know? "I fear I've been a fool and I don't know what to do. Will you advise me? I have suffered such misery these past weeks. The fear that I may have lost forever the one…the one I love."

His cheeks were glowing, and not with the warmth of the fire. Did he dare go on? Would she condemn him for having kissed the man he called his twin? For loving him beyond life?

Celestina gently cupped his cheek. "Misery? Oh, Angel-boy! What have I put you through?" She began to stroke, her hand caressing. "It's all right. I'm here now. I promise not to leave, nor ever to think of leaving again."

"Thank you." His hand closed over hers. "You have always been so good to me. A poor boy from nowhere, a peasant. A…a half-man." His throat grew tight.

"No." Celestina put a hand on each side of his face and turned it to look at her. "You have never been a peasant nor a half-man to me. You are the loveliest person I know, Carlo. And I am so glad you have finally decided to speak. So very, very glad."

For a moment, it seemed that Celestina had fallen and bumped heads with him. Then her lips were on his, soft and tasting of almonds. Her hands were on the back of his head, deep within his curls. It took a few helpless gasps for breath before he realised this was not the chaste kiss of a sister. Celestina was panting, moaning. Her kiss was hard and desperate, forcing Carlo's lips apart. He tasted something wet in his mouth and realised with horror that it was her tongue.

This was his soulmate? The girl who, not an hour ago, he had imagined a nun. This was the confidante to whom he had been about to unburden the chaste desire of his heart? How long had she...?

Oh, sweet Michael! Did she think he actually *wanted* this?

"Celestina." He prised her off him as gently as he could, fighting the urge to scrub his mouth, tongue and all, with his handkerchief. "Celestina, I'm afraid there has been some misunderstanding. I never..."

A sound at the door made them both look round. Carlo leapt to his feet. "What was that?"

13
Vulcan's Fire

Tammo heard the music before he reached the wicket gate. Fiddles and flutes playing a merry gigue. This was no opera music. It was the hand-clapping, foot-stomping music of the Angelian peasantry. It was coming from Count Pageno's courtyard.

The Pageno servants were holding their own Duke's Day ball in the coach house. Up and down the growing Mansion Quarter, there would be many of these impromptu balls today. Servants taking advantage of their masters' absence to drink and make merry. Good luck to them, Tammo thought.

He picked his way along the perimeter fence at the back of the mansion. The music was louder now. He caught glimpses of flags flapping wetly, smelled the tang of sweet-sour sauce wafting from the kitchen. Good. The servants might be dry and well-fed while Tammo shivered, but they were all gathered in one spot, well out of his way. This was going to be easier than he thought.

Tammo crept to the maple tree. Its boughs, still

flaunting a handful of sad-looking leaves, tapped against the balcony of the belvedere tower, entrance to Fenice's sewing room. Thank God Count Pageno had not had it pollarded!

Tammo grabbed the nearest branch and swung himself up into the canopy with a practised movement. He knew this tree like an old relative. Foot on that nub there, reach for that mossy fork, avoid that bough to the right, the one that bounced and creaked. It was as easy as climbing the stairs. Tammo let out a controlled breath as he stepped across from branch to belvedere. The clay floor was slippery, but not as much as it would have been, had he been wearing his good shoes. He had dressed for stealth and anonymity. Cloakless, and dressed in black with a plain black mask, he could have been anyone. Anyone with a squirrel's gift for climbing, at least.

He had a wonderful view of the gardens from here. Tammo pressed himself up against the door to Fenice's sewing room, in order to see without being seen. To one side, parterre gardens were laid out in symmetrical patterns: hexagons, circles, squares with rounded corners. Flower beds were cut into the shapes of leaves, and hedges were trimmed to resemble brocade. To the other side, he could see the open doors of the coach house and shadows of people dancing. The well at the centre of the courtyard had been dressed with rosemary and lavender: all wells were sacred on Duke's Day.

A caw from the maple made him start.

"Hell!" He bit back a curse, dodging. Outstretched talons clawed inches from his face. With a louder caw, the crow circled his head and made a second swoop, black wings fanning.

"Coronis?" Tammo couldn't believe it. "Damn it all, you nearly had my eye out! What's the matter with you?" Coronis made another attempt on his face. "You don't show up for days and then you come down on me like a harpy. Hell! Give it up, will you? You're going to give me away."

He hissed and windmilled his arms until Coronis retreated to the maple. With a look of utmost scorn, she gave a final caw and flew out of sight.

"Michael's dregs!" Tammo licked a scratch on his hand. What had got into that crow?

He glanced back at the coach house to see if anyone had noticed, but they were still dancing. He slid the dark flute from its case and breathed into it. He must calm himself for this to work. He gave an experimental trill.

Would Fenice hear him over the music of the dance? Would she need to? There was so much he still didn't understand about how people-charming worked. He just hoped she would come. He didn't know where Count Pageno's private library was. And he needed a lookout, someone to watch his back and make sure he didn't get caught.

The musicians in the coach house had moved onto a seductive sarabande. Tammo smirked. He could imagine what use Pompey and Caesar would make of that! They would have the maidservants lining up to dance with them!

The melody of the viol and oboe rose and fell, lingering over each phrase. Tammo used to be good at copying melodies by ear. It was one of the skills with which he had impressed Maestro Aquilla at the conservatorio. He put the flute to his lips and surrendered for a phrase or two to the power of the music and the flute's rich tone.

Then he focused his mind on Fenice: her hips, her scolding tongue, the glint of her eyes. She desired him, always had. Actually, she desired anyone with the right equipment between his legs, but he was going to ignore that for now. He pictured the last time they had met, him swinging her round and round, petticoats flying.

I'm right here, Fenice. You know you want me. Come and help me and there's a Duke's Day present in it for you!

For a breath, a tug of conscience tweaked at his heartstrings. Fenice had always been good to him. Was it right to use her in this way? But in the next breath, he remembered what the Marchesa della Pamina had told him. This was for the sake of Angelio. Lives could be at stake. Besides, it felt good to be desired. Virile. Manly. He would show all those lackwits from school who had ever called him Crow and Firebrand! And every well-heeled citizen who had tried to wither him with a glance. Citizen Capell was a man of the world.

That's right, Fenice. He drew out a trill, caressing each note like a lover. *Tammo Capell is here. And you're going to do whatever he says. Come and let me in, you little vixen!*

Was she coming? Playing like this was a drain on his energy. He could no longer keep watch on the servants. Every note was a struggle, a push against unseen resistance, as though he had to force the music through treacle. He made it a dusky tremolo. *Your gallant is waiting, Fenice.* The musicians below returned to the sarabande's opening theme. Tammo blinked sweat from his eyes. He couldn't keep this up much longer. The spell was going to break any minute.

Fenice!

He slid, breathless, down the closed door, his head leaning limply against the door-frame. Arches, maples and sky spun in a confusion of colour. Sweet Michael! It had better be Fenice that found him! He hadn't the strength to run. He sank his head to his knees, taking deep breaths until the sweat on his face grew cold and the gardens below returned to their normal proportions.

Squaring his shoulders, he hauled himself to his feet, replacing the dark flute in its case. He rubbed his backside. It was damp. Oh, holy Seraphim! Let that not be the first thing Fenice saw. He would never hear the last of damp breeches!

He held his breath, listening. Every bird call was a cannon shot. Was she coming? How would he tell? He scratched the back of his neck and blew out air. He couldn't bear this any longer. He was going to open the door and go in anyway. No, he wasn't. Yes, he was.

He took hold of the door handle. It turned of its own volition. The door opened.

"Tammo Capell. Fancy meeting you here," said Fenice.

"Well, aren't you a very Hercules?" Fenice reached above her head to squeeze Tammo's bicep.

Tammo grunted. "Get. Off. Me."

He strained to turn the brass wheel that brought the ascending platform to the ground floor. Fenice was irrepressible. In the short time he'd been indoors, her hand had already found its way to his left buttock, and threatened to seek out a more intimate spot. Had charming her been the best idea? At this rate, he would need a bucket of cold water over his head before he could concentrate on his mission.

It hadn't helped that, as they had tiptoed through the musicians' quarters, Fenice had seen fit to point out where Celestina was spending Duke's Day.

"Just through there. In her mama's salon." Fenice pointed to the wall of the musicians' rehearsal room. One single wall. The only thing between Tammo and his heart's desire.

"Set herself up like a queen in there, Giulio said. Let her have fun while Mama's out, I say. The poor darling will never run a household of her own."

She is a queen, Tammo had wanted to retort.

But he thought better of it. He pressed his lips shut, fighting the waves of adoration that swept over him. The Countess' salon. He would remember that for when he had completed his mission. First, get rid of the package. Next, get rid of Fenice. Then he would fly back up this shaft quicker than a demon in the opera.

The platform came to a halt.

Fenice led the way, hip-walking across the marble floor of the grand entrance hall. The rain outdoors made its marble walls look drowned, as though the whole mansion was underwater. A kingdom of mermaids and sea monsters. Tammo had heard the tales from sailors on the dockside. Mariners would sight a rock and a maiden combing her long, long hair, a looking-glass in hand. Nearer and nearer she would draw them with her siren song, until a chasm opened and the ship plunged down, down into the roaring fathoms below.

Tammo stumbled and shuffled in Fenice's wake, cursing the shortness of her legs. He just wanted this over with. The package of letters under his coat waslike hot coal; Tammo was sure anyone could see it, glowing through the heavy cloth.

He took a steadying breath. Pictured the Marchesa and Count Pageno meeting in the wedding-cake room, the Marchesa explaining how the bold Citizen Capell had risked all to deliver the precious letters. A hero of Angelio, she would say. Such a man deserved his own coat of arms, at the very least.

All sorts of fantastical scenes came tumbling after the first. Tammo Capell with a shield above the fireplace and a rapier by his side. Tammo approaching the Count with quiet dignity. Celestina's grateful smile. A marriage contract, in red and black ink. A wedding in the Pageno's private chapel…

"We're here." Fenice opened a door beneath an elaborate staircase. "All yours, Hercules. Sure you don't want to tell me what this is all about?"

He lifted her chin with a finger. "The less you know, the less you can tell. Secrecy is of the essence."

He tried to sound knowing, mysterious. Unfortunately, his voice abandoned him on the last word, which left him sounding like a man being strangled.

Fenice guffawed into her sleeve. "Man of mystery, are you now? Lackwit! I can see through you like a pane of glass, Tammo Capell."

That's what you think.

Tammo kept one hand on his breast pocket as he pushed open the door. Fenice might think herself worldly-wise, but he'd got the better of her this time. She had no idea of his mission. Nor what he meant to do later. Tammo chuckled to himself. It was as well Fenice could not read his mind. She would not like what she found there.

Oh dear, oh dear, Fenice. If only you knew! Good old Tammo Capell has snared the maid to catch the mistress.

Still, best not to hang about. Who knew how long the charm would last? Do the deed and then away. That was the best plan.

The Count's private library was a small room. It would be cosy of an evening, Tammo supposed. Right now, the candles were unlit and the fireplace cold; a musty smell of ashes and sour wine drifted on the air. Books stood from floor to stuccoed ceiling, and not formally as they did in the long library where he had eaten from time to time with Carlo. Here they stood higgledy-piggledy, large next to small. Leaning where neighbours had been removed, lying atop neighbours in hasty couplings. Tammo scratched his nose. These were the books the Count actually read. Not the ones he displayed to his friends for show.

Where to place the letters? Tammo turned on his heels, assessing his options. A hunt table made a half-moon shape before the fireplace; an empty decanter and wineglass shared the table top with open books. Against the opposite wall stood a bureau with drawers and a writing desk. A penknife, quills and sander jostled for space with a crucifix, rosary and horn-handled magnifying glass. A stiff-backed chair, upholstered in black, scarlet and blue with golden pheasants, was pulled up at an angle, as if the Count had just stepped outside.

Tammo took out the letters from his coat. There were four of them, tied with a red ribbon. The back of his neck began to prickle. He could be holding the entire future of Angelio in his hands. He, Tammo Capell, Knight-errant of the Marchesa! What would Celestina say to that? He shivered. Better get the blasted things out of his hands as soon as possible.

He tried one of the bureau drawers. Locked. Damn. What about this one? Locked as well. He chewed on his lower lip. The Count must keep a key somewhere. *Think, Tammo.* Where would a Pageno hide something secret? His fingertips fluttered over the scattered paraphernalia. In the sander? Inkwell? Box of spills? His eyes flickered toward the bookshelves. Propped against books of heraldry, there was a cameo in a deep, oval frame. A boy in profile, about ten years old, with the same noble forehead as the Count.

Orlando.

Tammo took the portrait down. As he'd suspected, there was a latch on one side of the frame. The portrait was a box. He pushed the latch to one side with his thumb. The box popped open. A brass key lay inside, a capital letter P at the centre of its bow. Tammo grinned to himself as he unlocked the lowest drawer. No one was as inscrutable as they liked to think.

The drawer contained many papers already. A number had huge seals hanging from them, with the Duke's crown-and-fountain sigil pressed into the wax. Another was in some kind of cipher.

Tammo gave a silent whistle. This was the real thing! All the secrets of the city-state could be under his hand. He swallowed hard and pushed the Marchesa's letters beneath a sheaf of calculations. He didn't want any more of this. It was too big. Lock up, put back the key and get out of here. Leave the aristocracy to their intrigues. He had business of his own to tend to. And it involved something much more pleasant than papers and politics.

"I thought you'd come here to make merry." Fenice slid a hand inside Tammo's waistcoat. He tried to hold back a shiver and failed. "I'm missing a hornpipe with Caesar for this. You should see his high cuts." She raised her eyebrows.

"Since when did you care about Caesar?" Tammo carefully extracted her hand, keeping a watchful eye on where the other one was going.

"Oh, he's nothing." Fenice tossed her head. "I only

accepted his offer to see the look on Pompey's face. Let him see what he's missing." She held onto Tammo's waist and looked up with narrowed eyes. "See what I'll be missing if you don't get your flute out."

"Fenice!" Tammo's cheeks flared. How thick were these walls? If Celestina had heard that, the Angel of Death could come and take him now. He was supposed to be a hero. Not some seedy rogue who popped in during Carnival for a quick tumble.

"I need you to stay where you are." He took a few steps backward, drawing the dark flute from its case. He played a low, enticing phrase. *Stay here. Don't speak or move unless someone comes. You can trust Tammo.*

Fenice smiled at him from beneath lowered lashes. Tammo nodded, flute at his lips, and retreated further.

That's right, Fenice. You stay right there.

The moment he was round the corner, he rammed the flute into its case and fastened the clasp.

He took a moment to straighten his cravat, squinting at his reflection in a lacquered cabinet. His hands were trembling. How did he look? Should he take the mask off? Leave it on? He scowled. There were too many decorations on the cabinet for him to make out more than vague impressions of himself.

He tugged at the cravat again and pulled down his waistcoat to make it straight. Just walk in there and get on with it. Bow. Kiss her hand. No, kneel at her feet, then kiss her hand. In that case, he would have to take the mask off. Bow, then take the mask off. Then kneel. On which knee?

He couldn't remember which was the correct one. And which hand were you meant to kiss? Left or right? What if she was wearing gloves?

Stop being such a lackwit. Just open the door and go in.

The door handle felt ridiculously slippery. What was the point, Tammo thought, of sweating from the palms of your hands? He tried to take a firmer grip. His heart was fighting to get out of his chest. *Just open the stupid door.*

He opened the door.

At first, he didn't understand what he saw. Two heads protruded from the back of a sopha. The heads merged into one another, chocolate curls tangling with nutmeg ringlets. Face was pressed to face. Hands caressed, searching, hungry. From the centre of the confusion came moans of pleasure.

A ball of fire burst in Tammo's chest. He slammed the door shut; his throat so tight he could scarcely breathe. He balled his fists, nails cutting into his palms, teeth clenched, arms shaking. His eyes burned.

Carlo.

Carlo and Celestina.

He paced the room, each breath coming harder, faster. He wanted to plug his ears, but the sweet moans continued inside his head. Celestina. His angel, his goddess. Tonguemaking with Carlo.

Carlo, the two-faced gelding! Hiding behind a mask of purity and piety. *Castrati can't marry, and some of us are glad to escape a duty we cannot perform.* Well, he seemed to be performing pretty well in there!

Tammo bit his lip until blood came. Everything that had happened since Carlo came home had been a lie. Carlo's drunken embrace. Celestina's letter to her knight-errant. She had never treasured the ring or the rosefinch because of him. It was all about Carlo, Carlo, Carlo. The two of them were probably sitting there now, laughing at him. Slow-witted Tammo, thinking they were still as chaste as brother and sister. And now…

Oh, God! Could castrati do it? Could paralytics? Tammo clutched at the door frame, bile rising to his throat. He needed to kill something or break something or beat something until his knuckles bled. Something was going to explode out of him at any moment and he couldn't hold it back.

"Tammo, you wild stallion. I'm waiting for you." Fenice put her head around the doorway of the Ming-styled chamber, her eyes bright with desire.

In three paces, he crossed the room and seized her by the shoulders. He propelled her backward until they were inside the booth of the ascending platform. Fenice's back was against the wall. Their breaths came hot and fast. Still grasping her shoulders, he lifted her up the wall until her face was level with his. His first kiss was savage, forcing her head back, crushing a sigh from her lungs.

"Oh, you bad, bad boy," she gasped.

Tammo didn't reply. He kissed her deeper, harder, and began to hitch up her skirts.

14

A Cruel Mistress

Carlo leapt to his feet. "What was that? Did you hear something?"

Celestina turned her head slowly. One of the pheasant feathers in her hair had broken and was hanging limp. Her eyes were unfocused, uncomprehending.

"The door." Carlo took a step toward it. "Where is Rinaldo?" It would be just like that little scoundrel to peep in at doors. If he had seen what just happened...... Carlo's stomach tightened.

"He went out riding with his tutor." Celestina's voice seemed to come from far away. Her lips quivered. "Carlo..."

He hesitated, looking back to the door. He was sure he had heard voices. Oh, sweet Michael! He could be horsewhipped for this. He would lose his job, his status. He would starve.

"Carlo." Celestina was watching him, her eyes pleading.

He went back to the sopha and sat as if it were made of eggshells. He took her hand in both of his. "Celestina..."

She leaned toward him again, her lips grazing his. That taste of sweet almond again.

He sat back and cleared his throat. "Celestina. My dear noblesse. This cannot be."

Her eyes flashed fire. "Fie upon that! We can neither of us conceive, neither of us wed. Why not take pleasure in one another?" She reached out her free hand to stroke his curls. "How long have we waited for this day, Angel-boy?"

She nuzzled against his neck, her feather-kisses drawing shivers from him. "I love you, Carlo," she sighed.

Carlo pressed his lips together. He hated to do this. He couldn't bear to watch her sweet face go from ecstasy to devastation. But to withhold the truth would be crueller still. He gently took her face in his hands, and tilted it until he could see her eyes.

"Listen to me, Celestina. You are a dear friend to me. A soul-mate. A sister. But that is all. I do not feel this kind of love for you."

She shook her head, the broken feather flapping. "No. No. You sent the rosefinch. You clung to me. You begged me to stay with you. You want this too."

She made to kiss him again. Carlo moved away. He summoned the spirit of Tancredi to add steel to his gaze. "No, Celestina. This is not what I want."

She stared, her eyes huge, her throat working. When she spoke again, her voice was tight. "No. You sent the rosefinch. You said... I refused the convent..."

"I did not send the rosefinch. I assure you, whoever was behind that gift, it was not I. If I have done anything to mislead you, my dear Noblesse Celestina, I beg your forgiveness. That was never my intention." Did she have to look at him with those sad eyes? "If this misunderstanding has influenced your decision about your future vocation, you must take time to reconsider."

"But…" She gave a little sob. "You spoke of love. Of the one you love." Tears welled in her eyes. "Do you not love me, Carlo?"

"I do. I do." His voice was catching now. His eyes stung. "But no man can have two masters, Celestina." He stroked her little finger with his thumb, looking down at the patchwork of her harlequin dress. "For me, there is a greater love. Another friend who is dearer."

A tear dripped down and glistened in the middle of a saffron patch, before soaking into the fabric. Carlo drew in a ragged breath. He could hear Celestina doing the same.

"A woman?" Celestina's voice was high and clipped.

Carlo shook his head, setting another tear loose from his eyelashes.

Celestina sniffed and turned away. She was vitrifying before Carlo's eyes, becoming hard and brittle as glass.

"I see," she said at last. "That is how it is with you. Achilles and Patroclus. Alexander and Hephaestion. David and Jonathan. How could a crippled girl hope to compete with a love celebrated by philosophers?"

"No, Celestina. Don't say that."

"I think I'd like you to leave now." Celestina's every sinew was rigid.

"Celestina, please…"

"Is that how you address your betters?" The voice had become her mother's. "Leave me, castrato."

It was as if she had pushed a blade of ice between his ribs. She looked him straight in the eyes, watching him flinch. Her expression was pure marble.

"Yes, noblesse." Carlo sniffled, his nose full of tears. "But please, I beg of you…"

Celestina turned her head away. "Just go, Carlo."

Castrato.

"Yes, noblesse. God save you." He fumbled out of the door. The Ming chamber wavered as he dashed tears from his eyes.

Castrato.

Sweet Michael! What had he done? His Celestina. His sweet, loving Celestina, who he would fight to the death to protect. He felt he had plunged a knife into her heart. Then turned the knife on himself. How could the familiar world become a hostile landscape in a matter of moments?

The ground beneath Carlo's feet had become uncertain. He feared to tread the mansion's halls, lest the tiles turn to marshland and swallow him whole.

He found a handkerchief and blew his nose, schooling himself to be calm. He must leave this place. Now. Fly back to his gilded cage, to the familiar Teatro and the opera. Back to his twin.

And tell him the truth, once and for all.

"Half an hour until curtain up!"

Carlo flinched at the sound of the boy's voice. The dresser, who had both hands in Carlo's hair, swore under his breath. Dislodged powder tickled Carlo's nose. He rubbed it and tried to sit still.

"May I come in?" said Scipione.

The dresser threw up his hands with an appeal to Michael, and left the room.

Scipione grimaced. "Oh, la! Forgive me." He walked over to the toilette table and balanced his weight on the edge. Carlo was sure he heard the table legs creak. "I just wanted to see how you were. We've seen so little of you lately. To speak to, that is."

From somewhere in the bowels of the theatre, Carlo heard Giovanni's voice, screeching. "Don't give me that tone of voice! I *saw* you with her!"

Another voice screeched back. "So, it's fine for you to act the harlot with the entire opera, but I must live the life of a monk, waiting for you to return? Is that it?"

Scipione closed the door, but not before Carlo's stomach had filled with chunks of ice. The world had become a hall of mirrors, reflecting his own pain at every turn. Was there no escape?

He drew up his knees and gazed at a hair on the floor. "Have you seen Citizen Capell anywhere?"

His voice barely carried the distance from chair to table. Scipione had to stoop to hear him. For a moment, Carlo thought he wouldn't answer.

The bass singer creaked to his feet and put a hand on

Carlo's shoulder. "No. But I'm sure he'll come tonight. He won't miss Duke's Day."

Carlo put his hand on Scipione's and squeezed it. "Thank you." He summoned a smile, and stroked his half-dressed hair. "To the Crusades, then! And heaven forbid we should face the Saracen unpowdered! Barbarossa himself would not have dared besiege Jerusalem without his beauty spot and half an ostrich on his head."

Scipione chuckled. "In the mouth of the wolf!"

It was all wolves. A pack of winter wolves, circling, circling. Waiting for the first sign of weakness before they pounced.

And Carlo without the strength to resist.

He couldn't find Tammo.

Carlo dropped scent onto a handkerchief and dabbed behind his ears. How did his hair look? After searching the stables, it might have grown dusty. He ran a brush through it, then turned to feed a pinch of seed to an oriole that twittered in its cage.

The candles of the tiring room had burned low in his absence; the fire likewise. Carlo shivered. He had begun his search as soon as he could dismiss the admirers that thronged to his door as the last curtain fell. He hadn't stopped to change his leg-revealing tunic for something more practical.

He put on his new mask, adjusting it in the looking-glass. Apollo's lyre sat on the bridge of its nose, between

Carlo's eyes. He took his Act Three cloak from the rail, and wrapped it about his shoulders. The scent of extinguished candles followed him out of the room.

Tammo must be in the building somewhere. The performance had ended over an hour ago, but the Teatro was far from deserted. The sounds of assignations were still to be heard within the tiring rooms of La Bellina and Il Cupide. Carlo walked down the backstage corridor. A sharp tang of sweat mixed with almond liqueur, lavender, and a growing smell of bird droppings as he came near the dove cages. The doves, exhausted from their performance, had their heads under their wings. A young lamplighter, slightly the worse for brandy, was sitting on one of the cages with his head against the wall.

"Where's Citizen Capell?" Carlo asked.

The boy forced his eyelids open and made a sound that might have been speech.

"The bird charmer." Carlo spoke each word as if to an infant. "Have you seen him?"

The boy leapt from the cage with a startled expression. "I didn't mean to sit on his birds, Signor Seraphini. I was just resting my legs a moment. I didn't mean any harm by it." The boy glanced around, as if expecting Tammo to appear through the wall. "You won't tell him, will you?"

Carlo assured the boy that he had more important matters to discuss. He hurried down the corridor, past the bursar's office and toward the light and music of the grand entrance hall.

He doubted his twin would be here. The Duke's Day

ball was in full flow. Couples were taking turns to display their dancing prowess in the glittering circle of Angelian high society. As Carlo bowed and apologised his way through the crowd, he saw the Marchesa della Pamina in her owl mask, stepping out with a gentleman dressed in black and silver. So, Tamino was not attending on her. Carlo dodged a flirtatious nun and a sultan eating smoked ham. Truly, there was no scene as fanciful as an Angelian masked ball! It was as if the opera itself had spilled over into the general populace.

As he reached the refuge of the staircase, he was met by the smell of cooked meat, mixed with that of unemptied chamber pots. Carlo touched his handkerchief to his nose. It was the usual post-opera chaos. Servants had been hurrying to and from their masters for the last three hours; no one had time to clean up. He tried to avoid stepping on chicken bones and oyster shells as he climbed to the first tier.

Still no sign.

Why had Tammo not been attending to his birds? Why hadn't he come to Carlo's tiring room? Carlo's chest squeezed tighter. He had to tell Tamino now, before he lost his nerve again. To look him in the eye and say, "I love you." To kiss him on the lips, just once. Whatever happened afterward, he had to let out the ardour that was hammering on the doors of his heart. He thought he would explode otherwise.

Had Celestina felt that way about him?

Carlo steadied himself at the top of the stairs, suddenly

light-headed as the memories rushed back. How had he failed to read the signs? All this time he had thought of her as a sister, a soul-mate who understood him. That kiss! Where had such passion come from? "Why not take pleasure in one another?" she had said. Carlo had thought she was like him. Was there no one else who shared his chaste desire? Was everyone he knew showing him their masquerade face?

A drunken roar from the card room recalled him to his task. Tamino *would* understand. He had to. Now where in the Teatro could he be? Perhaps he had gone up to the top balcony, to meet with other tradesmen? Carlo heaved a sigh. All those stairs! He should be lying on his sopha now, with Casale serving him wine and hot rosehip water. But he had to find Tamino. Squaring his shoulders, he began to climb.

Tammo was not in the Teatro. Carlo had looked everywhere, asked everyone. By the time he got back to the performers' corridor, he ached all over and there was a pounding in his temples. He was a lackwit. Of course Tammo was not in the Teatro. He would have gone straight to Carlo's apartment. It was obvious.

The first breath of frosty air caught in Carlo's throat and made him cough. Away from the shelter of the covered walkway, the cobbles were rimed with frost. His foot slipped more than once. He was still wearing theatrical buskins! At the front door, a snowflake landed on his nose. Well, he wasn't going back to change now. He had wasted too much time already. He could send Casale back for his clothes later.

Citizen Aldo yawned wine fumes in Carlo's face as he opened the door to the apartments. The little, green vestibule was dim, a single oil lamp casting greasy shadows on the walls. Carlo took a candle from the box on the wall and lit it from the lamp's flame. Despite his exhaustion, he took the stairs two at a time. How long had Tammo been waiting for him? He was surprised Casale hadn't come to tell him a guest was waiting.

"Carlo?"

"Sweet Michael!" Carlo clasped a hand to his breast. The stairs were pitch-dark above him. He could not see the speaker. But the voice was thick with tears, and unmistakably soprano.

"My dear Giovanni! What do you mean by sitting here in the dark and cold?"

Carlo raised his candle. Giovanni was sitting on the top step outside his apartment door, his arms wrapped around his knees. His usual alabaster features were blotched about the cheeks and nose, and his make-up had run, giving him a grotesque look. Even the famous ringlets looked dishevelled.

"It's all over, Carlo."

"I beg your pardon?" At first Carlo thought Giovanni was talking about him and Tammo. It was only by groping through clouds of memory that he remembered the overheard argument, the harsh accusations. "You mean, you and Angelo?"

Giovanni stifled a sob. Carlo felt a pang of guilt. His old schoolmate had evidently been waiting for him. By the state of his face, he had been crying for some time. But Carlo had to find Tammo. He might die if he didn't speak.

"I'm sorry, Giovanni. Why not come to my rooms tomorrow and drink some chocolate?"

Giovanni grasped Carlo's sleeve. His voice rose to a squeak. "Why would he abandon me, Carlo? He swore his troth to me. He gave me…he gave me this." Giovanni tried to pull a poesy ring from his little finger. It was stuck.

"I don't know." Carlo patted Giovanni's shoulder. "Venus is a cruel mistress. We cannot hope to understand her ways, or to pry into the hearts of others."

Never was a truer word spoken, Carlo thought. After today, he would never presume to understand the thoughts of others again. How many secret loves hid behind impassive faces? How many modest and mannered souls carried unspoken passions with them, day in and out?

"I must go." Carlo kissed Giovanni's hair. "I have urgent business."

Giovanni pulled harder at his sleeve and wailed. "But why go with Marie? It makes no sense, Carlo. He loved me."

"I don't know." Carlo used his fingernails to extract his sleeve from Giovanni's grasp. He must speak with Tamino, now. "Giovanni, why not get some sleep?" He flinched at Giovanni's look of distress. "Or what about Scipione? He's not abed yet, is he?"

Scipione might not understand Giovanni's particular taste in lovers, but he was kind. And discreet, unlike some.

"Or L'Amoricana?" Carlo suggested. "Forgive me, Giovanni, but I really must…"

With a groan, the dishevelled castrato rose and lurched back into his own rooms.

Carlo's heart sank. He hated to see a friend suffer, but he could not wait another moment.

Carlo let out a sigh as the apartment door closed behind him. At last! He walked into the parlour. Casale had got the fire roaring, just the way Carlo liked it, and set out wine and biscotti on a table.

One glass.

Carlo's stomach clenched. The room was empty.

"Casale!"

It was a moment before Casale appeared. His eyes were bleary, his waistcoat crumpled. Carlo couldn't begrudge his manservant a nap in his absence, but in the circumstances, it irked him.

"Where is Citizen Capell?" Carlo's voice came out a little sharper than usual. His head ached.

Casale blinked and looked about him. "Citizen Capell? He hasn't been here." He swallowed and spoke faster. "I wasn't sleeping, signor. Only resting a moment. I would have heard the door. He didn't come here tonight, signor. I swear on Michael's sword."

"Very well, Casale. You may leave me now."

His twin wasn't there. Had never been there. Not in the Teatro, not in the apartment. The swelling emotion in Carlo's chest welled up to his throat. There was nowhere for it to go. It would choke him.

Carlo lowered himself onto the sopha, slowly, slowly. His fingernails dug into the heavy brocade. The pounding in his head was now a whooshing, waves breaking on the shore. He reached for the glass. His hand shook; it fell to the floor and broke. He pulled off his mask and covered his face with both hands.

He sobbed.

15
Fever Pitch

Casale fussed with the hem of the tablecloth. "Signor, ought you to go outdoors? You've been sneezing all morning and the weather's getting worse." The manservant scowled at the frost-rimed windows as something un-Angelian and therefore untrustworthy.

Carlo blew his nose, and rearranged his sheet music on the spinet. "I am quite well. And I cannot leave Maestro Sarastro with no Tancredi."

He attempted a smile, although his head ached. He had a chill across his back too, despite Casale's burning what looked like half a forest in the grate.

Casale eyed his master, unconvinced. "You don't look well. If I may be so forward, signor?"

"You may not." Carlo blew his nose again and slid the music into a leather case. "You may bring a hot meal to my tiring room after the Angelus bell. Don't forget to clean out the birds' cages." He gave a fond glance at the fluttering finches and nightingales. "And get some new neck bands from the haberdasher's on Piazza Saint Jophiel. These ones look yellow."

"Signor." Casale bowed.

Carlo sighed as he closed the apartment door behind him and started down the stairs, wrapped in every fur and muffler he possessed. If Casale's armoury of elixirs didn't manage to stave off this cold, he'd be coughing through the next fortnight's performances. And when a primo singer coughed, the entire opera suffered from a cold. He could picture the bored chatter of the audience and the choler in Maestro Sarastro's face already.

His footsteps echoed around the green-walled lobby. He couldn't bring himself to care for his health. In his dreams, he had searched and searched for Tammo, going through room after room, in a mansion the size of a city. Finally, he had come to a velvet curtain and drawn it aside to find Celestina dressed in a nun's habit, advancing upon him with lips like flowers. He had run, but his feet had rooted to the ground, spreading out underground like the roots of trees. When he had tried to cry out, he had no voice.

"Oh, my little roast egg! Look at you! You look tired to death." Carlo flinched as Citizeness Aldo's inch-thick rouge and rotten smile loomed before him. If there was anything guaranteed to make him feel worse, it was the ministrations of his housekeeper.

"I still have plenty of that tonic I promised you. It'll only take a moment to fetch it." She pinched his cheek between thumb and forefinger. Carlo could feel the ragged edges of her nails.

He painted on a smile. "I assure you, I am quite well, citizeness. Never better." The lie came more easily every time he spoke it. He almost believed it himself. Carlo sketched a bow and made for the door before he was accosted by further pity. "God save you, Citizeness Aldo."

God save us all, he thought.

Carlo came stumbling into his tiring-room shortly after the Angelus bell. Sweet Michael, he was weary! Trying to counterfeit health for the Maestro's benefit was more exhausting than being ill. His voice had cracked a couple of times on the appoggiaturas, but thankfully Sarastro's gall had been directed toward Giovanni, who had lurched into rehearsal smudge-eyed and obviously drunk.

"Damn your eyes, Parnasso! Miss your cue once more and I'll take that handkerchief and ram it down your throat with the fire irons!" This outburst came after an hour of Giovanni sighing piteously and dabbing at the corners of his eyes like Saint Mary Magdalene in a painting. Even Carlo had begun to find it wearying by the time Giovanni started on his second bottle of almond liqueur.

Now all Carlo wanted was the sopha in his tiring room and a bowl of chicken broth. Perhaps he could sleep here, if the fire was well fueled. He sniffled and wiped his nose again.

Casale was putting a tray on the table Carlo used to apply his maquillage. "There's a jug of rosehip water and honey there. Drink it while it's hot and I'll stir your broth. Oh, and a package came for you. It's on the tray."

"A package? From whom?" Carlo flopped into his chair and searched the tray. In one corner was a blue velvet bag tied with a ribbon.

"Mistress Teresa from the mansion. I asked if she would speak to you, signor. But she just gave me the bag." He shrugged. "She seemed in an awful hurry."

"Teresa?" Celestina's body servant? A package delivered by her could only have come from her mistress. But why would Celestina send him gifts after the way they had parted yesterday? The word *castrato*—and the way she had said it—lodged in Carlo's chest like an icicle. He could feel it all over again. The opium. The knife. The stench of the barber-surgeon's hand. Then waking in that dreadful bath of ice…

"Did she leave a message?" His voice shook. He took the soup bowl from Casale's hand and sipped, grateful for the warmth.

"She said: *Your gift is returned. The time for childish toys is past.*"

His gift? Carlo wondered if he was too weary to understand. He hadn't given Celestina a gift.

He put down the bowl and took the velvet bag from the tray. Small. Heavy. Jewellery of some sort?

"Will you be requiring anything else, signor?"

"Put some more wood on the fire. I'll take a nap here shortly."

Casale turned and knelt at the fireplace, his fuzzy queue bobbing against his collar.

Carlo undid the ribbon and loosened the neck of the bag. Something shiny fell into the palm of his hand. Something gold with a smiling black face and jewels for eyes. A gift once made for a boy who was to be his father's heir and greatest joy. A boy lost before his time.

The carnival ring.

Carlo had not seen it in years. Count Pageno had given it to him when he had first become Carlo's patron. And when he and Tammo had broken the rules to taste Carnival for themselves—when everything had fallen apart and they were on the verge of separation—Carlo had given it to Tammo. It had been a pledge, the sealing of a vow. On that day, Carlo and Tammo had become sworn twins. They had pledged that their souls would be joined, even when apart. He had begged Tammo for a kiss and his newly sworn twin had granted it.

Carlo's throat tightened at the memory. A kiss for a ring. A boyish ceremony, and yet one Carlo had always thought as sacred as any marriage. In that moment, Carlo had bestowed on Tammo the most precious thing he owned, as a token of that greater treasure that had been Tamino's since the day they met: Carlo's heart.

He would not wear it openly, Tammo had said, lest folk accuse him of robbery. And Carlo had believed him. How many times had he consoled himself with the thought of that ring, concealed on Tammo's person? On tour, as he lay on his lonely bed in Lysfleur with no one but an embroidered Virgin Mother for company, he had imagined himself looking through its eyes, seeing that his dear Tamino was well.

Carlo's fist tightened about the ring, the little jewels digging into his palm. It had been a lie, all of it. The ring had been nowhere near Tammo in years!

How long had he waited before he gave it away? An hour? Two? Had Tammo walked in and handed Celestina the ring that same afternoon?

Masquerade faces. That's all there was. No truth. No beauty. Just a boyish dream. A pretty fancy, like Carlo's chambers with their birds and flowers and musical toys. A castrato's dream, doomed to fade with the closing curtains and dying roses.

No wonder Tammo could not be found. No wonder he had been so distant from Carlo this season, mocking his affections, telling him nothing. Carlo crushed the ring harder, until shards of pain pierced his flesh. When he thought of his first day home after summer, of his reunion with Tammo in the crypt of Sancti Michaelis, he wanted to howl like a wolf crying at the moon. All his hopes. All his daydreams. Snuffed out like candles after the opera, leaving nothing but foul smoke that brought tears pricking to his eyes.

He forced the ring onto his little finger, grazing the knuckle. His hands were plumper now than they had been five years ago. Castrato's hands. He pushed the soup bowl away, no longer hungry. Something unfamiliar and dangerous was rising in his chest, something he had feared since infancy.

His throat was tightening, closing. Two fingers on his throat, the barber-surgeon's chipped fingernails nicking the skin. *Let go of me. Let me go.* They were holding him down, pinning him to the board so they could hurt him. He pushed back his chair and stood. It squealed against the floor, a scream of agony.

"Signor?" Casale turned his head. "Is something the matter?"

"I…I must take the air." Carlo heard his own voice as if from underwater. "I cannot breathe. I need air."

He opened the door and wandered into the corridor. A seamstress was pinning scene numbers to a rack of tunics. Further along, that wretched dancer, Angelo, was attempting something extremely balletic against the wall with Marie. As Carlo stumbled past, he heard the crack of her stays, and his responding gasp.

"Signor!" Casale hurried after him. "You haven't touched your broth."

"Can I help you, Signor Seraphini?" asked the doorman.

"…take the air," Carlo murmured.

"But Signor, you have no cloak." Casale's voice tightened. "And you've got a cold in your head."

But Carlo had already left the Teatro.

Angelio had been transformed into a winter fantasia. Every

roof was topped with sugar. Snowflakes whirled this way and that with every gust, a host of white butterflies.

Between the Bridge of Glories and the customs house, citizens had set up a frost fair on the river. Masked and cloaked revellers were paying to play bowls, drink spiced wine, even to be shaved on the ice. Their laughter drifted on the wind like waves. A barrel organ churned out a tune that resembled *On the shores of Cythera*. Barges, ferries, skiffs and cutters stood frozen at tilted angles. White and silent, they were ghost boats, *memento mori* amid the revelry.

Carlo paced along the north bank, shivering in his indoor coat. Ice. Ice everywhere. Life was always forcing ice upon him. Ever since he first opened his mouth to sing for Signor Bernardi. It was the price he must forever pay. However fast he walked, he couldn't outpace the chill fingers that reached out to possess him. The ice would take hold of his soul. He shivered and walked and shivered, his nose streaming.

Yet he didn't feel cold. Hot coals had been kindled in his chest, his neck, his temples. Tammo had betrayed him. Tammo was the one with ice in his soul. Heartless guttersnipe! How dare he give away Carlo's ring? How dare he have the gall to feign twinship, kneeling in the crypt as if nothing was amiss? How could Carlo have kissed the lips of such a traitor? He wiped his mouth with a damp handkerchief. He must rid himself of the traitor's poison.

The traitor he had loved deeply. Oh, so deeply!

• • •

Dusk was falling by the time Carlo blundered through the stage door of the Teatro, chunks of ice in his hair. He was burning. Burning. The world was on fire. The lamp that lit the performers' corridor was a comet, its blaze stabbing the backs of Carlo's eyes.

"Where in Michael's bootstraps have you been?"

"Walking." Carlo cringed at the crow's voice that came from his throat.

Casale hurried toward him, the whites of his eyes showing stark in his head. "Signor, there's only a half-hour until curtain-up. You need to warm up your voice. I…there's some liquorice in the tiring-room. For your throat. And I'll put the kettle on for more rosehip water." He fluttered his hands about Carlo's shoulders. "Oh, signor, let me help you out of those wet things. Your poor hair is almost straight. A towel! A towel, someone!"

The comet shot lightning bolts at Carlo's eyes. He cradled his burning forehead. "Sweet Michael! Can you not hold your tongue? Or is the concept beyond your feeble wits?"

Why was he angry with Casale? He hated anger and arguments. They made him ill. But the words seemed to come on their own.

"Get me some almond liqueur." He lurched toward the toilette table. "I'm cold." Cold? Hadn't he been on fire a moment ago?

"But Signor, you never drink before a performance." Casale was staring at him like a confused child. This was exhausting. What had possessed him to employ such a lackwit?

Carlo flapped a sodden sleeve. "Just…go."

He braced himself against the toilette table and groaned. Who was he becoming? Maestro Sarastro? His father? A fit of shivering seized him. No, no, never. He had nothing in common with that drunken tyrant. Nothing.

"Nothing. Nothing." He repeated it to himself like a litany as he stripped the wet clothes from his back. His teeth chattered. He clenched his jaw and kept going. "Nothing."

A splinter stabbed under Carlo's fingernail. His hand went to his mouth before he remembered that he mustn't let go. His mad grab at the wooden cloud made the ascending platform wobble. Footlights rushed up to meet him. He gulped down frantic breaths. *Listen to the music. Wait for the cue.* The pulsing stars resolved into a row of candles, lined up in a trough of water. A boy was going along the front of the stage, trimming them. Distant. A doll-child in a toy theatre.

Breathe. Half-hidden by ropes and rafters, La Bellina and Giovanni argued in song. The plumes on their heads wobbled. The extreme vibrato in Giovanni's voice suggested he was putting all his fury over Angelo into the song. If he wasn't careful, he would lose control altogether.

Breathe. He couldn't breathe. His throat was full of mucus. He wanted to cough. *Don't cough. The voice; preserve the voice.* He swallowed, swallowed again, suddenly belched.

It tasted of almond liqueur. Why had he drunk almond liqueur? He never drank before a performance. Sweet Michael, how his head ached! That awful, heavy helmet. He pushed it up and wiped his brow. White powder came away in a sticky mess.

His life was a sticky mess.

Horses stamped impatiently at the foot of the ramp. Soldiers massed in the wings, their spears a golden thicket. La Bellina drew out the high note; soft, loud, soft, loud. The audience stamped and applauded. Roses fluttered down from the boxes. Bellina swept a magnificent curtsey; kissed her hand to the Duke, to her patron; spoke some flirtatious nothings to the box nearest the stage. A veiled lady leaned from a balcony and handed a rose to Giovanni. He put it to his lips in a gesture of utmost tenderness. The orchestra waited, poised, for Sarastro's signal.

"Take the strain, boys." The stagehands were ready.

Please, Michael, let there be no encore. He had to get this over with now. Stop gripping the wooden cloud like a hawk with its prey. He was a knight of the Crusades. A hero. Riding to battle in his chariot. Noble. Not sweaty. There: the introduction had begun. The twinkle of the harpsichord, violins scrubbing, bassoon providing a rhythmic *pom-pom-pom*. The platform jerked, sunk a span or two, jerked again.

"Easy, easy," came a voice from the rigging.

Carlo sang. Ridiculous words about how he was looking forward to great deeds of arms and chivalry. From some distant place, he could hear cracks and squeaks in his voice, but he couldn't concentrate on that because the platform and his stomach were going in opposite directions, and there were stars orbiting the candelabra, and his helmet was too heavy, and Tamino had given away his ring to Celestina, and the stage was full of horses and soldiers and crushed petals, and he couldn't breathe. He couldn't breathe.

He was walking toward the row of lights in the water trough. *God will lend me His aid to defeat the brutal foe.* Walking through a maelstrom of men and horses. His cloak dragged. His left ankle turned on his high heel so that he stumbled. The audience gasped.

Carlo shook his head, thrown by the sudden loss of applause. Why had it stopped? And why had the stage risen like a wave, then plunged him back to the depths? But he could see the row of harbour lights. He would be safe when he reached them.

There was a wire in the way. He knew what the wire was for, if he could just think. If he could stop walking toward it, stop singing, stop the waves from crashing in his ears.

He tripped on the wire. Fell. Something hit his face. Another something scorched his ankles. But that didn't matter because the clouds had come to welcome him with their chill embrace.

16
The Ravishment

It was inevitable he would end up at the Teatro. Like a great lodestone, the opera house drew Tammo back. Back to the stench and clamour of human life. Back to the masks and disguises, and the endless lies. *Like a dog returning to its vomit,* he told himself as he climbed the stairs, the sour tang of chamber pots finding a way through the rosemary-scrubbed veil of his batua.

But not backstage. Let someone else fly the doves; see how well they managed without him! He wasn't going into that bear pit of powder and machinery and tantrum-throwing capons.

Yes, he'd said the word. Capons.

He'd paid his silver lira along with the coachmen and link boys, and squeezed into the fifth tier balcony to stand between a fat coachman who took snuff every five minutes with the regularity of an automaton, and a greasy-wigged chairman with an oozing wen on the side of his neck. As for the rest of his neighbours, the ones who weren't sneezing from the coachman's snuff, were hawking and spitting on the floor or, worse still, over the balcony. Sweet Michael, how he hated them! Filthy, unnatural beasts. A crow or a magpie would never behave like that.

And it wasn't just the audience. He hated the preening warblers onstage, with their ostrich feathers and gold buskins. He hated the wealth-flaunters, the fan-signalling flirters, the exquisites, the orange-sellers, the swooners, the intriguers. He hated them all with a passion he could taste. He would stand here on the balcony and radiate hatred at every one of them.

He had crept away from the Pageno mansion in the early hours. Fenice was still snoring, curled against the wall. Three maidservants, squashed into a second bed against the other wall, were doing likewise. It was dark and his breath made clouds as he felt around for his breeches and shoes. There wasn't enough sky between the clouds for much starlight or moonshine, but the reflected snow gave the clouds a certain brightness. It had been enough for him to steal away, leaving his ill deed behind.

Damn it, why had he done the deed at all? *Never again.* That's what he had promised himself after Victory Day. And then to go up against the wall in the ascending platform… He felt dirty, like he ought to scrub himself in one of Fenice's laundry tubs. He had violated Celestina's memory, the purity of his devotion to her.

No. Carlo had done that. Carlo with his lying tongue and as many masks as the Night of Magnificence. Carlo had driven him to this.

The overture began. Scraping fiddles, doing the will of the fat Sarastro.

The curtains opened. Ridiculous processions with spears and banners and the full chorus marching backward and forward. The same stupid processions in every opera! This one had the novelty of a camel in it, although Tammo failed to see the draw of a beast that had to be dragged onstage by two handlers, and spent the whole time trying to eat their hats. If Tammo had had a musket, he would have shot it.

Then came La Bellina, in the creaking cloud machine. Self-obsessed virago! And Scipione, as the king. What was he wearing? He looked as if a giant pastry had been baked on his head. And Giovanni from school, the so-called Parnasso. Well, everyone knew he was a *femella*. He looked more of a girl than Bellina did.

Tammo ground his teeth until his ears ached. The hatred he felt for them was nothing to the wrath he was going to pour on Carlo. When Carlo appeared on that stage, the pit would tremble with his fury. Fire and brimstone would rain from the chandeliers. He had reserved for Carlo an anger that would make Armageddon look like a pillow fight.

The cloud machine began wobbling down. Here he came now. The false twin. The deceiver.

But what was wrong with his voice? Carlo never allowed such squeaks and slurs in his singing. Especially on his first entrance. He would have spent hours alone in his tiring-room, mewing and yawping before the looking-glass, sipping carefully measured throat tonics, exercising his body for the rigours of performance. He never stepped onto a stage with his cloak half-on, half-off, his helmet askew, his curls flat.

"Seraphini's in poor voice tonight." The coachman prefaced his comment with a hearty sniff.

Poor voice? That was an understatement. One might as well say that a roast goose was in poor health. Carlo had not even bowed to the Duke or acknowledged the Pageno box. He was tottering between the guardsmen like an infant of fifteen months. Was he drunk?

At the side of the stage, Il Cupide exchanged nervous glances with his page boy. This definitely wasn't normal. Carlo croaked out another phrase, turned on his ankle, staggered, coughed. Gasps and mutters rose around the auditorium.

"Devilish poor show tonight."

"I'm for the card room. Piquet, anyone?"

"I said we should have gone to the billiard hall."

"Got any more of that spicy sausage?"

Tammo searched in vain for his hatred, but something had dampened the coals. His world had shrunk to the two foot radius that surrounded Carlo's tottering progress.

Carlo limped upstage, his voice barely above a sparrow's chirp. He seemed not to see where he was headed.

The footlights. The flames. *Fire!* Tammo's throat constricted. He was ten years old again, beating on the burning door while his family slumbered toward death. The flames were licking up his hand, his neck. Smoke filled his throat.

He had to get out. The bodies were pressing too closely around him. The ceiling was oppressively low. Carlo was stumbling nearer and nearer the flames.

"Carlo!"

Too late. Carlo tripped on the wire meant to stop costumes from catching fire. The entire trough of candles tipped over as he fell headlong into the orchestra and struck his head against the harpsichord. Sarastro, who was sitting at the keyboard, leapt to his feet and swore, "Sweet Michael's dregs!"

Smoke and steam rose from the pit. Musicians scattered, desperately flapping sheets of music. A couple of violinists rushed to take Carlo's head. Stagehands ran from the wings, buckets of sawdust in hand. A horse reared and almost threw its rider.

"Get out of my way!" Tammo shoved the coachman and his snuffbox sideways, almost trampling the fellow with the spicy sausage. He had to get down to the pit. He had to save Carlo. That was his job.

He drew a deep breath and tried to bring some resonance into his crow's voice. "I said, make way!"

The forest of shoulders parted with a murmur of curses.

"Mind your manners, short-shanks," someone said, but Tammo wasn't listening. He'd made it to the staircase and was running downstairs as if he meant to break his neck.

"Let me through! Let me through, I say!" The assembly of

backs wedged more tightly together. "I'm a friend, damn you! Let me through!"

He hadn't run fast enough.

The fifth tier was a long way up. Every admirer, patron and general busybody on the first four tiers had a head start on him. As the staircase descended lower, so the press of bodies had become closer, with more and more people abandoning their boxes in the excitement of Signor Seraphini's fall. By the time the cavalcade had reached the ground floor, so many people had left their seats that it was only by Michael's mercy that there were no further accidents. To Tammo's relief, some of those surged onward toward the grand entrance and portico, to take comfort in describing the horrific sights to one another.

But many more forced their way through the doorway into the performers' corridor, where they were confronted by a counter-surge coming from the stage itself. The crowd of performers had arrived much sooner, having a shorter distance to travel. And being more intimately concerned with events onstage, it was far more hysterical.

"Some air, some air!" Tammo heard the stridor of a trained voice. "Egad, man! where are the smelling salts?"

There were rumours—although Tammo was too far back to catch more than the edge of them—that La Bellina and two dancers had fainted dead away and been carried to their rooms by guardsmen.

To some, this development was a greater lure than that of an injured Seraphini. Well-wishers were likely to force any door they came upon, in the hope of horrifying themselves with the spectacle of a swooning performer. They had already disturbed Signor Croci at his accounts and crushed a number of costumes beyond use. Neither the tirades of the wardrobe mistress nor the pleas of Signor Croci to "remain calm, good citizens" had the least effect. From where Tammo now stood, Carlo's tiring room might be as distant as the palace of the Caliph.

"A pox on this!" he muttered to himself.

He was going back to the old way of doing things. It might not be dignified, but it was simple and effective.

He jogged back the way he had come. Through the patrons' doorway, past the stairwell and into one of the little courtyards that dotted the Teatro's interior. It was covered in damp snow, and more was falling out of a charcoal sky. Slippery. But he'd known worse.

Tammo knotted his cloak about his neck like an extra muffler and hauled himself onto the windowsill. He kicked open the shutters and nudged the window with his knee so that it swung inward. He then grabbed hold of the lintel and swung himself after it.

A table containing Carlo's uneaten supper crashed to the floor, tipped over by his foot. Tammo stumbled in, grabbing hold of a clothes rack to steady himself. Several voices screamed. Caged birds twittered in a frenzy.

Something sharp jabbed inches from Tammo's eyes.

"Touch him and you'll have to go through me first!" Casale's voice was unsteady. Clearly, he had been crying. That didn't stop him taking a poker from the fire and using it to fend off Tammo as if Tammo was a mad dog.

Tammo gave a snort of exasperation. He unfastened his cloak, hat and batua, and threw them to the floor. "It's me, you lackwit! Tammo Capell."

"Tamino?" The voice was so weak, so cracked, that Tammo barely recognised it as Carlo's. He turned toward a velvet sopha, where a figure lay prone.

Tammo's heart gave a sick lurch. For a moment, he was back in the lime tree at the conservatorio, sharing a cloak while Carlo leaned on his shoulder. He bit his lip and swallowed hard.

"I'm here." His voice came out deeper than he intended. He cleared his throat.

Carlo tried to sit up. "I thought…I thought you…"

As his face came out of shadow, Tammo could see that his eyes were large with fever, his curls plastered to his forehead. The two dressers at his bedside had been applying damp cloths, leaving a grotesque marbling of theatrical paints and powders. One temple was swelling into an ugly bruise. His stockings had been removed, revealing a blister on his left ankle.

Carlo's efforts to speak brought on a fit of coughing. The two dressers, a man and a woman, began to flap with greater agitation than the orioles whose cages hung from the ceiling. The man pushed Carlo back onto the pillow, while the woman twittered in his ear.

"No, no, Signor Seraphini, you mustn't." The woman turned her head to scowl at Casale. She was a strong-featured woman, who reminded Tammo briefly of a Mother

Superior he'd known. "Why is there no physician yet? Or an apothecary, at least?"

Casale gave a helpless gesture. "Have you seen the pandemonium out there? A mouse couldn't get through."

"Well, he did." She jerked her head toward Tammo.

"And you expect a learned physician to clamber through the window?" Casale was incredulous. "Or do you expect Citizen Capell to summon one on the back of a flock of doves?" He went off into a whispered soliloquy of curses and *sweet Michaels*.

"He might as well do something useful," the woman muttered.

Tammo felt his blood begin to rise again. "Just let me speak to him, why don't you?"

The two dressers and Casale rounded on him with a tirade of objections. Casale's voice soon shouted down the other two, rising and rising in anger. What made Tammo think he could stroll in now when he'd been absent all week? Hadn't Casale's master been through enough without being upset again?

Tammo was on the verge of asking Casale how he dared speak to a citizen of Angelio that way, and did he wish to keep his job? He tightened his fists.

A faint sound from the sopha made them turn their heads. Carlo was trying to speak. The female dresser put an arm behind his head and lifted it.

Carlo drew several wheezy breaths. "Leave us."

The dressers looked at him in confusion. With difficulty, Carlo raised himself higher on the pillow. Sweat ran down his face. "Leave us. Please. I wish to speak to Citizen Capell alone."

"But signor…" A gesture from Carlo's be-ringed fingers silenced his manservant. Casale schooled his features before barking at the dressers, "Outside. Now. And find out if a physician is on the way."

As soon as the merest crack appeared in the doorway, the crowd tried to force its way in. Tammo assisted Casale in strong-arming the door while the dressers escaped, then slammed it after Casale's exit, not caring how many fingers he trapped. He made a show of bolting it shut, stoking the fire, tidying away his cloak and hat.

Now the others were gone, the atmosphere in the tiring-room felt close with more than fever. Tammo raked the back of his neck with broken fingernails. He felt dirty, soiled by his indiscretion. He was sure Fenice's scent was still on him, filling the tiny room.

He lowered himself onto the extreme edge of the sopha, avoiding Carlo's gaze. His friend's breathing sounded unnaturally loud. Did Carlo know that, less than a quarter-hour ago, Tammo had wished him to be struck by divine lightning?

Tammo glanced at the window. How easy it would be to simply climb back out and disappear into the night.

"Tamino."

That one word opened a yawning chasm in his belly. He forced himself to look into Carlo's face. Carlo was breathing hard. His eyes had a desperate, feverish light in them.

"What are the words of our vow? Say them to me."

"I…" This was not how he had expected the conversation to begin. He rubbed his hands on his breeches to stop them from sweating. "Carlo, are you hurt? I saw you fall. The footlights. I was up on the balcony. Are you hurt?"

He was talking nonsense. Of course, Carlo was hurt. He'd just fallen into the orchestra pit. But the thought of those flames… The whole Teatro could have gone up in smoke.

Carlo clawed at the coverlet, reaching for Tammo's hands. "Answer me, Tamino. Please, I must know. Does our vow mean nothing?"

His hands looked like spiders, crawling across the coverlet. Bejewelled spiders, glittering in the lamplight with rings and…

That ring. On Carlo's left hand. The smiling face surrounded by gemstones. Tammo's throat tightened.

When he spoke, his voice was so cold, he barely recognised it. "Where did you get that ring?"

Carlo's face became an emotionless mask. He lifted his hand with an affected gesture, examining the ring as if he had never seen it before. "Count Pageno gave it to me as a boy. I'm rather surprised you don't remember."

"I did. I mean, I do. But…"

"Oh, yes!" Carlo touched a finger to his Cupid's lips. "I made a gift of it, didn't I? To my dearest friend in all the world. As a symbol of our eternal love and friendship." His last words became a growl.

The dampened fury in Tammo's breast flickered back to life.

"Love and friendship! Don't make me laugh. I've done everything for you, Carlo Bianci. Everything. Protected you. Nursed you in sickness. Acted the part of a manservant. Written to you every week when you were touring. But that wasn't enough for the Divine Seraphini, was it? You had to steal away the affection of the only woman I've ever loved. Because God forbid that Tammo Capell should be happy, even in his dreams!"

A shadow of confusion passed over Carlo's face.

Tammo ignored it and raged on. "You don't honestly imagine that you can be with her, do you? Count Pageno would eat you for dinner! Signor Seraphini and the Noblesse Celestina? Huh! For all your airs and perfumes and fine clothes, you're nothing but a peasant. Do you hear me? Peasant!"

"Rather a peasant than a lackwit!" Carlo had gone deathly white, and tears quivered in his eyes. "How could you believe that I have ever loved anyone but you? And I was foolish enough to think you loved me back. Sweet Michael, what a notion! You know nothing of love beyond the lusts of the flesh. A mere rutting beast, that's all you are!"

Tammo stepped back. Carlo loved him? Loved him as in…*loved* him?

"I'm a beast?" His voice broke. "You're not even human! A monster, that's what you are. An unnatural, ball-less, lying monster!"

Carlo's voice rose to a hoarse shriek. "Get out of my sight! You are dead to me, Tammo Capell. I will never speak to you again as long as I live!"

Carlo's eyes rolled back in his head. He collapsed onto the pillow and began to shake and groan, thrashing his arms about.

"Carlo?"

Carlo groaned more loudly.

Tammo's stomach went cold. He dared to touch the eunuch's skin with the tips of his fingers. It was dry, like paper. Carlo started to foam at the mouth. The sopha creaked and rattled with his thrashing.

Damn. This was not good. When Casale came back and found Tammo had sent his master into a fit, he would go insane.

"Carlo, stop it."

The eunuch had gone from white to purple. Veins stood out on his neck. He writhed like a snake, his teeth gritting.

Time to leave. There was nothing Tammo could do here. His continued presence could only make things much, much worse. He unbolted the door for Casale's return. Then he scrambled back up the windowsill, out the window and into the courtyard.

Not a moment too soon. The door banged open; Tammo could hear masculine voices above the hum of the crowd.

"Quickly. Carry him to his apartment. I have sent the

physician ahead with a manservant. Sweet Michael, he's having a fit! Pray God we're not too late. The poor boy!"

Count Pageno. Tammo would recognise his voice among a thousand. He pressed himself to the window, shivering in the falling snow. Only now did he remember that his hat and cloak were still inside.

"Hurry," the Count said. "Pompey, set your young mistress down upon the couch. It will take two of you to carry him. Vittori, clear that crowd. Where is Teresa?"

"She fell behind, my lord." That was Pompey's resonant bass. "We lost her in the crowd."

"All is well, papa. I will be perfectly safe here until Teresa comes."

Tammo's heart almost burst out of his chest. Celestina was on the other side of this window! The damp snow matting his hair to his head no longer seemed so cold.

"No, no, my love, I cannot. If they were to force that door…"

"Then bar it behind you. Truly, papa. Do not think of me when Carlo is so very ill." Her voice broke on the last few words.

The Count murmured some words of comfort that Tammo could not make out. "Very well. We will shut you in. But I will send Vittori to you as soon as possible. And Teresa, when we find her."

"I know. Please go now, papa. My poor Angel-boy…"

Tammo waited for the room to fall silent. He hardly dared to breathe.

Celestina was alone and undisturbed in Carlo's tiring-room. He must go to her. After all that had happened, he wanted her so badly. The touch of her hand, her gentle words. The perfume of her soft brown hair. All he need do was climb back through the window. Surely this chance was a gift from the Archangel!

He was up on the window ledge the moment he heard the door close. Straight through the window, as before. And straight into the clothes rack again.

Celestina gave a sharp intake of breath. "Tammo Capell?"

Her handkerchief was pressed to her mouth. Both her voice and eyes betrayed that she had been crying, but there was no sign of fear on her face. A true lady, Tammo thought. She was braver than a barrack full of militia.

"Forgive me, noblesse." Tammo sketched a bow. "I was…trying to avoid the crowd." He looked at Carlo's sopha with feigned puzzlement. "Where is he? Am I too late?"

"Oh, Tammo!" The brave façade crumbled. "When he fell, I felt… I felt that it was all my fault. I have been cruel to him. I did not understand. If he should die…"

Her words were swallowed up in sobs. It was more than Tammo could bear. She was so beautiful, so fragile, so alone. Gently, he sat on the couch beside her. He reached out his arm behind her back, willing it not to shake. If she rejected him now, the Count's wrath would fall on him like Michael's fist.

Softly, softly as leaf-fall in autumn, he drew her into his arms. "All shall be well. I'm here."

She leaned on his chest, as she had done in the riding park. Tammo let his cheek rest against the velvet fontange on her head. So soft, so sensual. He quivered.

Celestina sat up and pushed him to arm's length. "No, this is not right. It was not right with Carlo, yet God will forgive me for loving him. But this… It is not right, Citizen Capell. Carlo lies dying, perhaps, at this moment, and I…I do not love you."

Tammo became perfectly still. His lips pressed so tightly, they went white. Inside him, a roar was building, a howl, a mighty gale. She did not love him. She loved Carlo but she did not love him. She must love him. She must. She would.

He had the dark flute out of its case before he knew what he was doing. He ran his fingers over the holes and leafy carvings, breathed deeply into the mouth hole.

"What are you doing?" Celestina looked at him as one might look at some strange insect creeping up the sleeve of a garment.

Tammo didn't answer. He began to play.

He played the call of the nightingale in twilit gardens. He played almond biscotti and sweet cream, the music room with its painted harpsichord. Lace fichus and fans and games of piquet. Sad poetry about lost lovers. Box forty-three at the opera. The music swelled and grew under his lips and fingers. It filled the tiring room, bringing new colours to Carlo's costumes and the flowers on his toilette table. The orioles in their cages harmonised a quivering descant.

He played childhood memories. Dolls and puppets and the Twelfth Night feast. Tears for poor, lost Orlando. He played Carlo's aria, *Dearest heart, beloved bride.* He played Carlo's voice, his Cupid's lips and chocolate curls. He put his own, unquenchable love for Celestina into Carlo's mouth. *I love you. I love you more than life itself. And you must love me too.*

Celestina gasped. A very different gasp from Tammo's when he fell into the clothes rack. Her cheeks were pink, her lips parted.

Tammo laid the dark flute on the sopha. He took Celestina's face in his hands, touching her ears, fingertips brushing pearl earrings.

Then he was kissing her. Deeply, hungrily.

She moaned and tightened her grip on him. Her tongue tasted of almond. Her lips were warm, and soft as silk.

With a deep sigh, he slid his hand down her neck, down her décolletage, inside her bodice. Her breasts were like a baby's cheeks. He had never felt anything so delicate.

She leaned back against Carlo's bolster. He could take her now. He could part her skirts and take her in a moment of glorious passion. She would be his, his alone. Celestina, Noblesse of the House of Pageno, the most beautiful woman on earth, surrendering her maidenhead to Tammo Capell.

A savage *caw* split the air.

The window flew open, bringing with it a flurry of icy

flakes. And riding on the back of them, dark wings and an angry beak. Tammo swore and covered his head.

Coronis was merciless. Her talons and beak reached for him in a screeching assault. Black feathers flew, like snow from Tartarus. Celestina lay on the couch and stared, like a person awakened from a nightmare. Coronis' talons tore at Tammo's cheek, beside the scar he already bore. He felt wet blood running, a second before he felt the pain.

"Tammo Capell." There was a face at the window.

It had no body, just hair of flame, and eyes that contained all the stars of the universe. Tammo cowered. He tried to cover his eyes, but the eyes of fire pierced his closed lids.

The voice echoed in his bones. "Tammo Capell, did I not warn you that no good would come of using my gifts for selfish means? But you have not heeded my warning, and you must face the consequences."

"Archangel." Tammo tried to speak, but his voice was sucked into his lungs.

The Archangel's face filled the room, an awful, impossible presence. He could not escape it. He grovelled to the floor, his arms cradling his head.

"Have mercy," he croaked, but the Archangel did not relent. If anything, the fire of his presence burned brighter. Crawling on his knees, Tammo gathered up his flute and outdoor clothes. He threw himself out the window, falling painfully onto his back in the snow.

He scrambled to his feet and ran for his life.

17

Feathers and Feverfew

Carlo's mind groped toward groggy half-wakefulness. Something cool and damp was patting his forehead. It smelled of lavender. And honeysuckle.

"There, there." A gentle voice. "Teresa, pass me a clean cloth. This one is drying out."

There was a pause, then the patting began again. Carlo winced. One side of his forehead was tender. He was shivering and sweating all at once. He tried to remember. Had he woken like this before? His memory was a shadow-play of lights and pain and worried voices.

"Let's try and sit him up, ladyship. Then we can cut off this tangle of hair. He'll be cooler without it."

A few drops of something warm and sweet dribbled into Carlo's mouth. It ran down his chin.

"I suppose you're right, but, oh, his poor hair! He'll look so forlorn without it."

"If the fever doesn't break," said a male voice, "we must put him in the ice bath."

Carlo's stomach clenched sharply. No. Not the ice. He

tried to move his limbs. Why was nothing working properly? His foot was burning.

"No ice!" Celestina's voice had the ring of absolute command. She took her hand from Carlo's forehead. "Come, doctor, and help Teresa to lift him."

Two pairs of hands eased their way between the pillows and Carlo's back. Cold silver touched his neck. He cried out in pain.

"Tamino! Tamino, save me!"

"He's calling on that accursed boy again." Teresa tutted as she snipped.

The cool cloth dabbed his forehead.

"Carlo, angel. It's Celestina. Do you understand? Do you know me, Carlo?"

"Tamino!" He cried again.

Something was tickling his throat. Through his gummed eyelashes, Carlo had the impression he was being made to swallow a goose's wing.

"Hold the bowl steady, man," said the physician's voice.

The tickling came again. Carlo's forehead throbbed. Saliva rushed to his mouth. His gut retched.

"There, there, signor." Casale's brown hand dabbed at Carlo's mouth. "Better out than in."

An acrid smell burned Carlo's nostrils. His throat was on fire. He retched again.

"Good God, is this necessary?" That was Sarastro's

boom. "You do realise this is our primo sopranist? His voice must not be damaged under any circumstances."

"It was either this or the ice bath." Carlo's eyes were open enough to see the physician flick a goose feather into the fire.

"No ice!" several voices cried together.

Was that Celestina perched on the alcove bed beside her maidservant? Celestina sitting on Tammo's bed. Where was Tammo?

"Where is Tamino?" He had no voice. "Water," he croaked.

"No cold water," said the physician. "Give him this bowl of warm milk." He unstopped a glass vial and tapped three brown drops into the bowl.

The milk tasted odd. Carlo groaned and turned his head away. His stomach hurt.

"Lay him back on the pillows. Pompey, lift me closer." Celestina's hands fluttered about him. "And remove that bowl, Casale. It stinks."

"No more opium, my master said." That was Vittori's voice, growling in the physician's ear.

"I do not give more." The physician's voice was clipped. "This dose replaces the one the patient just vomited." Glass clinked on glass as he replaced the vial in his medicine chest. "And I do not consult with manservants. Let your master speak with me himself."

"My master is at court," growled Vittori. "Where the situation is extremely delicate, as you well know."

Birdcages swung above Carlo's head. Orpheus. The

orioles. The linnets. Gold filigree gleamed, reflecting patterns of flame. Orpheus. The lime tree at school…

"Tamino is at the window. Don't let him in." Did he say that aloud?

Gleaming patterns of flame. Whirring wings. Birdcages swung.

Castrato. Have you lost something, castrato? You're not even human.

Carlo moaned. "There's a birdcage up there, mocking me. Tell it to stop."

"Hush, Carlo." Celestina stroked his forehead. "No one is mocking you."

A feather fluttered down.

The bluest feather fluttered down, a shard of lapis lazuli. Its downy barbs curled like fronds of ice leaves upon a windowpane. Freckles of golden light shivered over its surface.

The chamber was filled with golden light; it was like being inside a candle. Celestina, Casale, the physician, all were gone. There was a stillness to the air, a calmness like the last rays of sun on a summer evening, when the clouds blush low over the horizon, kissed by heaven's breath.

Someone was standing at the foot of the bed.

Carlo knew in an instant that it was a person he loved beyond measure. Yet it was not Tammo, or even Celestina.

It was a person he had seen in the crypt of the Sancti Michaelis Archangeli when he was thirteen years old. A person in a salmon frock-coat with lace at his cuffs. With a basket-hilted rapier and a wig like lamb's wool.

A person with the face of a castrato and the body of Achilles. And eyes like the sun at noonday.

"Archangel," Carlo breathed. "Am I dying?"

He spoke the words without moving his lips. He thought about moving his limbs but could no longer remember how.

When the Archangel spoke, his voice was like the sound of rushing water. It filled every corner of the room, and tickled the crevices of Carlo's mind. "Has my presence ever brought you death before? Or do you speak from a guilty conscience, my son?"

Something inside Carlo broke. "Where have you been? I have sought you all this season. I needed you. Why have you not appeared to me, as you did when I was a boy?"

"Because you are a boy no longer." The Archangel's gaze softened. "What is right for one season of life is unsuited to another. Your life no longer has the simplicity of childhood, Carlo. You must learn to seek me in doubt and confusion. To recognise me in forms you would not expect. I had hoped you would have learned that lesson."

The Archangel's voice grew deeper. His face and costume began to change, like a reflection when a stone is dropped into a lake. When his form settled, he was quite another person. Yet Carlo recognised him. He had the almond eyes, black queue, and silken robes of the merchant who took his coffee at Armide's.

Carlo's throat went dry. "The Mingguo merchant! You are he. But…you spoke to me."

"And warned you that your friend was in danger of tipping my scales."

At the mention of Tammo, Carlo's heart calcified. "A false friend. He betrayed me years ago."

The eyes of the Archangel burned. His two forms showed together, layered and transparent like two images projected through a magic lantern.

"Remember, Carlo, that a part of you lives in him, and he in you. That is how our bargain works. I took something from each of you to satisfy the other. To disown Tammo Capell is to disown yourself."

Carlo fought the many protests that clamoured in his breast. *He called me a monster. He deserted me.* The Archangel was not a person to be contradicted.

"Did you give Citizen Capell my warning?" The Archangel's voice was dangerously soft. "Did you tell him what you saw in the caffe that day? Of the spy Morestelli and the implication of the della Pamina family in the plot against the Duke?"

"He wasn't speaking to me." Carlo knew his tone sounded peevish.

"And why should that stop you speaking to him? Did you heed my second warning in the piazza of the mask makers?"

"He kept avoiding me. He wouldn't even look at me." Carlo could no longer restrain his frustration. It was unfair.

Tammo had sinned and yet he, Carlo, was being blamed for his shortcomings.

"Could you not have sought help?" said the Archangel. "From Count Pageno. From Citizen Grimaldi. What did you promise me in the crypt? To remain friends and brothers. To dedicate yourselves to my service. So short a time in which to break a vow."

Carlo moved his lips, trying to find words that would not come.

The Archangel sighed. "Alas, this cannot be mended as easily as when you were boys. Not only have you hurt one another, you have harmed my city of Angelio, and Celestina too. I fear she will not easily recover from this hurt. I must remove her as your companion. It is for your own good."

"But that was a mistake!" Carlo felt tears on his cheeks. "Signor, how is this just? When she spoke of one thing, I thought she meant another. I had no notion Tammo was trying to court her. Please. I never meant to tempt her. You cannot withdraw your gift, Your Excellency. Be merciful!"

"This is an act of mercy," said the Archangel. "Had you and your twin heeded my presence and my warnings, we would not find ourselves in this sorry state of affairs. As it is, your patron is now in danger of a kind that threatens both his future, and the future of all Angelio."

"Danger?" Carlo was finding the conversation harder and harder to follow. They had been speaking of Celestina, not her father. How could Celestina's disappointment in love endanger Count Pageno?

He looked at the Archangel, now solidly back in his

guise as an Angelian nobleman. The city's protector looked weary, despite his radiant beauty. "It was through the abuse of my gifts that this situation came about. Therefore, those gifts must be removed. And you and your twin must be the ones to put things right."

Carlo awoke to dim lamplight. He was lying inside the rosy curtains of his bed, propped up by bolsters and feather pillows. The sheets were clammy. The air tasted stale.

There was no doubt this time; he was awake.

He now recalled several such wakings. The chamber had been bustling with people. Going in and out of doors, mopping his brow, dosing him with laudanum, taking out his chamber pot. Asking him how he felt.

Asking, always asking.

Did he feel any stronger today? How was his throat? His chest? Could he sit up and cough, please? No pressure intended, but how long before he could return to the Teatro? Could he eat a tangerine? It had come from Count Pageno's own table. The nightingales missed him; would he like to see them? Was he giddy? Queasy? Constipated? Could he hold his arm still over the bleeding bowl?

Carlo pulled back his sleeve. A row of red slits stood out against the white of his inner arm, ranging from raw to scabbed. The raw ones itched. Carlo sighed. Gingerly, he touched the back of his head. The bristles of a clothes brush met his fingers. All his beautiful curls, gone! Shorn away during his fever.

He lay back against the pillows, exhausted by the effort. How could they expect him to get well? His heart was broken. He would never be well again.

Tammo had not visited once. Not even in dreams.

Carlo tried with all his feeble strength to recall one occasion on which Tammo had been at his bedside, or watching from his old bed in the alcove. Nothing came.

But Celestina had been there. She had sat beside his bed, mopping his brow. Her own fingers had mixed tinctures, the glass chiming as she stirred. Despite the hurt he had caused her, Celestina had taken pity on him.

But wait. Had not the Archangel told him that Celestina must be removed from Carlo's company? That it was an act of mercy.

Carlo's head swam. He could no longer discern what was a dream and what reality. Had the Archangel spoken with him at all?

He pulled himself up against the pillows. "Casale!"

His tongue was a piece of shoe leather. There was a foul-tasting glue at the corners of his mouth. He tried again. "Casale!"

A sudden snort told him his manservant had been dozing on the couch. The curtains parted. Casale's cravat was undone and his chin was covered with fuzzy, black stubble.

He looked at Carlo as a hound looks at its master. "Signor! What is it? Can I fetch you anything?"

"Water," Carlo croaked.

Casale put a glass to Carlo's lips. Rosehip water trickled down his throat.

"Noblesse Celestina," he said when he could speak again. "Is she here?" He glanced about the room, half-expecting to find her sitting in the shadows. No, that was foolishness. "I would speak with her on a matter of the utmost importance."

Casale looked at his shoes. "Signor, the noblesse has gone."

"Gone?" Carlo tasted the word in his mouth, trying to attach some meaning to it.

"Yes, signor. That is to say, she was here before. When you were very ill, humbly begging your pardon, signor. Quite concerned for you, she was. Visited several days and nights, if it's not disrespectful to the young lady to say so. But she wouldn't stay once the fever broke. Said she was going away."

"Away?" Carlo feared he was beginning to sound like a talking starling. "Where?"

"That she wouldn't say, signor. But she did not wish to be followed, she made me promise that. I do believe she wished to be away from society. To seek spiritual counsel, perhaps. Young ladies of her station sometimes do."

Casale scratched his nut-brown cheek and lifted his eyes heavenward, as if to say that the ways of young ladies were quite alien to him.

Carlo felt a wave of exhaustion roll over him. She was gone, just as the Archangel said. Perhaps forever. If the convent was her destination, that was certainly the case. The gift granted to him as a boy had been removed, leaving him friendless.

Unless…unless…noun, he could not face a confrontation with Tammo. He was not well enough. How could he bear to see anger and scorn in the eyes of his erstwhile twin? How could he bear the pangs of love that would torment him despite the disgust and resentment?

No, he would not demean himself by asking after Tammo's whereabouts. He would not allow Casale to think his master a pathetic, lovesick…

"Casale, has…?"

"Has Citizen Capell been here?" Carlo's cheeks burned. Was he so transparent? "No, signor, he has not. Never even sent a message. And you at death's door. It's a crying shame, if I may say so. I know you were childhood friends, but it's past time you were rid of him, signor. That's my opinion and I won't say it isn't. You have friends in higher places now."

"Fetch me some gruel, Casale."

Carlo turned his face to the wall, so the manservant could not see the working of his face as he fought back tears. It was truly over, then. Tammo had cast him off and Celestina had taken the veil. Carlo was alone.

He made a lacklustre attempt to eat the gruel. He could tell Casale was displeased by his efforts, but he didn't care. What did it matter if he starved? Tammo didn't love him.

Once his manservant had left the room again, Carlo

crawled to his escritoire and retrieved a ballad sheet, bought on the streets of Angelio for a few centesimi. The stanzas were embellished with cupids and cornucopias. Carlo knew the words by heart, yet he needed to see them with his waking eyes. It was the poem, "A Castrato's Love".

You ask me for my love: what can I give
When ours would be a fruitless union?
The angels do not wed as mortals do
And monsters among humans cannot live.

Which was Carlo: angel or monster? Celestina had called him by one name, Tammo another. Did he deserve to live among humans?

Perhaps his love, however chaste, was nothing but a sin. That was why the Archangel was punishing him. He was a hideous grotesque, neither male nor female. An abomination who brought disaster to all who came near him. Why would anyone want to be friends with such a monstrosity? Even the Archangel Michael had abandoned him.

Something prickled Carlo's ear. He reached into the pillow and pulled out a feather by its quill. It was the bluest blue, a shard of lapis lazuli. It might have been plucked from the wing of a peacock or a bird of paradise.

Or an angel.

18

Grimaldi's Secret

"Will you stop fiddling with that thing? You'll end up breaking it. And you can come and work the bellows if you're not going out to hunt. Might as well make yourself useful."

Tammo gave the dark flute another spin, watching it go round like a spinning-top, in ever-increasing circles, slower and slower, until it finally tipped sideways. He caught it and stood it up again. For a moment he toyed with it, contemplating another spin. At the last second, he snatched it up and swished at the air with the savagery of a bandit.

"Now then, lad. That won't make it any better." With gentle but determined hands, Grimaldi prised the flute from Tammo's fingers. "If you want to use up some anger, the forge is the place."

Tammo gritted his teeth. His fists clenched. He could knock the old man down. One satisfying punch to exorcise the storm raging inside him. He sighed, the fight leaching out of him. What would be the point of that? Would it bring back the time before he dishonoured two women, or his bird charming, or the boyhood days when he and Carlo were friends?

He dragged his feet over the frozen mud toward the forge.

His face hurt. Grimaldi had treated the wound with vinegar, and the claw-marks were fading to form new scars next to the old ones. He didn't care about that. Let him be disfigured, hideous even. It was less than he deserved. What hurt more was that Coronis hadn't returned. She clearly despised him as the rest of Angelio did.

He had fled to Angel's Wood directly from the Teatro. Grimaldi had raised an eyebrow to see him, half-dressed and lantern-less at the cottage door, with lumps of ice in his hair. But, apart from some muttering about the lateness of the hour, the old man said little. Soup for Tammo's belly, a blanket for his back and hot water for his feet were far more pressing concerns.

Tammo had lain awake all that night, staring at the ceiling of his box bed, convinced that the Archangel's face would burn through it at any moment. He couldn't believe what he'd almost done to Celestina. At one point, he had crawled out of the bed and retched into the night soil bucket for several minutes. He felt no better for it. If Grimaldi had woken at the sound, he hadn't said.

Next morning, Tammo discovered what punishment the Archangel had assigned him.

He had left the cottage early, unwilling to face Grimaldi in the revealing light of day. The snow had stopped overnight, leaving a thin covering on branches and exposed areas, with black mud showing through where trees provided the warmth of shade. A layer of ice floated on the surface of the water trough. It was one of those crisp, blue, winter's mornings that offered the prospect of new beginnings. He would take his flute and see what hunting the day had to offer.

Soon, he was in deep cover, surrounded by the music of the winter wood. The little sounds that pierced the frosty air. The call of the blackbird. The creaking of boughs. The crack of ice.

He found himself wandering toward the place where he had caught the rosefinch. That accursed rosefinch! All his troubles had begun when he caught that bird. Tammo halted and turned about. No more of that. No more intrigues with the Marchesa. No more forgetting his place with Celestina. The charm of the flute was not to be used on people. There was wickedness in that magic; no good came of it. He would do what he was meant to do. Charm birds and sell them.

The fluttering call of a waxwing caught his ear. Now, there was a handsome bird! Much sought-after in the winter months.

Where was it? Ah, there. Feeding on a crop of scarlet berries, its red crest and golden wing-tip standing out against the frozen white.

Tammo slid the dark flute from its case. One good catch would put his addled wits in order. Restore his dignity. A man could take pride in honest labour.

He knew something was wrong as soon as he played the first note. It didn't feel the same. He expected to feel something of the waxwing's little soul: its hunger, its furtive caution. There was nothing. It was just a bird in a bush.

"Come along, my pretty." Tammo trilled the waxwing's song back at the bird. He tried to find the right coaxing tone in his own mind, but all he felt were echoes in a hollow cave. He played again, more softly.

The waxwing froze, shivered its wings, and flew off into the glittering woodland.

Tammo sank onto a mossy root. He could feel the frost biting his thighs and spreading damp across the seat of his breeches. He put his head in his hands, and tore at his wiry hair.

Michael had taken his gift away.

Just like that, Tammo's ability to charm birds had vanished as if it had never existed. Fierce gasps of air burned his lungs and spewed forth in dragonish clouds. He could not begin to comprehend what this meant. For his future. For his livelihood. He didn't want to think.

So he hadn't.

He had ignored the whole stinking mess of outstanding commissions, bills at Armide's, crates of doves at the Teatro, and men in the pay of the Marchesa della Pamina, who may or may not be searching Angelio with cudgels in hand. He had pushed away every image of Carlo thrashing in a seizure, or Celestina staring as if Tammo had been unmasked as the prince of demons. He had stayed in

Angel's Wood like an exile, chopping wood, foraging for mushrooms and lichen, setting eel lines and rabbit snares.

And working alongside Grimaldi at the forge.

They were making axe heads that morning. Tammo worked the bellows, and held the head and wedge steady while Grimaldi wielded the hammer. Despite his wheezing and grunting, the old blacksmith had a formidable blow.

This was his life now, Tammo thought. He was the apprentice Grimaldi had always needed. The years to come would find him here, his beard grey and grizzled, swinging his lonely hammer, while old wives in Angelio told their grandchildren tales of the mad old smith in the woods.

His concentration slipped. The axe head came loose. Grimaldi's hammer clipped it and came down on the side of the anvil.

"Sweet Michael, boy! I could have taken your arm off." Grimaldi leaned on the hammer and wiped his brow with his woollen cap. "There's still plenty of time, you know."

Tammo chewed his lip, pretending they had not had this conversation before.

"Plenty of light left in the day to go to town and see how your friend is faring."

"I have no friends." Tammo's voice was a growl.

"So you say." Grimaldi let out a long breath. He scratched his beard, sniffed, sighed again. Then he put down the hammer and wiped his hands on his apron.

"Damp down the forge and come into the cottage. I need to rest my old legs." And when Tammo stared at him as if he had suggested they might dance the sarabande together, he lowered his brows so his eyes all but vanished. "You afraid, boy?"

Yes, Tammo thought.

Grimaldi never rested in the middle of a job. Something was brewing, and instinct told Tammo he was not going to like it. But that phrase, "You afraid, boy?" reminded him of his early days with Grimaldi. Tammo longed for the simplicity of childhood, when the worst of disasters could be erased by a puppet show or a sweet pastry. He followed his adopted father into the cottage.

It took the old man an infuriating amount of time to take off his outer clothing, stoke the fire and get comfortable in his chair. By the time he had settled to his own satisfaction, with his feet in the hearth, Tammo had chewed his bottom lip to a blister. Grimaldi cleared his throat and blew his nose with what would have been comedic deliberation in other circumstances. Could it be that the old man was nervous? Tammo had never seen him so.

When he began to speak, it was abruptly, with his eyes fixed on the kettle that swung from a chain above the fire.

"I wasn't always alone. Did you know that, boy? You'll find this hard to picture, but I was once a young whipper-snapper of an apprentice, even more scrawny than you were when you first washed up on my doorstep. I was apprenticed to a blacksmith at the age of ten, along with another lad. Amadeus, his name was. We used to call him Dodo."

Grimaldi sighed and shook his head with what might have been a chuckle.

"A right pair of scallywags, we were. Forever pranking the master and his wife. Eels in her Sunday shoes. Spiders in his hat. Sneaking away to the cock fights on half-holidays.

Many's the hiding we got from our old master. Our backsides were better tanned than his work apron. But we took it in good grace because we bore it together, you see. There was none of this dropping the other fellow in it. If the fault was mine, Dodo would insist he was to blame too. And I'd do the same for him."

Tammo tried to picture Grimaldi as an apprentice, slim, beardless, full of high spirits. He couldn't do it. Grimaldi was the old smith in the woods, from everlasting to everlasting. He was never a boy.

"We used to huddle in bed in the attic on winter's nights, and make plans for the future. We would have twin forges, we decided. Me on this side of Angelio and he on the other. And every Sunday afternoon, one of us would ride to the other's house in a donkey cart. Turn and turn about." Grimaldi sniffed and rubbed his beard. "The usual boyish nonsense."

"So, what became of him?" Tammo said.

Grimaldi gave a growl. "Don't interrupt your elders. God and Saint Michael know I've kept my silence all these years. Let me speak on, or I'll never manage it."

"Sorry." Tammo drew his knees up to his chin.

"Our master had a daughter, a year or two older than Dodo and me. Her name was Lucia."

Grimaldi's voice cracked. He coughed and went on.

"The best of the master's earnings was spent on her. Lace caps, collars, kittens, dancing lessons. He always made it clear that she had better prospects than a couple of apprentices.

"But Dodo and I, we couldn't help ourselves. We worshipped her. And, from planning our futures as master blacksmiths, our night-time talk turned to Lucia and her charms. The ones we could see and the ones we could only imagine. We would outdo one another with boasts of how we would woo and conquer her." Grimaldi snorted. "As if our master wouldn't have thrown us out on the street at the first hint of courtship!"

He sighed.

"But feelings run high when you're young. Aye, lad, just because I'm old, it doesn't mean I don't remember. I recall a time when a kind word from Lucia had me floating on clouds for days on end. I would have crossed oceans and slain giants for the touch of her hand. Any man who spoke ill of Lucia was my sworn enemy, destined to die.

"I never meant to turn on my best friend. Many's the time I've wished I could change what happened that day. We were in these woods, by the River Harmonica. Swinging on trees, showing off. Doing the things young men do, to prove themselves to each other. It was the time of the spring floods. You know how it is at that time, how dangerous the river can be. We were daring each other to go further along the branch, threatening to push each other in.

"And that was when Dodo told me. He said that Lucia had pledged herself to him. That they had exchanged tokens secretly. That he had kissed her in the larder—proper kissing with tongues—and she had let him open her stays to the bare breast.

"To this day, I don't know if he spoke truly. It may well have been an idle boast, the sort young men are apt to make. Lucia was scarcely allowed from her mother's side, and her father had already approved a suitor for her. A draper with his own house, who supplied cloth to the Ducal Palace for bed linen. But at the time, there was no doubt in my mind. Dodo had betrayed me.

"We fought. Right there, in the tree above the river. God forgive me, I never wanted to kill him. I was in a killing rage, yes, but he was my best friend. We had grown up together. Had we both walked home that day, we could have forgiven each other in time. As old men, perhaps we could have laughed about it.

"But Dodo never came home. He fell out of the tree and the river swept him away. You know the rocks in that river. By the time they recovered his body, it was... it was..."

Grimaldi made a helpless gesture with his hand. For a time, he sat like a statue, his eyes quivering with brightness. Tammo daren't move. The tale Grimaldi was spinning was like an old tragedy. If he so much as breathed, this whole episode, in which Grimaldi sat by the fire and spoke of love and betrayed friendship, would disintegrate like old cobwebs.

Grimaldi took out a handkerchief and blew his nose, slowly and deliberately. Tammo waited.

"It was never the same after that," Grimaldi said at last. "The coroner pronounced the death accidental, but I saw the way people looked at me. I heard the wagging tongues.

"As for my master's house, it was a house of torment to me. I saw the ghost of Dodo everywhere. In the forge, at the table, and especially in bed at night. Lucia had become the Angel of Death; I couldn't look at her without shame. The day she left to become the draper's wife was a day of utmost relief.

"As soon as I became a journeyman, I left that house. And as soon as I could set up shop on my own account, I came to the woods. I became the bitter, lonely old man you see before you. No family. No friends. No one to care whether I live or die."

"You have me," said Tammo, offended.

"Oh, aye!" The old man turned on Tammo, his birdlike eyes now bright beneath the fur of his eyebrows. "Citizen Tammo Capell, the bird-charmer who can no longer charm. A lovesick calf who'll never get himself a wife, afraid to face a sick eunuch because of his hurt pride.

"Don't think I don't know," he said as Tammo opened his mouth to protest. "Any man with the wits he was born with knows the castrato is your only true friend. Do you think such a friend is replaceable? Do you think that if he died on his sickbed tonight, you wouldn't torment yourself with it for the rest of your life? Look at a man who knows, boy! This is your future you're seeing. Old. Alone. Forgotten. And don't count on the blessed Archangel being good enough to send a runaway boy to your door. You'll die alone in a cold bed. Think about it!"

And with that, he got up and went back to the forge.

Tammo had thought about it fifty times, and come to as many different conclusions, when he heard the sounds of a carriage approaching. The jingle of harness, the snort of a horse, the steady, "Whoah, whoah," of the driver. From the rumble of the wheels, it sounded like a big, heavy thing. He scratched his neck. Carriages didn't generally pass this way, especially in winter. The road was little more than a pony path, liable to flooding and stones. Major transport went by water. The forest path was for foot passengers, cross-country messengers on horseback, and the mule carts of carriers.

The vehicle that emerged from the tangle of winter branches was to a mule cart what a peacock is to a sparrow. Every brass, every lantern gleamed. It was pulled by four horses, as alike as if they had come from a baker's mould. Not one had a single black hair out of place. The lead horse was being walked uphill by a groom, whose maroon livery was enough to set Tammo's heart thumping, even before he saw the coat of arms painted on the carriage door. A golden pheasant with its wings spread wide. It couldn't be! Not here in the woods.

The carriage drew to a halt. Grimaldi, who had limped from the forge to see what was happening, doffed his cap. He gave Tammo a clout on the shoulder to tell him to stop gaping and do the same.

A curtain was drawn aside by a black glove. The window opened. Two women looked out. They were dressed identically, in black veils and moretta masks. The first woman removed her mask to speak. Thick lace obscured her features, but that made no difference to Tammo. Had he not seen those features in his dreams a thousand times? Shame burned his cheeks.

"Tammo Capell." Celestina's voice was clipped and formal, as though she addressed the trustees of a charitable institution.

Tammo managed a rusty, "Noblesse."

"I did not intend that we should ever meet again," Celestina said. "I recall our last encounter only as I would recall a dream. It was not a pleasant dream." Tammo heard the increased hardness in her voice, and the tears that lay just behind it. "Were it not for my own shame, I would denounce you, Tammo Capell."

The woman beside her, presumably Teresa, rustled her fan in a manner that suggested she would like to denounce Tammo with her bare hands. Tammo lowered his eyes and stared at the golden pheasant. Something tugged at his mind about that pheasant, something uneasy.

He scratched his neck and cleared his throat. "No taint of shame is on you, my lady. The fault is all mine."

"Nevertheless." Her shoulders rose and fell. "I cannot

remain in Angelio at this time. I shall spend the holy season at the convent, in prayer and contemplation. I shall endeavour to find the forgiveness Our Lord demands."

She was so brittle, Tammo felt she was about to shatter. Why, why—when she must detest him above all people—did he long to enfold her in his arms and comfort her? Perhaps he should do it anyway and be damned? He was as good as lost anyway.

The tiniest movement at his side drew his gaze to the forbidding eye of Grimaldi.

"I pray you will find peace, noblesse," he somehow managed to say.

She would stay in the convent; he knew it. She would become a nun, just like her mother wanted. He would never see her again.

Celestina remained silent for so long, Tammo thought the conversation over. He started wondering where the carriage would find space to turn about. And why the sight of a golden pheasant filled him with such dread.

When she spoke again, it was so sudden that Tammo flinched. "However, I have not come on my own behalf, but on behalf of one who needs you."

Carlo.

Every muscle in Tammo's body twitched with the desire to walk away. Only the knowledge of Grimaldi just handspans away kept him standing.

"How is he?" Tammo feigned carelessness.

Celestina shook her head. The black veil swayed.

"Frail. Fragile. Sorry for himself. You know Carlo."

There was the hint of a smile in her voice, but it was a smile akin to tears. She put a hand on the window and leaned closer. "He needs you, Tammo."

"I doubt that."

The words were out of Tammo's mouth before he could stop them. Memories of the argument flared red-hot. Hurtful words flung like volleys. *Peasant. Rutting beast.* Carlo's long, white hand, flaunting the carnival ring. Its gemstone smile, laughing in his face.

Carlo thrashing on the couch in a fever fit.

The black veil quivered.

"Don't you think I would make him well if I could. My dear Carlo!" She fought to steady her voice. "If my love could have saved him… But mine is not the love he desires. He has made it clear to me that he loves another." She breathed deeply and shook her head again. "I don't pretend to understand it, but I know he won't get well until you come to him."

Tammo ran his fingers through his bristles, trying to aerate his brain. Carlo had rejected Celestina.

Carlo had *rejected Celestina?*

Other memories came barging in. That night when Carlo had tried to kiss him. Words spoken during their argument. *How could you believe that I have ever loved anyone but you?* What was the noblesse trying to tell him? That Carlo was a *femella* like Giovanni? Was that it? He had heard it said that eunuchs desired men, but surely Carlo…

There must be another explanation. All these years they had been together, eaten together, slept together. Carlo loved him like a brother, like a twin. Didn't he? *As much woman as man.* Tammo shuddered. Did he really know Carlo at all?

But frail and fragile, Celestina had said. Carlo had abandoned good health long ago, sacrificing it to grant Tammo the gift of the dark flute. No matter that Tammo had now lost that gift. Carlo suffered for a gift Tammo had abused. Didn't Tammo at least owe him an apology for that?

But didn't Carlo owe him an apology for the same reason? Carlo had been granted entrance into Celestina's family, along with all that meant for his career, at the price of Tammo losing all chance of true love. If Carlo had no designs on Celestina, the least he could have done was say so. Tammo was damned if he would apologise unless the eunuch apologised first. He balled his fists.

"You must go to him," Celestina said. "That is all. God save you."

The window of the carriage slid shut. Tammo was left bowing in a patch of snow, as Grimaldi helped the groom find a space to set the carriage on its way again. Despite the cold, Tammo continued to stand until it was well out of sight.

A heavy hand on his shoulder awoke him to the material world. "That was a real lady, that was," Grimaldi said.

Or rather, that was what his words said. The look in his birdlike eyes said to Tammo, I told you so.

19

"Do you love me?"

It was the Feast of Holy Innocents. The frost patterns that had grown up the window in the night showed no sign of melting, despite the roaring fire. Crystals more fragile than gold leaf curled up the pane in a silver filigree. How Carlo had adored their beauty as a child! He had believed they were painted by the finger of the North Wind herself. Now, all he saw was ice. The ice of cold hearts. The ice of rejection. He had Casale close the shutters and light every candle they possessed.

He should have been in the Sancti Michaelis today. Singing above the high altar as Angelio honoured the child martyrs of Bethlehem by crowning a boy bishop. A hundred white-clad boys would process down the aisle carrying candles. And Carlo would give voice to the heart-rending words of Holy Scripture.

In Rama was there a voice heard,
lamentation, and weeping,
and great mourning.
The congregation of worshippers would be moved to

shed tears, as the beauty of the music lifted its soul. It should have lifted Carlo's soul, had him soaring alongside the seraphim in their flight.

Instead, he was alone in his apartment with a cough that hurt his chest and made him wheeze when he lay down. *This* was the sopranist who could stretch out a *messa di voce* for a whole minute and give three encores back-to-back! This feeble worm who could scarcely draw breath! What if he never recovered, never sang again? What then? Retrain as a priest? Face a future as a Carnival freak? A capon, a cripple, a man-seemer.

There had been a eunuch boy at the conservatorio whose voice had failed. Nicolo. Carlo had pitied him above all people. Imagine undergoing the cut—the knife, the opium, the bath of ice—only to discover that it was all in vain! There was no way to undo the process, no way to un-castrate oneself. Everyone knew you for what you were. They had only to look at your figure or hear your voice to recognise a eunuch. And the world could be cruel, Carlo knew that. If there was no adulation from an audience to temper the cruelty, what then?

Lamentation, and weeping,
and great mourning.

He had shed enough tears to fill a lake. Every time he looked at the empty bed in the alcove. Every time he caught the glint of the carnival ring on his finger. He had sobbed until the sobs had turned into coughs that rattled his bones. He had wailed with a hoarse voice at the ceiling of swinging birdcages. Despite finding the angel feather beneath his pillow, the hollow hours of the night brought no consolation.

He had no tears left. They had frozen, along with the rest of the water in Angelio.

Carlo wrapped his dressing-gown closer. He had been sitting at the spinet for the better part of an hour, trying to learn some new songs Maestro Sarastro had left him. To speak honestly, he had spent more time staring at the ships and sirens painted on its lid. He had to keep stopping to cough into his handkerchief. Sometimes, mucus came out. It disgusted him.

He blew on his fingertips and tried once more to play the opening section of the aria. His fingers stumbled over black-and-white keys.

There was a knock at the door. *Not again.*

"Tell them I'm sleeping," he croaked, as Casale swaggered past to answer it.

Twice today, Scipione and Giovanni had disturbed him, saying that a game of scopa and some Teatro gossip would make him feel better. Twice, Casale had seen them off, saying his master was not in a mood for games. Carlo doubted he would ever be in a mood for games again. The world was empty, grey. Even the caged birds were subdued, catching their master's ill humour. The music box had long since been removed and put away. Carlo never wanted to hear the tune of "Where are you, Beloved?" again. His life was bleak enough without his being mocked by clockwork automata.

"I said, no!" Casale's voice was strident. It hurt Carlo's

head. "How have you the gall to come here after what you did to my master? Citizen Aldo should have known better than open the door to you."

Carlo's heart contracted. He knew whose voice would answer.

"Watch your tongue, manservant! I don't answer to you. If your master wishes me gone, tell him to come here and say it to my face."

Sweat broke out on the back of Carlo's neck. His stomach writhed and twisted. He couldn't face Tammo now. He hadn't the strength.

"My master does not converse with liars and traitors." Casale was at his most cavalier.

"Stow it, Snowball! I won't listen to this. God save your master. You can go to Hell!"

The door slammed. Carlo's skin began to tingle all over. Breathe. Just breathe. His head swam. He felt close to swooning.

Casale came in, his cheek twitching with fury at the insult to his rank and skin colour. Snowball! Tammo must be in a foul mood to use such language; it made a hypocrite of him. He hated being called Firebrand, that old schoolboy nickname that drew attention to the scar on his skin.

"Good riddance," said Casale.

He wiped his hands together, as though removing dust. Then he picked up the poker, and was about to stoke the fire when he happened to glance up. "Why, signor, you're as white as a church candle. One moment. I'll fetch your elixir."

Carlo clung to the case of the spinet, willing away the spots that invaded his vision.

"Drink this, signor." Casale spooned out the mixture.

Carlo swallowed. Breathed. Swallowed again. That was better. His head was clearing now. The invisible hands had left off squeezing his lungs.

But his heart ached.

Now the nervous fit had passed, the memory of Tammo's voice gave him exquisite pangs of love. Tamino had come so close, only to leave again.

"Shall I warm the bed-pan, signor?" Casale asked.

There was another knock on the door.

"I'll throw him downstairs," Casale said between his teeth.

"No." Carlo held up a hand. "If it is Citizen Capell…" His voice trembled on the name, despite his best efforts to prevent it. "Ask him to step inside. I would speak with him. Alone."

Casale went to the door, muttering something unfit for such a holy day.

Immediately, Carlo was seized by an urge to call him back. The tingling and the faintness began again. He should have waited until he was stronger. What if the sight of Tammo threw him into a seizure again?

Too late. His former twin strode into the room, chin thrust out. The door clicked shut behind him. Carlo gathered the scattered threads of his courage together and looked up.

"Sweet Michael!" Tammo swore.

For a minute or two, Carlo thought that was all he was going to say. Tammo took in Carlo's wasted figure, the dark smudges under his eyes, and the shorn curls that an embroidered nightcap could not disguise, with an expression that could have been pity or disgust.

Carlo twisted the carnival ring on his little finger.

Tammo cleared his throat. "God save you, this holy day."

"God save you," Carlo replied automatically. If one of them didn't begin a conversation soon, this could go on all day. "I trust you enjoy good health."

It was the wrong choice of words. Tammo's face flushed, making his scar stand out pale pink. "Come off it, Carlo! I know you're ill. There's no need to make a five-act opera about it."

Carlo shrunk into himself. "You never came to see me." It came out more peevishly than he intended.

"I'm here now, aren't I?" Tammo scratched furiously at his neck and paced about the room. "Michael's dregs! I came here to apologise."

"For which sin?" Carlo looked away. "For giving away my love token after you'd sworn eternal twinship? Or for calling me a monster?"

Tammo flinched as though he had been struck. "That's not fair and you know it, Carlo. I spoke in anger and so did you. If you can't take an honest apology, I shall leave now."

I haven't heard one yet. Carlo plucked his lips to prevent the unwise words tumbling out. This conversation exhausted him. He wanted to go back to bed, but feared he lacked the strength to rise.

A sudden coughing fit seized him. He bent double with his handkerchief to his mouth. Tammo fell silent and came to sit beside him. An uncertain hand touched his shoulder.

"Are you all right, Carlo?"

Carlo gasped once, twice. The hand rubbed his back, gently, gently. Air returned to his lungs. With it came a warmth of feeling Carlo could no longer deny. His twin had touched him, comforted him. Whatever angry words came from Tammo's mouth, his hands told a different story.

Carlo dabbed at his mouth and nose. "I shan't give you my Tancredi just now." He tried to smile and coughed again. He felt about ten years old. He was awfully afraid he was going to cry.

"You ought to be in bed," Tammo said.

"Then I'm afraid you will have to help me, dear twin."

He used Tammo as a lever to help him stand and limp to the bedchamber, and up the three stairs into bed. Tammo pulled up the blankets. Carlo wished he could curl up with his head on his twin's shoulder. Couldn't they forget the arguments and misunderstandings? Could they not go back to the way it was before?

"Tammo." Carlo's voice sounded very small. "Do you love me?"

He could see at a glance the discomfort his question caused. Tammo was chewing his lip and scratching his neck and blowing out air all at once.

A weight grew heavier and heavier on Carlo's chest. The answer was no.

Tammo took a deep breath. "Do you want to lie with me?"

"I beg your pardon?" For one terrifying moment, Carlo thought his twin had made a proposition.

"I spoke with Celestina. She said you loved another. And you said…" Tammo's face was beetroot red. "You said you loved me. You tried to kiss me. So, what is it, Carlo? Are you like Giovanni? Is that what this is all about?"

It was a long time before Carlo was able to answer. His heartbeat sounded in his ears; his stomach was full of serpents.

You ask me who I am: what will I say?

He could hide the truth behind another mask. Pretend it was all a jest. But jests didn't break your heart like this. He was tired, so tired of pretending.

"I don't want to lie with you, Tamino. I don't want to lie with Celestina. Or Giovanni or Casale or La Bellina or anyone else. I don't want to lie with anyone; I never have."

"So, Celestina was wrong?" Carlo could hear the relief in Tammo's voice.

"No." How could Carlo explain this when he barely understood it himself? "She was not wrong." Oh, this was so difficult! He felt as if he stood naked on the edge of a precipice. "I have no desire for the rites of Venus, but that doesn't mean I can't be in love. Deeply in love." His voice shrank to a whisper. "With you."

He turned his face to the pillow, waiting for the blow to fall. When nothing came but silence, he dared to look.

Tammo's face was that of a schoolboy baffled by Pythagoras' theorem. "With me?"

Carlo gave a watery smile. "Who else, dear twin?"

"But you don't want to lie with me? Then… What do you want? Kissing? Carlo, what do you want of me? Because, whatever it is, I'm not that way out. You know I'm not. It isn't fair."

No, thought Carlo. It was not fair. But then, many things weren't. If only he were not so weak and weary! Every word was an effort.

"Oh, Tamino!" He sighed, willing it to not turn into a cough. "Of course I want to kiss you. Of course I want to be held in your arms and be called beloved. But I can live without those things. Have I not lived without them all these years? But I cannot live without your friendship. All I want is to be near you. Just to be near you."

"Just to be near me?" Tammo spoke as if he expected a hidden clause to surface.

"If that is all you can offer, my dearest twin, I shall be content with that."

Tammo scratched his bristles until they crackled with sparks. "But, how can you not want to, you know, stab your stiletto?"

In spite of himself, Carlo felt a spark of the old humour. "How you do harp on that theme! Love comes from the heart, not the breeches. I have as little taste for thrusting my appendage into someone—or having someone's appendage thrust into me—as you would have for eating a cat."

Tammo scowled. "So, wait... Is this a eunuch thing? I mean, would you if you could?"

"No." Carlo's eyelids grew heavy. "I can't explain it any better. I don't feel anything lacking. I simply have no inclination for it, and never will. I don't know why I'm like this. I don't know if it's because of the cut. It's just who I am."

He gave a shuddering yawn that brought tears to his eyes.

"You need to rest," Tammo said. "I should leave you in peace."

"Stay." Carlo's voice was a gossamer thread. "Just until I fall asleep. Please."

He watched the conflicting emotions battle it out on his twin's face. Disgust. Loyalty. Shame. Resentment.

Tammo gave a growl from deep in his throat, and yanked at his neck bands. "Very well."

Carlo wondered if he spoke in such an offhand way to try and trick himself into believing he had not agreed.

Tammo threw himself into a chair at Carlo's bedside. "Sleep well," he muttered.

Dreams plucked at Carlo's mind the moment he closed his eyes. Dreams in which the Archangel appeared to him with an important warning, something he ought to tell Tammo. But clouds closed around him. He couldn't recall the message.

In the last moments of consciousness, he felt the brush of something, half prickly, half velvet-soft against his forehead.

Tammo's kiss.

20
Mea Culpa

The bells above the portico were chiming Matins as Tammo jogged down the marble stairs into Saint Michael's Square. Flocks of pigeons took flight, scattering over the heads of hawkers and mummers. The Morningstar Fountain was dressed in evergreens for the New Year's Dash, when young men would race at midnight to drink the first waters of the year. Everywhere he looked, citizens were walking arm-in-arm, wrapped in thick, felt cloaks and wearing the thousand faces of Carnival. Music played. Frost glittered. The city was alive.

For the first time in weeks, Tammo felt alive with it.

He had been to confession, and felt like a child who had resisted the soap and hot water of the bathtub, only to discover the joy of warm, clean skin. It had been such a relief to unburden himself to the faceless presence of the duty priest. He wasn't sure the priest had believed some of the stranger details of his confession, but the man had pronounced God's forgiveness all the same, and Tammo had prayed out his penance under the pendulous swing of the great winged censer.

All he had to do now was decide what to do with the rest of his life.

He had left his twin sleeping, and promised to return. He was unsure what to make of Carlo's confession to him. Any attempt to think of it made his cheeks burn and his head spin.

He would also have to face Fenice, but not today. There had been too many confrontations with wronged lovers recently. He would collect his wage from the Teatro and pay off his debts to Armide. He would think no further ahead than that.

He crossed the square and began walking down the Street of Perfumers. Here, the frosty air was fragranced with rose, lilac, bergamot, and vanilla. Behind ice-rimed mullions, glass bottles of every colour sparkled in the winter sunlight. A hundred ceramic pots and jars held pomades, powders, dried lavender and rosemary. Soaps so delicious you wanted to eat them, nestled in baskets on beds of pine shavings. Everything imaginable to tempt the red-heeled customer.

Tammo shrugged his collar up to his batua mask, praying he wouldn't run into any of his old patrons.

Hanging above one of the shop doors, Tammo noticed a coat of arms whose paint was still fresh. A jewelled quail emerging from a crown: the personal arms of the Nobilissimo. Gaetano Elisei, Perfumer of Quality, now supplied scent to Angelio's heir, and was keen to advertise the fact.

A line of verse plucked at Tammo's memory.

That plucky little fighting bird, the Quail,
Seeks water from the Well, to no avail.
An arrogant gold Pheasant guards the way,
And never leaves his post by night or day.

It was the animal fable the Marchesa della Pamina had made him learn and interpret with the dark flute. Why had it not occurred to him at the time to associate the characters with coats of arms? Sweat prickled the back of Tammo's neck. If the Quail was the Nobilissimo, then the Well must be the Duke. And the gold Pheasant…

"Sweet Michael! No!" Tammo stopped walking as suddenly as if he'd been turned to a pillar of salt. "Hell! Seven spike-wheeled circles of Hell!"

A manservant walking two greyhounds, who had come within an arm's length of tripping over Tammo, threw back some inventive curses of his own, along with a withering stare.

Tammo's vital organs had forgotten how to work. He pressed his back against a locked doorway, as much to hold himself up as to be out of the way.

The golden Pheasant was Count Pageno. The Quail, the Nobilissimo, wanted him out of the way, so there was no one to limit his influence at Court. But that meant—oh, sweet Michael have mercy!—the Marchesa and the Nobilissimo were in it together.

At his departure, Rose and Quail both laugh.

Three bells and a rose: that was the Marchesa's sigil. She was the Rose.

She had played Tammo like a virtuoso. The letters he had planted weren't information for the Duke. They were fake evidence of a scandal involving the Count. Evidence the Marchesa and her allies could bring to light at any time.

"Sweet holy seraphim! I charmed them all into this." Tammo recoiled from the flute at his hip as though it carried smallpox.

Every time he had played for the Marchesa's guests, hers was the tune he had made them dance to. Hers and the Nobilissimo's, against good Count Pageno.

Against Celestina's family.

Oh, hosts of Heaven! Why not dash his brains out on the cobblestones right now and be done with it? Confession? Repentance? Cleansing from his sins? Might as well put a lump of charcoal in the bath and say you'd made it white.

"Devil's arsehole!" Tammo slammed his palm into the wall. Then, deciding it didn't hurt enough, he took off his glove and punched it with his fist.

The Archangel should have struck him down with lightning. He should have chopped him into a thousand pieces with Grimaldi's axe. Then burned the pieces. Then fed the ashes to…

A breeze lifted his batua cloak, blowing wig powder into his mouth. Something landed on his shoulder. Something with needles on its feet, that dug into his shoulders. It couldn't be…?

The something gave a joyful *caw.*

"Coronis!" Tammo's throat tightened. "You came back."

He ran the back of his finger along her spine. So soft. So fragile. So strong. "Coronis."

His Coronis. Come back to him. He'd never felt so pathetically grateful for anything. She had come. It wasn't too late to change things.

Coronis stretched her wings, flexing and testing their strength. She cocked her head, fixing Tammo with one bright eye.

"You're right," Tammo said. "It's no good standing here, bloodying the wall."

But where to go? Not to the Pageno mansion, that was for sure. He could just imagine knocking on the door and admitting he'd broken into his patron's house to plant evidence against him. That would be like handing himself over to the hangman. Back to Carlo's? What could the eunuch do from his sickbed? Tammo mentally ran through names and faces like a card sharp shuffling the pack. The priest he'd just confessed to? Maestro Sarastro? Armide??

Armide. The Mingguo merchant at the coffee house.

Tammo slid down the wall, his lungs battling to inflate. The eyes from his visions, the almond eyes. The foreigner was the Archangel. He'd been there all the time. Damn it, he'd given Tammo a warning with that fortune-telling card. The scales of justice. And Tammo had just blundered on as usual, ignoring it all.

Well, there was no time for blundering now. He

scrambled to his feet, ignoring the stares of passers-by. Coronis caught his mood, cawing and circling his head. Without even troubling to dust down his cloak, Tammo set off at a run, picking up speed as he raced through the narrow streets toward Piazza Giustizia.

"The merchant of Mingguo. Where is he?" Tammo bent over, hands on knees, panting and coughing.

The look Michelangelo gave him had all the eloquence of a mullet on the fishmonger's slab.

Tammo waved his arm in the direction of the table which, up until now, had accommodated the merchants with no intention of giving them up. It was empty.

"The Mingguo man? The silk merchant? The fellow with the pigtail and the wide-sleeved coat?" Surely the lackwit knew the man who had been drinking his master's coffee since the Feast of Seraphim?

Or pretending to, Tammo thought, his innards twinging. Was it blasphemous to think of an Archangel sampling coffee and liqueur? Could angels drink? He supposed those other two were lesser seraphim in disguise. Unless they were the Archangels Raphael and Uriel. Oh, merciful heaven! How had he got into this mess?

He raked his hands through his hair, lifting the wig from his scalp. Coronis flew from his shoulder to her accustomed perch on the dado, and got on with the business of beak-wiping as if nothing had happened. At least someone kept a level head. Tammo felt his was about to combust.

"Oh, I know the man you mean." Light came into Michelangelo's eyes, rendering him fractionally less fish-faced. "Sallow chap. Narrow eyes. Generous with his coin, he was." The lad grinned, and patted the pocket of his apron.

For a moment, Tammo relished a little scenario which saw Michelangelo's head, in close connection with Tammo's hands, making violent contact with the dado rail.

He took a deep breath and let it out by degrees. "Yes. I'm sure he was. Where is he now?"

Michelangelo rubbed at something sticky on the table with the corner of his apron. "Paid his bill and left a couple of weeks back. Same time you did, in fact. Are you coming back for good now, Citizen Capell? Because Citizen Armide has had to let your room to someone else. He says he can't keep it open forever, not when he's waiting to see the colour of your coin. He says he's only kept it this long out of the goodness of his heart. And the grille is full up with letters for you. He threatened to burn them last night. I hope you don't mean to cross him again, citizen. It's not too comfortable for me, if you get my meaning." He rubbed his posterior with a forlorn expression. "Can I get you a drink while you're stood there, Citizen Capell. We've got..."

"Stow it, for sweet Michael's sake!"

There was an awkward silence. The other customers

stopped speaking and stared. Tammo blew out air and scratched his leg with his batua mask.

"Damn. Damn. Damn." He spoke under his breath. His gaze darted from one wall to another, as if the retired castrati were likely to step from their portraits with offers of help. "Damn the Marchesa. Damn her salon and her footmen and her stupid chequered floor. And damn her ridiculous bosom as well. Ten to one it's stuffed with lambswool. And damn—"

"That's enough damnation for now, young man."

A hand gripped Tammo by the shoulder. His first instinct was to turn and throw its owner to the ground. But something stopped him. A calmness to the stranger's tone. The ease with which Coronis watched from the rail, not ruffling a feather.

"I believe we can help one another. But no more shouting out. These are delicate matters." The stranger's whisper was so close to Tammo's ear, it tickled. A heavy perfume of vanilla and cloves draped itself about the pair of them like a scarf.

Tammo suddenly realised that he knew the man. Not by name, but he had seen him at Armide's before. He was the one who was always sitting in the corner, writing in his pocket book. Tammo took a firm grip on his flute case.

"Waiter, we'll take a private booth, if you please. Closed shutters." There was something odd about the stranger's voice. He sounded like a girl impersonating a boy.

"This way, signor." Michelangelo made a bow and led them along the dim corridor usually reserved for waiters.

Coronis followed, a silent shadow. They reached a booth decorated with frolicking satyrs and almost-naked dryads, a favourite haunt of young exquisites and their mistresses. The stranger indicated for Tammo to sit, but neither spoke until daylight was banished by the shutters, and a candle and coffee pot sat on the table between them.

The stranger removed his mask. He was no stranger at all.

Last season, those plump, androgynous features had been on every news sheet and playbill in Angelio. Carlo had carried a cheap engraving of that face all through his time at the conservatorio, hoping one day to fill this man's beribboned shoes. And he had.

"Signor Morestelli?"

The former primo had been in Angelio all this time. Watching. Writing. But for whom? Tammo squinted in the dim light, checking his exit routes. His muscles tensed, ready for action.

Morestelli put a finger to his hairless lips. "Hush. You must not speak my name aloud." He was using his own voice now, unbroken despite his forty years. "I heard you speak of the Marchesa della Pamina. Tell me what you know."

Tammo squared his shoulders. "How do I know you're not on her side?"

"Wise man." Morestelli gave a tight smile. He reached into his pocket and drew out a silver medal. It had the Duke's crown-and-well engraved on one side. He showed it to Tammo before returning it to his waistcoat.

"I trust that proves my allegiance. The Duke has employed me to discover plots against him. You have heard of his break with the Nobilissimo, no doubt?"

Tammo nodded.

"We have long suspected the Paminas were of that party. But it is no small thing to bring an accusation against a family of such pedigree. And we have no proof. The Marchesa's salon is notoriously hard to infiltrate. But you cursed the House as if you knew it. What can you tell me?"

Sweat trickled down Tammo's back. Morestelli had the connections that could end the Marchesa's plans and save Count Pageno. But he could also hand Tammo over to the Duke's guard for planting the letters.

Tammo took a deep breath. "Do I get imm…whatsit? Immunity. For helping you. Because, let me tell you straight. If you send me to the gallows, Carlo, I mean Signor Seraphini, will die. Of a broken heart. He's looked up to you all his life, signor, and you'll have broken his heart."

Tammo's knees were shaking under the table. The coffee bowls were rattling. The candle looked in danger of falling over.

Morestelli smiled, wider this time. The action caused a small avalanche of face powder to fall from the corner of one eye. The vanilla scent grew stronger. "I never reveal my sources. Just tell me, citizen."

So Tammo told him.

The coffee bowls were drained to black sludge. The candle

had acquired baroque curlicues. Morestelli leaned on his elbows and tapped one forefinger against the other. Ruby rings winked.

"This is a troublesome situation, citizen. I could send men to warn Count Pageno, but he is unlikely to take such an affront to his honour quietly. There could be duels, vendettas, armed factions. The Ducal court is like a tinder box at present; it would only take a spark such as this, and the next step would be riots in the street and burning effigies. And that could be the very opportunity the Nobilissimo's party is waiting for."

He examined the lace on his cuff with needless intensity.

"It would be better to approach the Marchesa in private, but without sight of these papers, we have nothing with which to accuse her. They could be copies of famous sermons, for all we know. Cryptic rhymes about pheasants and wells are not enough. Not where a family like the Paminas are concerned."

"Do you want me to retrieve the letters, signor?" Tammo's stomach twisted as he forced the words through his damaged throat.

This was the very fate he had been hoping to avoid. There was no way he could seduce Fenice again, even if he still had the gift of charming. He'd just been absolved of that sin, for crying out loud! He bit his lip and picked at the veneer on the table. Seduction had got him into this hole. He would be better off like Carlo, with no desire for pleasures of the flesh. Tammo Capell had charmed his last human. He would have to trust to stealth, as though he were a charity boy again.

The relief was palpable when Morestelli said, "No thank you, citizen. You've done quite enough."

Tammo couldn't tell if that was praise or rebuke. He decided he didn't care.

Morestelli stood, and put on his cloak and mask. "I must take counsel with my fellows. If you have any more useful information, ask for me here by the name of Signor Nero. In the meantime, pray to the Blessed Michael to confound the wits of this treacherous faction before they can act against His Grace. God save you." Morestelli slipped out into the crowded piazza.

Coronis flew to Tammo's arm. He stroked her, taking comfort in her smooth feathers, her delicate spine. Pray to the Archangel! That might have worked when he was a boy. Tammo had come here hoping to plead with the Seraph Prince face to face. Instead, he had been given Coronis and a castrato spy.

"I suppose you might be a gift from him." Tammo fondly ruffled Coronis' head. "If only he had sent a message with you, telling me what to do. Perhaps he has, and I can't understand it. Tell me, Coronis: do birds really speak the language of angels?"

Coronis cawed and preened a wing.

"I don't know what that means." He glanced down at the flute case. "It's all gone now. All my charming skill. All those bird voices in my head. If I could play this now, the way I used to, I would tell everyone in Angelio to be faithful to the Duke and Count Pageno. Do you hear me? I would!" he shouted to the ceiling. "But it's not for use on people. Never was. I misused the gift and got my just desserts. But why should other people suffer for my sins? Tell me that, Coronis."

Coronis cocked her head. Her eyes reflected the light of the dying candle, swirling orange against indigo. Such large eyes she had, just like Carlo. Carlo, who knew nothing of lust and seduction. Who thought love was a feeling in the heart.

Tammo picked up a feather that had fallen from Coronis' tail. "If we all thought that way, we wouldn't be in this mess. We'd all be as chaste as a marble Diana."

Coronis gave a loud caw and bobbed her head. Tammo narrowed his eyes. Was that a nod? Had he finally said something that made sense?

Tammo leapt to his feet. He grabbed his hat and mask, scattering small change as he raced out the door and across the piazza.

He knew what to do. He had to get to Carlo's.

21

The Language of Angels

"I don't understand you, dear twin." Carlo dabbed his sticky eyes with a handkerchief. It smelled of jasmine. Such a delicate scent. "Forgive my sleepiness, but did you say that Coronis gave you a message from the Archangel?"

"Sort of." Tammo scratched his neck in the old, familiar way. "Look here, can you just trust me? There's not much time. Morestelli said the court was like a tinderbox waiting to explode."

Carlo couldn't help a pang of envy that Tammo had been the one to speak with the great man. If anyone deserved to hear Morestelli's secrets, it was the singer who had taken his place in the Duke's opera!

But that didn't explain why Tammo had come bursting into his apartment with a force Casale couldn't stop, waking Carlo from his sleep and demanding that he help restore the balance of Michael's scales.

"Could you tell me again, just a little?" Carlo sat up and supported himself with pillows and bolsters. Tammo perched on the edge of the bed, leaning on one of the four posts. Part of Carlo wished he could draw the curtains around them both, enclosing them in their own fairy grotto.

The other part flinched whenever Tammo's voice rose above a sedate mezzo-piano. Would he ever completely trust his twin again? Would he always half-expect the hurtful blow, forever cradling his heart against rejection?

"Yes, well." Tammo scratched his neck again and cleared his throat in a manner that sounded like the growl of a beast. Carlo flinched. "What you said to me before. About how you feel toward…well, me. No stilettos, and all that."

Carlo would no longer need candles if his twin's cheek burned any redder.

"Well, I need some of that. To undo the…um… seduction. That I practised on the Marchesa's guests. With the dark flute."

Carlo's eyes opened wide. Clearly, there was a great deal his twin had kept from him.

"Yes, well. I'll tell you about that later." Tammo coughed. "What we need now is some kind of…essence of eunuch."

In spite of himself, Carlo smiled. "I cannot suffer to be bled any more. I fear I shall grow flat."

"No. No, that's not it." Tammo scrubbed hard at his bristles. "We need a new song. An un-seducing song. Feelings of chastity, you know."

"Alas, I cannot sing at present."

Tammo kicked the bedpost. "We need a set of verse.

That's what *she* gave me. A set of verse to interpret in music. Sweet Michael, I should have burned the thing! None of this would have happened."

He continued under his breath, with what Carlo suspected was a recitative of curses. Coronis added a *basso continuo* of caws.

Carlo plucked at his lips. A set of verse. Did he have such a thing? He possessed many volumes of poetry, it was true. Libretti for operas. Poems he had set to music himself. But could any of them be said to contain the essence of a eunuch?

Yes. There was one. Bought for a few centesimi on the streets of Angelio. The verse that had been haunting him all season.

Carlo sat up straighter. "Tamino, look in that drawer. Yes, that one. There's a paper. That's it. Can you read what it says?"

"*A Castrato's Love?*" Tammo held it to the candlelight.

"Not a piece of my own writing." Carlo lowered his eyelashes. "But one from which I have taken much comfort."

Tammo's gaze ran along the lines of print. "Yes. I see what you mean. But what shall we do with it? We have to get this right, Carlo."

Carlo blew his nose. "I think perhaps if I read it aloud… I'll try not to cough too much. You could interpret it on the flute. Interpret the sentiment, the feeling, as you say, of chastity."

Tammo gave a heavy sigh. His face was that of a man defeated. Carlo longed to embrace him. "That's no good. The flute no longer works for me. The Archangel has taken away my gift."

"He's taken away my gift, too," Carlo said. "Celestina has gone to the convent. But the Archangel told me we must put this right ourselves." He flinched at Tammo's sharp glance. "Yes, I saw him. In a dream. He must have had something like this in mind."

He leaned further forward, wincing at the pain in his chest. "Let's try it. What have we to lose that we have not already lost?"

He saw affirmation in the twitch of Tammo's lip.

Carlo pulled the carnival ring from his little finger. "Wear this when you play. Maybe it will bring our souls closer together?"

Tammo shrank back. "No, Carlo. I don't deserve to wear this again."

"No you don't," Carlo agreed. "But I think that might be the point." He held out the ring at full stretch. "Just while you play, Tamino. You can give it back afterward. In fact, I would prefer it if you did."

"Very well." Tammo took the ring and put it on his own finger.

Carlo refamiliarised himself with the lyric. Tammo went through the little rituals of a flautist preparing to play. A stranger might have seen the practised movements and assumed confidence in the player, but Carlo could hear a hesitancy, a slight loss of rhythm in the fluttering fingers and voiceless breaths.

His twin feared the flute. Just as Carlo feared his twin.

He would have to let that go. At least pretend an open heart. He would be Prince Octavian again, but this time he would be an Octavian without Venus. His would be the voice of chaste Daphne, issuing from the body of genderless Hermaphroditus.

Tammo gave him a nod, and Carlo began to read.

You ask me for my love: what can I give
When ours would be a fruitless union?
The angels do not wed as mortals do
And monsters among humans cannot live.

You ask me who I am: what will I say?
I cannot answer "man" or I will lie.
And "woman" is still further from the truth,
The mask of gender but a part I play.

I am a castrato, Angelian born.
I glory in my youth and in my song.
I let the flowers gather at my feet,
For hidden in my rose there is no thorn.

Carlo was still reading when the changes began. Coronis began to flap her wings and leap about on the bedstead. At the same time, a whirr of wings came from Orpheus' cage, and the song thrush began a melodious cadence: *up-down, up-down.* The sound rippled through the apartment, a fluttering, fluting, twittering ensemble.

Casale's voice came from the parlour. "The birds, signor! They are crazed! What shall I do? They will injure themselves."

Coronis lifted her head to caw. But what came from her beak was a sound Carlo had heard but once in his life. A voice with the purity of starlight, the clarity of cut glass, the mellifluousness of liquid gold. And a tone and timbre unlike any voice on earth.

"Open the windows." Tammo's hoarse voice cut across the music. "Open the windows!" he yelled into the parlour. "And the birdcages too!"

He was already battling with the bedroom shutters. Wooden boards banged against the walls. Carlo gasped and coughed as a blast of icy wind lifted the bed curtains, making them flap like sails in a storm.

"They're going! They're going!" Tammo called above the choir. "The birds are flying away."

Bent double over his handkerchief, Carlo was aware of rushing wings and dancing feathers. Wingtips brushed past his ears. The chamber was alive with birdsong…

The windows banged shut, hard enough to blow out the candles. Carlo picked a shred of feather from his nightgown. Another round of coughing seized him.

"You all right?" asked Tammo from the window. He was peering through the slats, looking out into the winter sky. "Well, they've gone," he said, turning back into the room. There was a sheen of sweat on his brow.

"Yes, but where?" Carlo forced the words through shallow breaths. "And to do what?"

•••

Count Pageno shifted his weight from one red heel to the other. How much longer?

The Nobilissimo's court masques were as tedious as they were tasteless. Half an eternity of the heir and his cronies posing in ridiculous costumes around an indoor fountain, beside a grove of saplings that leant drunkenly in their pots. And no one was permitted to sit but the Duke and Duchess. If only one of them would stand and leave! Then the ridiculous pantomime would cease.

Highly improbable. The Nobilissimo had offered the masque as an olive branch to his parents, and they were willing to accept the gesture. A formal show of unity within the Ducal family. Count Pageno had his doubts. The Nobilissimo's known intimates had been seen sniggering behind their hands. Whatever came of this apparently harmless allegory of birds around a well, it did not bode well for harmony at the palace.

The Count stifled a yawn. He didn't need this. There was more than enough to worry about with young Bianci sick and Celestina taking herself off to the convent. He sighed. He ought to devote more time to family matters. These last months, he had thought more of the Duke's family than of his own. Young Rinaldo sorely needed a father's hand. Yet what was a man to do? Lose his position at court and he would lose all that kept his household so well-provisioned.

The viols struck up a minuet. The Nobilissimo strutted through the steps, hand-in-hand with the Marchesa della

Pamina. Both were wearing more feathers than the whole cast of the opera. The Nobilissimo had a peacock tail protruding from his coat-tails, the fop!

Still, the coxcomb could dance, the Count would give him that. As elegant a pair of calves as one might see anywhere. His leaps and high cuts made the peacock feather bounce violently. One of them fell off and was trampled underfoot.

Across the room, a nobile lowered his sequined mask and stared at Count Pageno with undisguised hostility. The Count's features tightened. The man was a mere cavalier. A social inferior. How dare he?

The Count returned the look with a toss of his head. There was an odd atmosphere at court today. As if frost had invaded the marble hall, and the hearts of everyone within.

A scent of vanilla and cloves wafted into the Count's nostrils. "Beware the Nobilissimo." A soprano voice spoke in his ear. "We have reason to believe he employs foul means to bring members of the court into his favour."

"That does not surprise me." Count Pageno was well aware of Morestelli's move from sopranist to spymaster. He and the Duke had discussed the eunuch's last report only yesterday. The Marchesa della Pamina's was a name that cropped up all too often. The Count narrowed his grey eyes at her dancing figure. He would personally discover what she was up to and put a stop to it.

"It would be well, my lord," said Morestelli, "if a third party checked your correspondence for the time being.

Merely as a precaution, you understand. I myself would be happy to oblige…"

He never got any further. For at that moment, all the windows of the palace flew open. A rustling of wings like the roar of the sea drowned out every other noise. And the whole room was filled with birds.

"And then," said Count Pageno, "as sudden as you may please, the windows opened and a flock of birds flew in."

Carlo sat up straighter. A flock of birds. His birds?

"A moment later, they looked like angels. The Host of the Seraphim, as God is my witness. And the song! Should I live a thousand years, I would never hear the like again. It put an end to the masque, I can tell you! The whole court repaired to the Ducal chapel and fell on their knees in prayer, myself included. Some are saying it is the judgement of God for all the factions we have allowed into our society."

"Do you think that, my lord?" Carlo's voice was a breath.

"I know not what to think. I'm only grateful I lived to see it." The Count gave a wry smile. "But anything that halts the Nobilissimo's scheming is palatable to me. Angelio's protector is not deaf to the cause of the righteous."

"Indeed not, my lord.

Carlo hugged himself. The plan had worked. Tamino's instinct had been right, Michael be blessed! Relief washed through his body, relaxing his limbs.

• • •

Afterward, Carlo remembered the day of the birds' flight as the one on which his health began to return. He napped in the afternoon and awoke with an unexpected hunger for pigeon risotto. The joy with which Casale watched him eat it could not have been greater had his manservant been made a cardinal.

The next day, he put on his outdoor clothes and asked Casale to dress his hair. Not that there was much hair to dress. The mirror revealed a thin-faced person, whose schoolboy crop and shadowed eyes made him look both younger and older than the primo castrato Carlo remembered. He'd need a wig for his head when he went back into society. It befitted the muted persona he now wore, along with his clothes. Both fitted him ill, but he was grateful for the semblance of normality.

And now his patron came to call.

When he heard Casale's formal tone in the hallway, Carlo guessed the cause. Pompey and Caesar marched in, standing on either side of the parlour door like maroon velvet bookends.

Carlo was glad he was fully dressed and out of bed. He had, in fact, been looking over the manuscripts of some new arias, humming the melodies under his breath. He had not yet returned to his nightingale's form, but his cough was mending. And he had regained enough balance to stand and make an elegant bow as his patron came through the door.

"Carlo, my boy! God save you!" The count's warmth was genuine and brought the sting of a tear to Carlo's eye. "Sit down, sit down. Don't wear yourself out by kneeling."

"My Lord Pageno." Carlo returned with gratitude to the sopha.

The count looked around the room with an air of approval. Was it Carlo's imagination, or were the lines in his face more deeply entrenched? Carlo plucked his lip. How big a part had he played in the count's troubles this season?

"The stench of sickness has gone. The air of life is in this room again." The Count reached over and patted Carlo's knee. "It's good to see you so much improved, my boy. Don't let Sarastro rush you." His gaze fell on the manuscripts. "It is true that Angelio has mourned the loss of Seraphini from its opera these past weeks. Although, from the behaviour of La Bellina, you would think the pieces had been reworked solely for her glorification. Sweet Michael, the vaingloriousness of that woman knows no bounds! She went on stage as Cleopatra with both pugs in her arms. Did you know that?"

Carlo laughed softly.

"And that simpering schoolfellow of yours isn't far behind. Parnasso. Smouldering at the audience so violently last night, I thought his fake bosoms were going to fall out."

Probably a sign that he and the dancer were paramours once again, Carlo thought. A sudden snort of laughter provoked by the image of Giovanni's bosoms set him coughing. Count Pageno waited for the fit to pass before speaking in a gentler voice.

"You gave us all a nasty fright, Carlo. Not just when you fell, but when it seemed you would not recover. Michael knows, I cannot afford to lose any more boys. You know that." The Count cleared his throat. Carlo looked politely out of the window. "You mean a great deal to me, Carlo. I know your health is delicate at times, and it concerns me. That is why, when the season is over, I am sending you to Minervia, to take the waters. Say nothing," he said, as Carlo began to speak. "I would do as much for anyone in my care."

"Then all I can say, my lord, is thank you."

For a time, there was silence, broken only by birdsong.

"And what is the news of the day, my lord? I feel quite rustic, living apart from polite society for so long."

The Count stroked his chin. "Well, young Angelino di Fosco lost his father's entire brood stable at the Marquis of Parini's gaming table…

"Oh, and I shall tell you of a very strange happening at court. A miracle, I dare say…"

Count Pageno continued to talk, but Carlo was no longer catching every word. He managed to cover one yawn with his sleeve before the Count noticed, but the second caught him unawares.

A fatherly look came to the Count's eye. "I'm tiring you. I will leave you to rest." His hand hovered over his breast pocket. "I am reluctant to give you this, but my daughter insisted."

"Noblesse Celestina?" Carlo lifted his head.

The Count suddenly looked a hundred years old. "She

has not been herself lately. You know, I suppose, that she spent the Holy Nativity at the convent?"

Carlo nodded, although his heart leapt. Spent? Had she come home, then?

The Count shook his head. "I wonder, should I blame myself? Her mother is so preoccupied with Nobile Rinaldo. And matters at court have been…pressing…this season. I fear I have not given enough time to a daughter's needs. Especially one whose future is not… That is to say, her mother had expected to be matchmaking by this stage, but…"

"It's not your fault, my lord," Carlo said.

"It is kind of you to say so." The Count prepared to leave. As he and Carlo made their final goodbyes, he pressed a sealed letter into Carlo's hand. "I am sending her to…well, you'll see."

After the Count had left, Carlo broke open the seal. The scent of honeysuckle brought tears to his eyes.

Celestina's pretty handwriting ran across the page in neat lines.

My very dear Carlo,

I cannot face you in person, and doubt I will for some time. Yet I must speak my mind.

My time at the convent has brought new clarity to my thinking. As I long suspected, I do not believe I have a vocation, and shall not take the veil. Yet the sisters have such need of help in their works of mercy that I feel a great desire to assist them. I shall think on this further during my exile.

Yes, dear Carlo, I am leaving Angelio. My parents think,

and I agree with them, that a prolonged stay at our country villa will do me good. I leave as soon as the weather permits. The events of this season have done much damage to my heart, and while I believe you are innocent in the matter of my great folly, others are not. In short, I must be apart from the familiar places that have been the scenes of so much suffering.

Before I leave, however, I must tell you of a matter that may mean more to you than it does to me.

Two days ago, my rosefinch, Carlino, brought in his beak some letters from my father's study, the seals broken by his pecking. These contained details of the most abhorrent plot against the Duke, implicating my father as a traitor. I burned them. Later that day, my father told me of certain occurrences at court, by which birds had become angels and stopped an offensive masque. I perceive the hand of the Archangel in this. And, also, that of one whom modesty forbids me to name, but who is dear to you. May God forgive him.

Dear Carlo, I pray you will forgive any offence I have done you. In time to come, I hope we will be friends, as we were of old.

Pray for me.

I remain your devoted and most affectionate friend,
Celestina

For quite some time, Carlo forgot that there was anyone or anything else in existence. Then he blew his nose, wiped his eyes, and said: "She is not lost to us, thank God."

He would have sat for some time more, had there not been a sharp rap on the door. This was followed by the swaggering entrance of one who filled the entire room with his presence.

"Bianci!" Maestro Sarastro hollered. "God save you, if He hasn't already. When are you going to stop moping and come back to the Teatro?"

22
A Castrato's Love

The cold snap had broken at last. While no one would call the weather mild, it no longer gripped your lungs with merciless fingers. The forest pathways had softened, and the tips of branches showed the tight, black buds of future leaves.

Tammo made his way up the pony path to Grimaldi's cottage. The winter sun was palely beautiful, turning the sky Madonna blue, and the dewdrops to crystals. He had cut a switch, and was carelessly rattling it through the brush. Coronis flew a few paces ahead, stopping every now and then to crow at her lazy master.

"Give over, you ill-omened bird."

Coronis cocked her head, not the least bit fooled by Tammo's gruff outburst. Tammo grinned. He couldn't even fool himself for long. He was so glad it had all come back to him. Coronis. His birds. The song of the dark flute. He didn't dare think himself wholly forgiven. Not yet. But to have his corvid friend by his side, that was something.

• • •

It had been several weeks since his abilities returned to him. Not that he had noticed straight away.

When the miraculous flight departed from Carlo's window, Tammo's first thought was to rush into the street below, to see where they went.

No such luck. The flock was long gone by the time Tammo burst out of the Aldos' front door. He was forced to return, panting and stomping, to a breathless Carlo and his astonished manservant. They were all too awed by the miracle to say much beyond the occasional, "Michael's dregs!"

Not long after that, the birds had returned.

Tammo and Casale had chased about the apartment with an indignity that made Carlo giggle. They had finally caught Orpheus and his companions, and returned them firmly to their cages. From what Carlo could tell, they were their normal selves again. Carlo had coaxed Orpheus back out onto his finger, much to Casale's dismay, and the little song thrush had chirruped his aria and pecked at Carlo's lace cuff with great contentment.

Tammo had eyes and ears only for Coronis. The moment her dark wings appeared at the window; he sensed her bewilderment. Had she been granted the power of speech, she would have said, "What in Michael's bootstraps just happened to me?" But far more important in Tammo's mind was love and loyalty for her human companion, and a sense that coming back to him was coming home.

"Coronis! To me, girl!" Tammo stretched out an arm and Coronis landed on his shoulder, nudging his neck with the top of her head and croaking. Tammo stroked her and made kissing noises. "Where have you been, my pretty maid? That's what we would all love to know, isn't it? And how about you singing like a lark? You should teach me how to do that. Yes, you should. I could duet with Carlo here."

At first, he feared to test whether the return of Coronis meant the return of his affinity with bird-kind, and skill with the dark flute. More than once, he persuaded himself that the life of a blacksmith was enough for him. That he didn't need the hassle of patrons and trade cards and endless pots of coffee at Armide's.

It didn't last long. The pull of the dark flute was too strong. The smell of warm wood. The feel of curling vines beneath his fingers.

In the end, he had stalked into the depths of Angel's Wood at first light. Closed his eyes, put the flute to his lips and played. With the very first note, he knew. The voice of the forest, the trees, the sense of deep time. The myriad little lives that fluttered and chirruped in its branches.

"I'll only play it in the forest from now on," he said to no one in particular. "Wood to wood, nature to nature. Nothing more."

Then he abandoned himself to wild music.

At first, he had felt the need to charm something at every strike of the cathedral bell, just to make sure the change was permanent. It took two linnets, seven starlings and a whole flock of doves to convince him. After that, he left a huge offering at the Sancti Michaelis and captured a pair of golden orioles out of sheer joy.

He now had a surplus of stock and, according to Armide, a new reputation as a man of mystery, who might disappear and reappear at any moment.

"And you know how the ladies like that," said Armide. "They'll be eating out of your hand come spring."

It hadn't taken the jovial shopkeeper long to forgive Tammo his debts. He could have been a touch less forgiving, to Tammo's mind. Tammo had had to bear with the man's interminable bonhomie as he informed Tammo, minute-by-minute, it felt, of everything that had passed during his absence. Why, in the name of sanity, would Tammo want to know what weather Father Clementi's barometer had predicted during each day of Christmastide, let alone whether it was correct?

Tammo had felt an increasing desire to cut his own ears off, until Armide suddenly said, "And the Marchesa della Pamina has gone away in a huff. You heard of the miracle at court?"

"Yes." Carlo had told him all he needed to know; he wasn't about to discuss it with Armide.

Armide fidgeted for a few moments, frustrated by the lost opportunity to demonstrate his knowledge of current affairs. When it became obvious that Tammo would drink in silence unless Armide filled the void, he went back to his first topic. "Some say the Marchesa has gone into seclusion. She was not to be seen at the opera, nor at Count Pageno's Twelfth Night banquet."

Someone would have poisoned her if she had, Tammo thought. He could not see the Marchesa being welcome at the Pageno mansion ever again. Still, it was a relief to know she was no longer a threat. Carnival season was flying by, and Tammo didn't fancy having to lurk in his mask and tabarro come summer.

"And her salon has not met for weeks, so the papers say. Although some say the Nobilissimo meets with her secretly. They're planning to build a new theatre."

"Pleasure garden, I heard," said a priest.

"No, no, Father. That's the Marquis of Parini. The Nobilissimo's building a racecourse."

The same old gossip as usual. Tammo had left them to it.

He could go about his business again, that was the main thing. He would start with that pair of orioles he had in stock. He knew a patron who would all but bite his hand off for them, given the right behaviours.

His own behaviour had been far from ideal this season. And while he'd apologised and confessed until his soul resembled a rag on washday, there was one apology he'd been avoiding out of sheer cowardice.

It was Epiphany when he finally approached the servants' entrance of the Pageno mansion. The count always gave his staff New Year's gifts on that day, and Tammo hoped, somewhat desperately, that this might soften up the mood.

He decided to wait in the courtyard, hat in hand. He

even considered kneeling, but decided at the last minute that the posture might be taken for mockery.

A faint whickering of horses from the stables and a smell of chestnuts from the kitchen were the only signs of life. Tammo scratched his neck and polished his shoe on the back of his stocking. How long should he wait? Maybe he should just sneak off quietly? He glanced toward the maple trees, considering a hasty climb over the wall.

"Well, if it isn't a rake shaming blackguard come calling." Fenice's stare came direct from the depths of a glacier. She was half his size and still put Tammo in terror of his life.

She flicked her fingers, as if wiping dust from them, and leaned on the doorpost, one hand on her hip. "This ought to be instructive. Out with it then, Capell! Let's hear your inspired reasoning as to why you couldn't move fast enough once you'd navigated my creek."

Tammo cleared his throat. "Fenice…"

"I'm not your strumpet, Capell."

"Fenice, I'm so sorry. There was this patron and she… That is to say… I shouldn't have used you, Fenice. It won't happen again."

"Too right it won't!" The ice turned to fire. "I'm back with Pompey, for your information. So, I suggest you show your heels. Wouldn't want him to break those clumsy little fingers of yours."

Tammo opened his mouth to reply, but decided it wasn't worth the effort. At least he had tried. Fenice would come around eventually. He hoped.

"I'm sorry," he said again, before abandoning his quest altogether.

He was unsure how often he would visit the Pageno mansion from now on. Carlo had told him about Celestina going to the countryside, so she wouldn't be here. He didn't ask himself how that made him feel; some things were best left undisturbed. Fenice had always been a welcome distraction, a gaudy burst of colour among the grey. He hadn't realised how much he had enjoyed her friendship. He found himself praying he wouldn't lose it forever.

Water dripped from the trees. Beneath Tammo's feet, the thawing ground cracked. Coronis had settled on an ash tree, away from the path. She turned her sentinel's glance this way and that. Not for the first time, Tammo had the feeling that she knew things far beyond his comprehension.

Between the bare trunks, something glittered. Metal caught by the sun. The outline of what looked like a human figure. Tammo blinked his eyes and yawned. The woods played tricks on you all the time.

No. There was someone in the clearing. Tammo heard them clear their throat. He narrowed his eyes against the sun, trying to see the stranger more clearly. From this distance, they looked to have come directly from a masquerade. Or the stage. They wore a tunic and breastplate, with a plumed helmet. A sword was in their hand. And there was a strange white cloud behind their shoulders. Almost like…wings?

Tammo's mouth went dry. The person took a step toward him, and for a moment, Tammo saw their face clearly. Liquid eyes. Golden hair. They said nothing; they simply looked at Tammo and smiled. A smile that made Tammo's eyes water.

Every bird in the forest was silent. A strange warmth filled Tammo's belly. He doubted he could have moved, had he wanted to. But he didn't want to. He had never felt so happy in his life. He might have been standing there for a minute, or hours.

"Tamino?"

Tammo blinked rapidly, causing tears to spill down his cheeks. For a moment, he couldn't recollect where he was. Why was he standing, staring into the wood? He felt oddly peaceful, as if he had woken from a beautiful dream. He put a hand to his cheek, wondering why it was wet.

"Tamino, what is it? Are you crying?"

He turned, wiping the tears away. "No. I don't think so." His head was clearer now. His feet were cold. "Where did you come from, all of a sudden?"

Carlo was leaning on a staff, panting slightly. Out in the open, it was obvious how much weight he had lost. His clothes no longer hung from his shoulders, as they had at the time of the miracle. (His tailor would have seen to that.) But he cut a much slimmer figure now. A paler one, too.

"Shouldn't you be at the Teatro? Sarastro won't like you being outdoors." He scowled. "I'm not sure I do, either."

"Oh, stop being such a nursemaid!" Carlo came nearer and leaned on Tammo's shoulder. Heavily. "It's bad enough that I have Casale, Citizeness Aldo, Count Pageno and the maestro on my back. I wanted to breathe the fresh air and smell the fresh earth." His voice softened. "And to see you, Tamino."

"Well, it's too late to send you back." Tammo linked his arm with Carlo's, and they began a rather lopsided walk in the direction of Grimaldi's cottage. Their height difference always made walking together an uneven affair, and Carlo was leaning on Tammo more than usual. Coronis flew ahead, cawing her approval.

"How was opening night?"

"Ah, so kind of you to remember." Carlo batted his eyelashes. "I thought I would weep when I saw how they stood for me and called my name. I coughed onstage three times, but I think they forgave me. One person came to my tiring room, masked, and gave me a silver rose."

"Forgave you? They worship you. And you love it; don't pretend you don't."

Carlo blushed, as prettily as only he could. "A little. But not as much as I love…good company."

He pressed his Cupid's lips together. Tammo was certain he had intended to say something else.

"Not forgetting good food and good clothing," he grunted.

"Ah, so you've noticed my new wig." Carlo turned this way and that, to show it to best advantage. "A New Year's gift from the maestro. For some reason, he dislikes bald singers upon the stage."

"I gave Grimaldi a new apron," Tammo said. "He didn't like it."

They lurched in companionable silence for a while. Tammo recalled the many gifts Carlo had lavished on him over the years. They had seemed so embarrassing at the time, as if he were Carlo's pet.

But no gift from Carlo had arrived this New Year. It left a hole that Tammo felt as a physical ache. He didn't know how to talk about it.

But it put him in mind of something else. He released Carlo's arm and pulled a leather thong from around his neck. Celestina's scapular came with it; he covered it with one hand. With the other, he held out the carnival ring.

"Sorry I've kept it so long. I meant to give it back to you on that day, after the birds flew. I know how much it means to you."

"Yes, it does." Carlo's voice had gone tight.

The weight of years hung between them. Two young boys in a sanitorium with tears on their faces, afraid they would be parted forever. An impulsive gesture in a young girl's chamber, following a miraculous healing. A forbidden kiss before the fire. Jealousy. Anger. Hurtful words neither had meant to say.

"Keep it." Carlo's voice was so quiet, Tammo wasn't sure he had heard right.

"Are you sure that's what you want, Carlo?"

"No." He could hear the tears in Carlo's voice now. The eunuch blinked hard, forcing them back. "So put it away now, before I change my mind."

Tammo fumbled with his clothing, tucking both the ring and the scapular out of sight. Something significant had happened.

He reached for Carlo's hand.

Palm to palm, fast-clasped, fingers intertwined with fingers. He stroked a thumb across the back of Carlo's hand. Carlo squeezed, ever so gently. The words of "A Castrato's Love" came to Tammo's mind. *You ask me for my love: what can I give?* Tammo had no answer to that. Not right now. Maybe not ever.

Maybe it didn't matter. Maybe what mattered, on this blue winter morning with the sun slanting through the trees, was that his friend was by his side.

He didn't look Carlo in the eye. If he wept, there was no need for Tammo to see it. Instead, he cleared his throat, and fixed his eyes on the horizon.

"Come on," he said. "Grimaldi's waiting."

Glossary

Amazon - a mythical female warrior.

Angelus - a prayer recited three times daily, signalled by the ringing of bells. In Latin, it begins, *Angelus Domini nuntiavit Mariæ* (The Angel of the Lord declared to Mary).

Apostolic Empire - a group of countries with an elected emperor, bound by ties of religion. Angelio is part of this.

Apostolic Father - the Pope.

Appoggiatura - a short, ornamental note, which delays the main note of the melody.

Aria - a solo song in an opera.

Bas-relief - a sculptural technique that makes a picture look like it is raised from the background.

Basso continuo - instruments providing a bassline and harmonies in baroque music.

Batua - a white mask with a strong chin and no mouth; usually worn by men, with a hat and cloak.

Belvedere - beautiful view; a piece of architecture with a roof and open sides, usually high up.

Blackguard (pronounced *blaggard*) - one who behaves in a shameful way.

Brocade - heavy fabric with a raised pattern, often in silver or gold.

Buskins - theatrical laced boots, resembling those worn by ancient Greeks and Romans.

Cadence - sequence of notes or chords that bring a section of music to a close.

Caliphate Empire - a large empire to the east of Angelio.

Capon - a male chicken that is castrated at a young age, and fed on a rich diet to make it fat. An abusive term for a castrato.

Carnival - a season of celebration in Angelio, lasting from the Feast of Seraphim until Lent.

Castration - removal of the testicles.

Castrato - a singer who has been castrated at a young age to preserve his high voice.

Centesimo (plural **centesimi**) - a copper coin.

Chairman - man who carries a sedan chair.

Citizen/Citizeness - a polite term for a working-class person born in the city of Angelio.

Conservatorio - music school where Carlo and Tammo were trained.

Council of Nine - Angelio's ruling council, headed by the Duke.

Coxcomb - a man overly concerned with his appearance.

Cupid - the Roman god of love; Venus' son.

Cythera - Venus' island in mythology.

Daphne - a nymph in classical mythology who escaped being amorously pursued by Apollo by becoming a tree.

Denaro (plural **denari**) - a copper coin.

De Rigueur - required by fashion.

Eunuch - a man or boy who has been castrated.

Exquisite - see **fop.**

Femella - an abusive term for an effeminate man (a person who today might identify as gay, transfeminine etc.)

Festeburg - a city whose main trade is in automata; Celestina's house carriage was made here.

Fichu - a large, square kerchief, worn to fill in the neckline of a low bodice.

Fontange - a high headdress or hairstyle at the front of the head, supported by a wire frame, and decorated with ribbons and lace.

Footman - a male servant in a grand house, whose duties include admitting visitors and waiting on tables. Often chosen for their good looks.

Fop - a ridiculous man, obsessed with his dress and manners.

Gallant - a man who is attentive or flirtatious toward women.

Gigue - a lively, baroque dance, with a swaying feel.

Glissando - a seamless glide between musical notes, going either up or down.

Grace note - a short, ornamental note in music.

Hermaphroditus - a figure in classical mythology who was both male and female.

Intermezzo - a short, light piece between the acts of a serious opera.

Jackanapes - a cheeky or impertinent person; a monkey.

Lackwit - an idiot.

Lira - a silver coin.

Loggia - a covered gallery attached to a building, often on an upper floor.

Lysfleur - a country to the north-west of Angelio; the main rival to the Apostolic Empire.

Maestro - master; a teacher or respected musician.

Man-seemer - an abusive term for a castrato.

Mantilla - a light, lacy shawl, worn over the head and shoulders.

Masque - a court entertainment, with members of the court dressed as allegorical characters.

Maquillage - makeup.

Mea culpa - Latin phrase from a prayer of confession, meaning "through my fault." In other words, "It was my fault. I apologise."

Messa di voce - placement of the voice. A singing technique that involves holding one note, while gradually making the voice louder and softer.

Mezzo-piano - moderately quiet.

Mingguo - a large empire to the far east of Angelio.

Memento mori - a reminder of death; for example, a ring in the shape of a skull.

Moretta - a rounded, black mask, held in place by clamping a button between the teeth; usually worn by women.

Night soil - excrement.

Nobile - son of a noble family.

Nobilissimo - the Duke of Angelio's heir.

Noblesse - daughter of a noble family.

Oyoa - a country to the far south of Angelio, on the western Afric coast.

Overture - music before the opera begins.

Paramour - lover.

Parterre - a formal garden on the level, with ornamental flower beds.

Pediment - triangular shape at the top of a building or cabinet.

Phaeton - a light, four-wheeled carriage.

Piazza - a town square; often named after a church.

Pillicock - penis; an insult.

Portico - a covered porch or walkway, supported by columns.

Prie-dieu - a kneeling bench with a raised shelf for a book or icon, where a person may kneel to pray.

Prima donna - the leading lady in an opera.

Primo castrato - the leading man (castrato) in an opera.

Queue - a long, tightly-bound pigtail.

Rakeshaming - degraded; an insult.

Recitative - a chanted speech in an opera; usually leads into an aria.

Reliquary - a beautiful container for the remains of a saint.

Salon - a private gathering, where people of a similar class and outlook gather to discuss literature, philosophy, politics and current affairs. Usually hosted by women.

Sancti Michaelis Archangeli - Angelio's cathedral, named after the Archangel Michael.

Sarabande - a stately dance in triple metre.

Scapular - a monastic outer garment like an apron, hanging front and back from the shoulders; for ordinary people, there is a smaller version, which is two small pieces of cloth, hanging front and back on a string or ribbon. The small version is often embroidered.

Scopa - an Italian card game, played with suits of coins, swords, cups and batons.

Sedan chair - an enclosed chair, carried on poles by two men, one in front and one behind.

Settebello - the seven of coins, an important card in scopa.

Shabbaroon - a scruffy person; an insult.

Signor/Signora - sir/madam; a term of respect.

Sirrah - a term used to express contempt for social inferiors.

Seraph - a six-winged angel; Saint Michael is the Prince of Seraphim.

Seraphini - Carlo's stage name.

Snuff - powdered tobacco, taken through the nose.

Soldo (plural **soldi**) - a silver coin.

Sonnet - a type of poem, often in praise of someone.

Sopranist - a male soprano.

Stanza - a verse of poetry.

Strumpet - a woman who has many casual sexual encounters.

Stiletto - a slender dagger; slang for penis.

Stow it - shut up.

Seamstress - a woman whose job it is to sew and mend.

Stays - traditional corset, fastened with laces.

Stucco - plaster covering walls and ceilings, often in decorative patterns.

Syncopation - off-beat rhythms.

Tabarro - cloak usually worn with a tricorn hat and batua mask.

Tancredi - a mediaeval knight of the Crusades, played by Carlo in an opera.

Teatro - a theatre; short for *Teatro di Palazzo*, Angelio's opera house.

Tiring room - dressing room.

Tokay - sweet, white wine from the borderlands between the Apostolic and Caliphate Empires.

Tremelo - a trembling effect in music.

Toilette - the process of attending to one's appearance.

Venus - the Roman goddess of love.

Vulcan - husband of Venus; god of smiths; jealous of her lovers.

Warming pan - a metal container on a stick, filled with hot coals and placed between the sheets, to warm a cold bed.

Wicket gate - a small gate, built into a larger gate, wall or fence.

From the Author

When *Cage of Nightingales* came out, it was the fulfilment of a dream that had been over ten years in the making. I first had the idea for the story of Tammo, Carlo and Celestina in 2011, the year I first fully identified as asexual, after reading a brilliant book, *The World of the Castrati* by Patrick Barbier. This got mixed in with a dream I once had in the form of an anime (the first and only time!) about a beautiful, paralysed girl and a chancer boy with a magic flute, and hey, presto! The Angelio series was born.

I want to thank everyone at Deep Hearts YA for loving Tammo and Carlo as much as I do. I cried in Specsavers when I got the acceptance email! A big thanks to Craig, Cali, Francisco, Margaret, and, of course, Ave who made the amazing cover design. Thank you for letting me be my British self, and for accommodating my suggestions.

Another huge thank you to the indie bookshops who stock and sell my books. I will get round all the ones in the UK eventually (I can't promise the same for the international ones, but I thank you). Thanks to the local libraries (especially mine), the LGBTQIA+ groups, the online book reviewers, the online community in general, and most of all, you the readers. I'm so glad for everyone who has taken Angelio to their heart. Do come and find me on Threads (@angeliocitystate) and we'll enthuse about it together.

The world of Angelio is fictitious, but the castrati were

real. Carlo and his friends are inspired by the real lives of singers such as Caffarelli, Senesino and Marchesi. And in particular, the greatest of them all: Farinelli (Carlo Broschi), who had a lifelong friendship with the poet Metastasio, they called each other *Gemello* (twin). They are our queer elders, who lived as a third gender long before terms such as trans or nonbinary were widely used. If you want to know about them, Patrick Barbier's book is still a great place to start. There's also the 1994 film *Farinelli Il Castrato* (rated 15 in the UK and R in the USA) which isn't exactly a true biography of Carlo Broschi, but sensitively portrays the many contradictions of a castrato's life (and has a great soundtrack!).

I've read many books and visited many museums, theatres and historic buildings in my research. For disability, I recommend *Disability in Eighteenth-Century England* by David M. Turner. For insight into Black lives in this period, try Paterson Joseph's novel *The Secret Diaries of Charles Ignatius Sancho*. Thanks to Opera North in Leeds and the Sky Arts channel for the operas I've seen, and the Sam Wanamaker Playhouse, London, for the brilliant play *Farinelli and the King*. Hearing countertenor Iestyn Davies sing his music live was the closest I will ever come to hearing Farinelli for myself.

I also want to thank a couple of artists: Kirsty Rolfe for the picture of myself and Farinelli as BFFs, and Nes Lee for the "tinification" of Tammo and Carlo. Both of these pictures feature a lot in my online life, and hang on the wall above my desk.

Big thanks, as ever, to my friends and family, especially those who have supported my writing from the start, and come to all my book launches. Sorry I don't say it enough.

Lastly, shout out to the *OFMD* fandom, cast and crew. You came into my life right in the midst of all this taking off, and totally gave me Angelio vibes. The two are now inextricably linked in my mind, written on each other in permanent ink. I hope my tiny bit of representation continues what we have begun, and that I never stop learning how to do it better.

Elizabeth Hopkinson, Bradford UK, 2025.

About the Author

Elizabeth Hopkinson (she/they) is the author of the Asexual Fairy Tales and Angelio series. Both sell in indie bookshops in the UK and around the world. *Masquerade of Finches* (Angelio #2) was shortlisted for the inaugural Tempest Prize (Northern Writers Awards).

Elizabeth lives in Bradford, West Yorkshire, UK (home of the Bronte sisters and the Cottingley fairies!) with her husband and cat.

Elizabeth is a greygender romantic asexual and is committed to asexual representation in fiction.

Find her/them at elizabethhopkinson.uk or on Threads as @angeliocitystate

Books by Elizabeth Hopkinson

Cage of Nightingales
Masquerade of Finches

More From Deep Hearts YA

Dreamers
T.J. Baer

The week of Leo Torres' sixteenth birthday, he decides to finally start living as the boy he is. Armed with a new haircut, a chest binder, and a stack of notes declaring his new name to his teachers, Leo shows up to the first day of school ready for a brand new start.

But the ghosts of the past aren't so easy to overcome. As word about him spreads around school, Leo has to deal with confused classmates, a furious sister, and recurring dreams featuring his long-dead father, who promises he can teach Leo how to "dream walk." Leo is almost positive the dreams are just that—dreams—but when they take him into the dreamscape of the soft-spoken new kid, Robbie, Leo realizes nothing is as it seems.

Leo never expected to spend his sixteenth year coming out, falling in love, and walking into other people's sleeping minds, but he's learning that pretty much anything is possible. Anything he can dream.

More From Deep Hearts YA

Broken Arrows
Nanouk Kira

Marian despises her life in Nottingham Castle. She feels confined—trapped—especially with her upcoming forced marriage to the sheriff's cousin. She longs to escape, but has nowhere to run.

She also has a talent for getting into trouble.

When she goes out riding and is captured by outlaws of the notorious Robin Hood, she is stunned to learn that Robin Hood is, in fact, a woman of the same age. She hopes for some help from this outlaw, but Robin only wants to use Marian as a tool to steal the sheriff's seal.

As she spends time with the outlaws, Marian finally feels freedom she'd never felt before. And she also feels…something for the outlaw Robin Hood. Then an opportunity arises. Rather than Robin using Marian, Marian could work with Robin, team up, and take down the sheriff together.

But…is it wise to trust an outlaw, especially when her heart's involved?